BRING ME HOME

Copyright © 2023 Genevieve Jasper

All rights reserved.

The characters and events portrayed in this book are fictitious. Any similarity to real persons, living or dead, is coincidental and not intended by the author.

No part of this book may be reproduced, or stored in a retrieval system, or transmitted in any form or by any means, electronic, mechanical, photocopying, recording, or otherwise, without express written permission of the publisher.

Editor: R. A. Wright Editing
Formatter: KB. Row

BRING ME HOME

Genevieve Jasper

Foreword

Bring Me Home portrays a fictitious motorcycle club. This book contains mention of crime, parental death, anxiety, physical and attempted sexual abuse, as well as other themes that some may find distressing.
If you have anything you'd specifically like to check, please don't hesitate to reach out to me.

CHAPTER ONE

ISABELLE

When you're young, people always talk about what you'll be when you grow up. What you'll do and where you'll go . . . Kids want to be marine biologists and teachers and firefighters. They'll be heartbreakers and world leaders and forces of nature. I never wanted any of that. It never mattered to me. All I wanted was to be happy, because that's all *he* wanted for me. And I truly thought I would be. Naive, clearly. Realistic? Never.

What has brought on this melodramatic monologue, you might ask?

They're currently preparing us for graduation. Mrs. Peploe drones on like we care about gowns and how to walk and setting ourselves up for the future. Some do, I guess. Those who know what they want; those who get good grades. Then there's the others—the ones who don't give a fuck. Maybe they have no ambition. Maybe they have other journeys that don't involve college.

Me, though . . . why would I care about my future when I don't care about life?

Don't worry, I don't want to die. I just don't care to live. Not like this. Not with this huge ball of nothing inside me. I wonder if I'll ever actually be happy again. Will it come? Maybe it's something you need to nurture, but I'm just too tired. Ridiculous, really.

Eighteen years old, nearly nineteen, and too jaded to work on contentment. Why have I given up so early? I'll tell you, but you'll get the wrong end of the stick. It's because of a guy. It's always a guy, isn't it, in some way or another . . .

Either way, Mrs. Peploe isn't holding my attention, my gaze out the big window propped open next to me as the warm breeze drifts across my skin.

"Hey," Betsy whispers, her fingers hovering over her phone. "You coming to the pool after school?"

"Nah, not today." She doesn't mean to go swimming—she means the derelict, abandoned pool where we go to drink and hang out. Well, the others do. I can occasionally be convinced to go, but only when I'm really wanting to drown my sorrows. It's not often I join my classmates. I prefer to do the real wallowing alone.

"You sure? Dan'll be there." I shake my head, not even bothering to reply. As if that's an incentive in any way. The guys at my school hold no interest for me, not that much does these days. And even if Dan did, I've got plans today. Plans I can't miss.

I don't go back to the house first. She'd probably keep me there out of spite, and I don't want the hassle of walking out. I'd only take the chance if her partner wasn't there anyway, and it's not a risk I'm willing to take. Not today. Instead, I visit the drive-thru and pick up my usual—a peach iced tea—before continuing on to my destination, which sits in the pretty outskirts of the town. Not so far that it makes it a journey I can't complete after school, but not so close that I pass it every day, as I live in the center.

I park in a hurry, then slam my door shut and grab my blanket from the trunk. I'm eager to get there, especially today. It's the only place I feel close to him now. I don't have our old house, and I avoid the places we used to go together. This headstone is the only thing I have. It's small and neat—so unlike him it makes me smile every time I see it. He wasn't a small, neat person. He was larger than life; loud and clumsy. He had so much love inside of him that it spilled everywhere.

I smile when I think of him, as I always do. He'd hate for me to be sad, and I hate to disappoint him . . . even when he's not here to know. Spreading the small blanket on the grass, I plonk myself down and lean back, feeling the warmth through my thin tee as I rest my head where his name is carved. I let my body gradually relax against the stone and feel peace for the first time since . . . probably the last time I sat in this very spot. These days, it feels like the only time I can breathe is when I'm here, with him at my side again.

"Fuck, I miss you, Dad," I say, and the words are carried into the air. I know what you were thinking when I admitted to being messed up by a guy back there, but there's no sleazy ex. Just the most important man in my life . . . *gone.*

I can hear his voice so clearly in my head, admonishing my language, and I think that's why I say it. Anything to seem closer to him at this point, however sad it is. I think back to the talk at school today and wonder what he'd want for me, want for my future. I'm trying my best to live it right but I feel so lost.

I know for sure he'd have been one of those embarrassingly loud parents, whooping and hollering as I walked the stage for graduation, but I can't recall a single time he pushed me toward a career or had any expectations for me. He never made me feel like I needed to be anything other than myself, because I was already good enough. That's what I miss most about my dad. He accepted everyone; made them feel they were exactly who they should be as long as they were happy. All he wanted was for me to be happy.

Well, ditto, Dad. Shame that seems like too much to ask these days.

Awareness trickles over me as I bask in the peace this place brings. I feel them before I see them, as I always do. A second of apprehension and the hairs on the back of my neck stand to attention, followed by intrinsic calm. You'd think knowing strange men were following me would have the opposite reaction, but nope.

Maybe it's the lack of eagerness to live. Maybe it's because I've felt them for years and I'm used to it. Maybe it's because they remind me of him. Remind me he was alive.

I pull the now empty ice-cream spoon from my mouth with a pop.

"Dad, why do the big men watch us?"

"You think men watch us?" he asks carefully.

"They definitely do," I say, in that pious way only a six-year-old can, which earns me a chuckle.

"These men, do they want to hurt us?" he presses.

I shrug. "No one can hurt me with you here."

His eyes shine with pride. "But do they want to, you think?"

"They haven't so far. Maybe they're protecting us."

"Maybe they are, Belle. Do they scare you?"

"No. They're like silent knights," I declare.

"The best damn knights in the world." I don't understand the pride in his voice, but that doesn't matter.

"Or princes—the kind that saves the princess." I'm deep into my fairy-tale phase at this point, something he's only too happy to indulge with bedtime stories.

"Good thing you don't need saving then, sweet girl, because you deserve a knight."

And that's how I've seen them ever since. They haven't hurt me, even now that my king has been slain . . . although they've been doing a pretty shitty job of protecting me recently.

I don't turn to see who it is today. I'm already with the only guy I want to spend my time with, though it doesn't stop me wondering. It's a little game I like to play before I find them in the distance as they stand in the crowds, watching me. Which protector is here today? I'm so used to them I've got them numbered, classified in order of who is around the most.

Is it One? The lean guy who looks more angel than human, his blond hair so light I thought it was white the first time I caught a glimpse of him?

Is it Four? The shorter, stocky man who I'm not convinced isn't actually square, with a shaved head on top of a meaty neck?

There are more, of course.

I ignore whoever it is anyway, soaking up the last of my time here. I don't come very often, wanting to keep it special—or I'd camp out here and never leave—but the day before May Mayhem starts seemed like an apt occasion.

Tomorrow marks May 1st. Dad's birthday. Mine falls on the last day of the month, and we treated it like our very own public holiday that lasted thirty-one whole days. Forget March Madness; May Mayhem was my dad's idea, and it used to be my favorite month of the year. Excessive, yes, but it wasn't about money. It was about spending time together and gaining new experiences. My most treasured memories were made in the month of May.

I think about the plans I have for this May. Nada. I could make some with my friends from school, but I think I'd rather be alone. Truthfully, calling them friends is a bit of a stretch. They put up with me, and I put up with them. It seems to be an unspoken high-school rule that conventionally attractive people become popular, so as soon as the boys noticed me, I was indoctrinated, but we're not exactly close. I wonder what they've got planned for tomorrow. Anything has to be better than spending it in the house. The house I now need to head back to as the sun sets.

"Bye, Dad," I say softly, with a last glance up at the orange-streaked sky before I pack my stuff away. As I throw it into my trunk, I finally sneak a look at which knight we have today, knowing he'll disappear the second I drive away.

Six. The one with deep skin and unruly curls that make him seem young. It doesn't really mean anything to know, especially as I got it wrong. I guessed Seven. That's my guess most of the time, though it's hardly ever right. Most of the time, I hope for it to be him. Seven is my guilty pleasure.

He comes the least.

She's screaming before I even get my shoes off, but I let it wash over me. There's no point in shouting back; it'll only prolong the dramatics. At least Gary isn't here. She may scream, but he hits, and I'm tired and bored of covering bruises.

I stand placidly with my hand on the banister, waiting for her to get it out of her system. Her face becomes redder and more putrid with every word, but I stay silent, ready to make my escape as soon as she decides she's had enough. Probably when she realizes the glass in her hand is empty.

Her normally pale face is unrecognizable when it's screwed up in anger, her dark-blonde hair wild as she hurls abuse my way. We actually should look quite alike, with our similar willowy statures and wavy blonde hair. Way more similar than my dad and me, which I hate, and is the main reason mine is now dyed a silvery gray.

My dad didn't have many relatives—in fact, *Celia* is the only one he'd named in his will to care for me. I'm not surprised he stayed away from her. What I am surprised about is that he'd leave me with her, not having any other plan. Or that she said yes in the first place.

But then, who thinks they'll die at thirty-one?

CHAPTER TWO

Isabelle

Sadness engulfs me. I normally coast through life, feeling numb. It's far preferable to this grief that stabs my chest like hot pokers, making my bones heavy before I've even opened my eyes.

Another birthday without him.

All I want is to jump out of bed and do our whole routine. I want to be starting the month of birthday celebrations like we're royalty. I want to be getting ready to cook him waffles. Waffles on the first of the month and pancakes on the thirty-first.

What I *don't* want is to be waking up in this house, more alone and untethered than I've ever been. And I certainly don't want to have to see my aunt or Gary—her partner—today. He doesn't live here but seems to be around at all the worst times.

If I escape the house early enough and sneak back in when they're preoccupied, I can go the whole day without talking to them. That's enough motivation to drag myself up and into the shower. I can probably get out while Celia's still sleeping off her hangover.

After getting dressed in black jean shorts and a cropped T-shirt, I slip on some Vans and creep out of the house. Without plans or anyone I want to spend my time with, the only thing I can think to do is park up on the hill and sketch the day away, although, as I close the door behind me, disappointment hits at the sight of fog blanketing the streets. Hopefully it clears out, because the view is all I sketch nowadays. If I can't see it, I can't draw it. My creativity died along with my will when Dad left me.

My rumbling stomach is a welcome distraction, and I decide to take a detour. I drive until I spot a little strip mall off the highway that I've never visited before, but it does have a diner, so that's good enough for me. The bell dings as I make my way in, but no one pays attention, the cacophony of noise drowning it out for everyone else. The chrome fixtures and bright red booths look old but well cared for, giving the diner a warm, welcoming atmosphere, but despite finding an empty table tucked in the back, the sound quickly becomes too much. The clinking, the scraping, the laughing, the talking, the chewing . . . I'm so used to being alone and my mind being quiet that it's overwhelming how busy it is in here. I'm about to get up and leave when the waitress appears at my table.

"What'll it be, love?"

"Erm, waffles and an iced tea, please," I say on autopilot, my subconscious remembering what day it is, and I instantly regret the choice. I haven't eaten that meal in five years. "To go," I add quickly, knowing I can't sit here and enjoy it.

"Sure," she says easily, moving away to the kitchen. I space out once she's gone, working on keeping my breaths even and my mind calm before I start spiraling, and mercifully, she's back again not long after she left. With a kind smile, she hands me a brown bag and a to-go cup, and I take them gratefully, swapping them for enough cash to leave a decent tip. Then I all but run from the room, making it back to the safe confines of my car before the emotions can assault me.

Once I'm inside, I let out a long breath. I'm officially cracking up. Can't even cope with being around other people for half an hour to enjoy a birthday breakfast. When did I get so insular?

The smell emanating from the bag is enough to have my mouth watering, so I unwrap it, then tear off chunks of warm waffle to eat with my fingers. A plus to being alone in the world—there's no one around to judge me and my feral food habits. The waffle is crispy on the outside and fluffy on the inside, close to perfect, but it still lodges in my throat, not allowing me to truly savor the taste. Waffles on the first feels so wrong without him. I give up only halfway through, washing the lump in my throat down with my tea.

The fog still lingers heavy in the distance, so I sit in the lot, killing time on my phone. The seats in here are comfortable, and the sun coming through the windows warms me nicely, even if the fog is killing most of the sunlight. The only nice thing my aunt has ever done for me was to buy me this car for my seventeenth birthday and pay for driving lessons. I'm pretty sure it's so she didn't have to take me anywhere, but I'll take a win when I get one.

I check through social media, scrolling past posts from people I don't care about until I'm bored and searching out the windscreen, hoping for something to strike my interest. I should head over to the hill anyway. At least the view is better than here. What a choice—a strip-mall parking lot or a hill clearing that's not so clear.

I need something—anything—to jolt me out of this. I'm so sick of the nothingness that envelops me constantly. The lack of interest, the absence of caring . . . it's draining.

The sweet smell from the bag of food is making me nauseous and spiking my anxiety, so I grab it to throw away before I leave. I'm at the trash can, dropping the remnants of my breakfast inside, when my attention is caught by sudden movement across the lot. A rusty metal door is pushed open, and two people, wrapped up in each other, stumble out in a burst of music. They're laughing as he presses her clumsily to the wall, both of their smiles so wide it makes my cheeks ache. Then my heart joins in as I try to remember the last time I even *looked* that happy, let alone laughed as carefree as they both are. I'm missing that—missing connections with people that are alive; the joy of feeling free.

The door creaks behind them as it swings, music still spilling from the doorway, not that they seem to notice. The hinges must be as old and battered as the door looks, because it won't close alone, and as it sways back and forth, I make a split-second decision. It suddenly seems imperative that I take their place, see if I can gain some of the happiness they've taken from wherever they've just come from.

Despite very much knowing better, I move toward the building before the door can close on me. The couple are too consumed in one another to notice me slip inside and pull the door closed.

Leaning back against the rusty metal, I take in my surroundings and wonder what the hell possessed me to do this. I don't know, but I do know that my heart is racing under my top, and I *feel* something for once. I'm so sick of feeling numb. That's what convinces me to stay on this side of the door.

But now what?

I'm at the end of a dimly lit corridor with signs for cleaning cupboards and toilets lining the doors, the only unmarked one at the other end of the hall, directly opposite me, where the music seems to be coming from. My heart races further as I stare at it, willing it to open as much as I hope it stays closed. But I'm not here to hang out in a hall.

What *am* I here for? I don't quite remember, but my feet are carrying me toward the noise whether I do or not. Here goes nothing, I guess.

I wander toward the sounds and pull the door open slightly to peek through the crack. My feet might be keen, but my brain is still cautious. Through the sliver of doorway, I see a long, mostly empty bar, with grease streaks visible along the walnut wood. There are people filling the booths and tables, though, even though it's still morning. The walls are a deep red, the stools that line the bar old and rickety, and the booths a dusty-looking velvet. Everything is deep brown or red, accentuating the dingy basement vibes, even though it's light outside.

No one comes storming toward the door demanding to know who I am and why I'm here, so I let out a breath, pull the door all the way, and make my way into the room as it swings shut behind me. Not one person bothers to look up from what they're doing, and my shoulders relax slightly. As if any of them care that I'm here—I could be invisible.

Grabbing one of the wooden stools, I look up to find the bartender already waiting for my order. Right. I panic and order a Long Island iced tea. It's the most adult-sounding drink I can think of, although I don't need to worry, as he slaps it in front of me minutes later without asking for ID.

With a thanks and some cash, I spin and lean back against the bar top, content to nurse my glass and people-watch for a bit.

Truth be told, it's my favorite thing to do—making up stories for strangers—and this place is fascinating. The stripper, who looks bored beyond belief: maybe she's a struggling college girl looking for easy money. The keen young guy shoving ones in her underwear: an eager virgin? The older gentleman watching the door while trying to act nonchalant from the booth: he could be on the run. The one slurring and mumbling to himself at the other end of the bar ... recently single?

I've only been here a little while when I feel the energy change around me, like a tidal wave rippling as someone makes their way closer. I can hear the mutterings, even over the loud music, as every head in the room turns to face the intruder. I don't know if the wave is pushing me to get away or pulling me into the current, but I stay where I am, determined to not show any reaction. Not when someone sits next to me, not while I wait for the room to regain its easy atmosphere, not even when I get that prickly awareness of someone watching me. Then I feel the calm.

I dip my gaze to my now empty glass, catching a drop of condensation that runs down the side with my finger as I try to surreptitiously get a glance at the person everyone seems to know . . . and I think I might, too. Well, as much as you can know someone who has been watching you for years.

He, of course, is pointedly not looking in my direction, which at least allows me to get a glimpse of him without locking eyes, but I'm reluctant to look at him now that I have the chance. For the first time, he's so close. So real. Instead, I take in his jacket—the same one he always wears. I've never been close enough to any of them to get a decent look, although it's so dark in here I still can't make out much of the detailing. Just a dark leather jacket.

They all wear it—my *knights*, the men who watch over me. At first, I thought maybe they had similar fashion sense, but it's more than that. I've never once seen any of them without the dark leather attached to their backs. It's practically a uniform, even in the heat of summer. Each of them interchangeable except him. The guy who sits next to me now.

If they're angels, he must be God.

His knights. Their commander.

Seven.

His face stars in many dreams, and even more showers, so I don't need to look again to make sure, although I really want to. I want to take in his square jaw and strong nose, his short-cropped blond hair. The only thing I can never conjure in my mind is his eyes, yet I still don't dare peek above his chest.

Why today? Why is he here?

Does he think I'm that stupid I don't recognize him?

He's so close now that his scent—like warm earth and gasoline—overwhelms my senses. He's tense. I can tell by the way his fist is clenched on his thigh. Like this is the last place he wants to be. Suddenly, I want to know so much more than what his eyes look like. I want him to know that I know about them—my knights—and I want to know why they stay so far away. If they're all I have in some way, I want to know more. Everything.

However, sitting in a seedy bar when no one knows where I am, with a random older man that everyone here seems wary of, doesn't seem like the best place to confront him. Then again, what else do I have to lose?

Game on, Seven. Game on.

CHAPTER THREE

AXLE

She doesn't look at me, her gaze moving from where it was taking in my cut to watching over everyone else, as usual. It's probably for the best, even if I do crave her eyes on me. What the fuck she's doing here, I have no idea, and she's lucky I was so close or I'd be losing my mind.

The guys know to alert me if there's anything out of the ordinary. It's why she has the tracker on her phone in the first place. They've seen how their usually calm-and-collected president can go apeshit if she's not where she's supposed to be. But this dump of a bar, alone, drinking underage? That's a first for her.

Turning to put her empty glass on the bar top, she barely glances at me before spinning back to watch the room as she flicks her long silver hair over one shoulder. It basically goes to her waist these days, having grown steadily over the years.

I haven't seen her in a while, and she's done that changing shit again, where I blink and she looks so much more like a woman. Where I notice her long legs and plump lips and curse myself for even fuckin' looking.

She's a stunning girl. That can't be denied. The unusual hair color only highlights the darkness of her almost-black eyes, and I'm surprised no deadbeat has tried to come up to her in the ten minutes it took me to get here, but maybe it's my lucky day. Or maybe it's theirs, since that means they get another day breathing.

The bartender picks up her empty glass and opens his mouth to no doubt offer her another, but when he notices my withering glare, he snaps it shut. Isabelle goes to stand but stumbles off the stool, pitching forward without both feet on the ground. I wonder how much she managed to sink before I got here. It probably only took me ten minutes, but what eighteen-year-old isn't a lightweight? I know she drinks sometimes, but barely enough to turn her into a seasoned pro, or even someone who can handle it.

Then again, what do I know? I'm the coward who can barely bring himself to check on her these days. She could be a whole different person.

I put a hand out to steady her so she doesn't end up plastered to the floor, and she takes it, setting herself upright. Then she looks at me, and I regret every decision I've made today. I should've sent someone else to the meet; someone else would've been closest to her. I should've checked she was okay and then waited outside. It makes so much sense why I've stayed away recently, although that sacrifice is all down the drain now.

Her big, deep, trusting eyes lock on my face as her hand burns an imprint in mine, and in an instant, my world tilts. I'm fucked.

I told myself that when she hit twenty-one, it'd all be fine. She'd be an adult, have what she needs, and I'd have done my duty to him. We'd all back off, and she'd go about her life never even knowing we existed. But in a split second, it's no longer about him. My world flips on its axis and makes it clear everything is about her.

She blinks for a second, then grins widely. The alcohol must have diminished her inhibitions, because she normally walks around with a severe *fuck off* aura. Or she used to.

"Thanks," she beams. I grunt in response as I snatch my hand back, but that doesn't put her off. "I'm Issy." I look up at her again with a blank biker stare that would scare away most men, but her grin grows. "You're hardly about to save me from falling off a stool if you were gonna hurt me yourself."

She must be able to read my fucking mind or something, because even if that logic is deeply flawed, the conclusion is correct, and she knows it.

"Axle," I offer gruffly.

"Nice to meet you, A."

"Axle," I repeat tersely. I hate people shortening my name, but she giggles irritatingly in front of me.

"You don't mind, do you, A?" She lays a hand on my arm as she bats her eyelids in an obvious way. This is not who I thought she'd be, and although the same scorching feeling comes from her touch, I'm not feeling the flirty persona. Maybe I'm not drawn to her in the way I thought. I've kept away so long I don't actually know her at all. I've built her up in my head, or maybe her looks have short-wired my brain. I'm filled with a weird mix of relief and disappointment. But this is good. I have no business feeling for her what I thought I was, or what my body is still trying to convince me I do.

"Is it time you went home?" I ask sternly. I can do stern. I have bikers shitting their pants with one look. *Issy* doesn't seem to give a fuck, though.

"Are you coming with me?" she asks, twirling some hair around her finger. It draws my attention to her full lips.

God, she really is gorgeous.

Everything about her screams effortless. The casual but sexy outfit of a relaxed tee and shorts, the way she carries herself so confidently in everyday life, not giving a fuck if she's being watched or judged or wanted. Everything except this superficial personality she has. She wouldn't have got that had she grown up with us.

But no, although I do need to see her back home safely, I am not going with her the way she thinks. I could drag her out of here—no one would care; it's my bar and the patrons know to look the other way when a biker comes in—but that would give it away to her. Better a rejection from someone she thought she was gonna fuck than to give the whole game away after all this time. I just hope she's drunk enough to not register the patch on my cut, which really would tell her way more than I want.

"Sure," I grumble. She blinks coyly up through her lashes, and for the first time since she looked up at me, I thank fuck I was the closest. The guys know where the line sits with her, but a look like that is enough to tempt even the most loyal man into betrayal.

After throwing a couple notes on the bar, I gesture to the door, and she moves ahead of me, stumbling as she goes. Grabbing her to keep her upright, I'm surprised when she tucks herself into me, her arms around my waist. She feels too fucking good there.

"My car's over here." She points to one on the other side of the lot as the lights flash. No way is she driving in this state. I hate to do it, but I'll have to get in the fuckin' cage to take her home. I could put her on the back of my bike and she could get it tomorrow, but I can't trust she'll hold on this drunk.

"Let me drive," I huff when we reach it.

"Of course, chauffeur." She giggles, pulling herself away from me as we reach the car. "Let me grab something first."

Yanking the driver's door open, she bends over to lean across the seat, wiggling her hips as she does. It might be over-the-top obvious, but I fall for it anyway, staring at that round ass as she searches for whatever she needs. The wrong thing to do in so many ways, but especially as when she straightens up, all signs of drunkenness disappear and she holds a gun pointed straight at my chest.

Distracted by a fucking eighteen-year-old's ass. I almost want to laugh at the situation. I look back to her with a cocked brow and marvel at how much fucking hotter she looks when her eyes light up with defiance. Out here in the sunlight, you can tell they're a rich brown rather than black, and the darkness practically shimmers without the alcoholic haze she was putting on not two minutes ago. Bimbo to fighter in seconds—fuck if my dick doesn't take immediate notice of the change.

I keep my tone bored. "Is this some kind of game I don't understand, Isabelle?"

"Are you not having fun?" she asks, tilting her head slightly to the side. "You prefer the drunk young girl that lets you take her home?"

The scowl that overtakes my face isn't for being tricked; it's for her stupid fucking plan.

"Is this you playing vigilante? Do you know how dangerous that is?" She rolls her eyes as if I'm being unreasonable, while *she's* the one that lured a grown man she knows nothing about to her car. Even with a gun, there are a million ways this could've gone wrong for her.

"Should we not be less concerned with *my* actions and more about *yours*?" she says.

"Don't put yourself in danger," I growl at her. We've watched over her her whole life to ensure she's not, and she walks into it willingly?

"Isn't that what you're for?" She stares straight at me, and I realize she's smarter than I ever gave her credit for. "Or that's what I assumed, but now you're taking little old me, underage and drunk, home," she muses.

I know how this looks, and if it wasn't me she was holding a gun to, I'd applaud the way she was looking out for herself—but it is me. Not to mention how fucking dangerous this situation is for her.

Knowing she could do this to someone else—anyone else—and the outcome be wholly different has my skin crawling. I step into her, the barrel pressing into my chest as she hardens her jaw, her eyes like steel on my face, and fuck me if that look doesn't go straight to my dick. Still, she doesn't back down.

"Why do you all follow me?" she asks.

"How long have you known?" I counter.

"I asked first."

"Then I guess we're both shit out of luck."

"I'll call the police," she warns, not expecting the smirk that tilts my lips.

"No you won't," I say cockily, and her lips part in outrage. "If you were going to, you would have long before today. You're sulking because I'm not telling you what you're demanding to know."

Her brows drop in anger as I belittle her fight. "I deserve to know."

"Trust me, you don't want to, because if you realized who the fuck you're threatening with a gun right now, you'd regret it."

She tightens her grip on the handle, refusing to show any weakness, and I'm pretty sure I'm leaking pre-cum like a fucking virgin. "I sincerely doubt that."

My teeth grind against each other as I clench my jaw, my hands flexing as I get the overwhelming urge to touch her. Things would be so much easier if she was the vapid bimbo she pretended to be, rather than the girl demanding her answers with a gun trained on me like a fantasy come to life. *Fuck.*

"Go home," I say dismissively, as if she's not fucking up my every feeling and thought, then I turn and walk away before she can tear her angry eyes from mine and read exactly who I am from my patch.

"Hey!" she calls in outrage, but I ignore her as I hop onto my bike and the engine comes to life. I pull out onto the road, leaving her behind.

Or so she thinks.

Instead, I pull over a block away and call in reinforcements to make sure she does as I say and gets away from the bar.

CHAPTER FOUR

Isabelle

He turns, taking those icy blue eyes away from me, and it pisses me off. Almost as much as when he walks away without a care in the world, as if there isn't a loaded gun pointed at him. His confident gait and my intrusive thoughts call for me to shoot the cocky fucker. As I lower the weapon to my side with a disgruntled sigh, I take in his jacket.

The dark leather looks like it was tailored to fit him. It's old, but well kept. Form-fitting over his large frame, but not tight. But it's the stitching on the back that holds my attention, my eyes drawn to it the instant I register it. There's a guy wearing a leather jacket and jeans, much like Axle is now, except he has his face hidden by a metal helmet as he sits astride a motorbike. Except it's not just any guy—a shield sits propped against the wheel, and a sword is held aloft in one hand. It's a knight.

I stare until he's too far for me to see the image properly and then watch as he climbs onto a motorbike and peels away from the bar, the roar of his engine giving me goosebumps. I guess the music from the bar covered his arrival. I don't blink until he disappears from view, the sound fading with him. Anger simmers in my veins, along with a million other emotions I'm not practiced enough with recently to decipher. Most importantly, I feel *alive*. I don't want this feeling to end.

Stashing my gun back under my passenger seat, I lock the car and strut determinedly back to the bar. He'd interrupted my drinking, after all. I use the main entrance this time, but as I step inside, the bartender gives me his full attention and folds his arms.

"You can't be here, girl."

"What? I was just in here!" He didn't seem to care about having me inside or even serving me alcohol half an hour ago.

"That was then," he says, with a shake of his head.

"But—"

"You heard him." I spin to see the man the voice belongs to, ready to tear him a new asshole for interfering, but my words get stuck in my throat when I see who it is.

One.

I roll my eyes so hard I nearly strain something.

"Is this some kind of teleporting machine? Do I summon one of you by stepping inside?"

He doesn't answer, just continues watching me with that infuriating smirk that reminds me of Seven. I'd love to wipe it off both their faces. I sigh and storm past him, but he follows me, calling out as I reach my car. "Don't be mad."

With my hand on the door, I turn to face him as he pushes his pale hair out of his eyes. "Why would I be mad?"

"You're not?" he asks, confusion crossing his face. His eyes are denim blue, completing the boy-next-door vibe he has going for him, but I'm pretty sure he's not innocent.

"Oh no, I definitely am," I clarify stubbornly, "I'm just wondering if you know why."

He smiles at that, but there's something akin to sadness lingering in his tone when he speaks. "I knew you'd be a spitfire."

"Then you have me at a disadvantage, because I know absolutely nothing about you." I narrow my eyes at him.

"I know," he says, almost apologetically. His smile turns weary as he walks back to climb onto his bike, showing me the same emblem on his jacket as Axle. He sits there and waits, though, until I pull away, and then the loud rumble from his bike follows me. Even once I lose him in my rearview mirror, I can still hear the steady roar of his bike's engine. I can't see him, but he's not far.

Finally, I head to the hill, resigned to spending the rest of my day in a slump, redrawing the view I must have committed to memory a thousand times by now and yet still can't draw without seeing it in front of me.

Surprisingly, though, the moment I pull out my pencils, my hands are itching to move across the paper, the view far from my mind. I let them lead the way, sketching something from memory for the first time in years.

A bike rears out of the page, with a knight confidently lounging on top, knuckles clenched around the handle of a sword. My hand is cramping by the time I have the shading right—the whole image mainly dark, with highlights glinting off the metal for contrast. Blowing the excess graphite off, I lean back, stretching the muscles of my back out as much as possible after being hunched over in the car seat for so long.

My gaze lingers on the finished product for a long moment before I close the sketchpad with a sigh and drop it on the passenger seat. It's the first drawing I haven't torn into tiny pieces and given to the wind in longer than I can remember.

When I pull up at the house a little while later, Gary's car on the drive is the first thing I notice. The pit in my stomach deepens, and I can only hope for them both to be black-out drunk, which would allow me to sneak past, but the moment I enter, I know the wish is fruitless.

"Where the fuck have you been?" he demands, from where he's pouring another drink in the open kitchen to my right. My aunt is nowhere to be seen, but it normally doesn't take her long to join in.

"I went for a drive."

"Just a drive? Looking like that?" he asks disbelievingly as he makes his way toward where I hover in the doorway, wishing I could turn around and get back into my car.

"Like what?" I ask, rolling my eyes as I close the door behind me.

"Like a two-bit whore," he spits, his eyes blazing. Fuck knows what has him so angry, but no one speaks to me like that. I'm in shorts and a slightly cropped tee, for fuck's sake.

"Fuck yo—"

His hand lashes out, halting my speech as my head whips to the side. The vicious crack of his skin against mine rings in my ear, and I stumble back against the door before the blistering sting starts to burn. That fucker.

My anger simmers to a boiling point inside, but I force it down. There's no point in fighting against him. He's drunk and a lot bigger than I am, his bulky frame putting me at a disadvantage. Instead, I steady myself and make for the stairway to my left, but he doesn't like that either.

"Don't ignore me," he calls, as I climb them two at a time. "You think you can go sleeping around, then come back and think you're better than me?" Hearing his footsteps behind me, I try to quicken my pace. If I can just get to my room—

His hand snatches at mine as I reach the top, tugging me around to face his aggressive scowl. He sways dangerously but doesn't seem to notice, his face a snarling red mess. "You're old enough to give it up now, huh?" He pushes me to sit and covers my body with his before I can push him away, crushing me against the last couple of steps, my back bent over the landing.

"Get. Off!" I grit out, shoving against his immovable weight, but he chuckles darkly. I was expecting the hit—maybe another one or two—but I wasn't expecting this. He's normally full of vile things to shout at me, but I have no idea what's made today so different.

"Maybe you're just old enough for me to take it," he says with a sneer.

The words are like ice through my veins, and I flail desperately. He pulls away slightly, reaching for his belt buckle, and my panic skyrockets. There's no way this is happening.

He grabs for my thrashing limbs as my feet connect with his shins, my hands punching at his torso within the limited room I have. He stumbles back from a knee landing near his groin, and I think I have enough room to spin and scramble away from him, but still, his sole focus is getting to me—getting me. He's leaning back too far, too close to the edge, and his feet fight for purchase on the stairs, but he manages to snag my wrist and his grip doesn't falter. I manage one good kick, and then he topples back . . .

Everything moves in slow motion as his momentum pulls him over, and me with him. I'm not strong enough or heavy enough to counterbalance, and although I struggle against his hold, it's pointless. His eyes widen, his drunken brain finally realizing what's happening, but it's too late. We're already in the air.

He hits the stairs first, his body contorting grotesquely as I'm pulled over his head and the stairs rush to greet me. I screw my eyes shut as if somehow that will save me, and we fall, weightless then winded by the impact as we tumble and crash, one over the other, repeatedly down the stairs. I get a blur of the ground floor rushing toward us, then pain sears through me, and everything goes black.

CHAPTER FIVE

Isabelle

A soft hand over the top of my head makes me open my eyes slowly. When I see the eyes that are as familiar to me as my own looking down at me, so full of love, I choke out a sob. I must've made it to heaven after all.

"Dad," I whisper through my tears. "I missed you."

"You miss me, Belle. You can't stay." I'm too preoccupied with seeing him again to register his words.

"But—"

"No buts. You don't belong here. Not for a long time yet."

"Neither do you." He belongs with me. I try to grab for him, hold on tight enough to stay with him forever, but I can't seem to move.

"I'd die a million times over to keep you living. I wish you would."

"Would what?"

"Start living." His words are said gently, but his eyes are determined.

"I can't do it without you," I admit.

Suddenly, it really feels like I can't. Look at how it's gone downhill since he left. I have no real friends; no one who I love or who loves me in return. No home to feel safe in.

"You'll always have me," *he promises.*

"But you're not there. I need you to tell me how to do it without you."

"You already know. I taught you everything I could. You're an incredible girl, Belle. Please give life a chance again. For me." *That's a low blow, and he knows it works, if his small, lopsided smile is anything to go by. It highlights the crinkles around his eyes, and my chest aches. He gently cups my cheek.* "Thank you. Grab every opportunity with both hands, sweet girl. Everything happens for a reason."

"I love you, Dad." *He lays a soft kiss on my forehead as I close my eyes, trying to commit his touch to memory.*

"I love you, Belle."

Monotonous beeping makes me frown, and the world is blurry as I try to blink away the dampness in my eyes. Staring up at the plain white ceiling, I wonder what awaits me now, as realization and disappointment war for space inside me. I survived. *Damn.*

I take inventory of my body and feel a dull ache *everywhere*. I should probably be grateful that's all I feel, so maybe they've got me dosed up on something to stop the pain from getting worse. The door clicks open, and I strain to see who's there.

"Oh, hello! Nice to have you back with us." As she moves closer, I see a petite and friendly-looking nurse. She gives me an indulgent smile as she comes to my bedside, then slowly helps me rise to sitting. I look around at the room. There's not much to see—some comfortable looking chairs, a coffee table, and a TV. There's a used mug on the table, and I wonder who it belongs to. Who's been here at my bedside while I've been out.

"What happened?" I ask the nurse. What I actually mean is how did I get from the house to here? Did my aunt find me and drive me here? Doubtful; she doesn't give a shit. But perhaps the nurse thinks I've lost my memory, because she looks away and flicks awkwardly through a clipboard at the end of my bed before answering.

"You had a nasty fall." I know that's true. I remember the sickening feeling of flying, bracing for impact. Pain.

"But how did I get here?"

"The ambulance brought you in," she replies, as if that's obvious . . . which I guess it should've been. "Try and get some rest. The doctor will be in soon."

I want to quip that I've been resting for God knows how long already, but the dull ache starts to recede, and suddenly, I feel weightless and slip gently back into sleep.

Her screeching pierces through me, and if I thought I'd woken up in heaven before, this time, I'm definitely in hell.

"They said you were awake, you little bitch."

"Hi," I sigh, wondering what she's even doing here. I was sure I wouldn't see her until I went home.

"Don't *'hi'* me," she spits, leaning over the side and into my face. "It's *you* who deserves to be in a coma, not him."

"No, it's definitely him," I say, gritting my teeth. I didn't know he was, but I have not an ounce of sympathy for his predicament. "That sounds a lot like karma for someone trying to do what he was doing."

"Oh, please. You might think the little innocent act works, but not with me. He rejected you, so you pushed him down the stairs." My mouth gapes at her version of events, considering she wasn't even there. "And now you think you can take everything from us? Just you wait—"

She doesn't get to finish whatever riddle she's spewing before the same nurse as before is in the room, pulling her away from the bed.

"You're not supposed to be in here," she says sternly. My mind whirls with confusion and my head thumps. Snarling viciously at me, my aunt opens her mouth to say something more, but the nurse quickly ushers her out of the room, leaving me in silence for a moment. What is going on?

"How are you feeling?" the nurse asks kindly when she pops back in shortly after. I think it through, glancing down at myself before deciding I feel pretty good, all things considered.

"Not bad, thank you."

"I'm sorry to do this so soon, but the police want to talk to you. They weren't happy I didn't let them know you were awake last time." To her credit, she looks royally pissed that she has to tell me this at all.

"That's fine," I tell her. I've got nothing to hide, and the sooner it's over, the better. Maybe then they'll let me out of here. Although I have no idea where to call home now. It doesn't seem like Celia will be welcoming me back with open arms.

The nurse gives me a friendly pat on the arm before she leaves, and in less than a minute, two officers are taking her place in the room instead. They both look as young as me, honestly, but they seem nice enough as they introduce themselves and get started.

"Your uncle—"

"He's not my uncle." That won't stand. Can't have them thinking I'm related to the scum.

She nods in understanding, her eyes kind when she continues. "Gary is under investigation, although he is still unconscious."

"Good. He attacked me."

"You remember?"

"Yes, he—" Shivers pass over my skin when I think of what he tried to do, and words fail me. Verbalizing the act is way harder than I thought it would be. Thankfully, they let me off the hook, moving on without me confirming.

"We have the video from the foyer security camera. You disappear at the top of the stairs as it's focused on the front door, but the rest is quite clear."

I have no idea how my aunt has chosen to blame me if she's seen the footage—does she think I like a quick slap as foreplay?

"So, what do you need from me?"

"We know you've just come round, but we'd be grateful if you could come to the station once you're discharged to provide a formal statement?"

I nod, thankful I don't have to go through the details just yet. I've only been awake a couple of minutes, and I already feel drained. All I want to do is to curl up and lose myself to sleep.

"That's great, Isabelle," the female officer says. Thank you for your time."

"My aunt thinks it's my fault," I say, though it's pointless. I doubt they care, and I have no idea why I do. Not once has she acted like she liked me, let alone loved me, but it hurts to think that the only person I have in the world would turn on me so easily for such a piece of shit.

"She's been quite vocal," is all the officer says back.

"I'm surprised she's letting me be treated."

"That's not her decision."

I guess I'm technically an adult, but she is my guardian. There isn't anyone else who could have spoken on my behalf while I was unconscious.

"How long have I been out?"

"Three days. We'll let the nurse come back in to fill you in. Get some rest, okay? Please give us a call if you need anything from us." The other officer leaves a business card next to my bed, gives me a kind smile and a nod, and they exit swiftly. I sigh, my eyes locked on the ceiling. Just when I'd thought this May couldn't get any worse.

"How are you feeling?"

I turn to the door as the same nurse comes through again.

"I'm fine."

She gives me a knowing look, her years of training no doubt telling her my body is starting to ache again. Fiddling with the drip next to me, she stays silent.

"Three days, huh? What's wrong with me?"

"You were very lucky. You have some heavy bruising, but nothing was broken." Wow. I remember the way we tumbled down the stairs, rolling over the top of each other, and do feel lucky. Sounds like he got most of the injuries. *Good.* "Get some rest," she murmurs, and the world goes hazy again.

It's lunchtime two days later when they finally agree to let me go. I've made absolutely no headway on deciding what the hell to do once I'm released, but it's not like I can camp out in the hospital forever.

My aunt thankfully didn't make another appearance at my bedside, but I doubt I can avoid her forever, especially as my first stop has to be her home. Hopefully she's not in and I can grab some essentials and some cash, not that I have a lot of it. My phone, which was in my pocket, has a cracked screen but is still in working condition, so I can at least call a car when I'm outside and not have to hike all the way back.

The only clothes I have are the shorts and cropped tee I was admitted in, although the nice nurse did manage to find me some new underwear. Dressing quickly in them, I escape the suffocating room and head to the front desk. I start to stress about not being able to pay for my treatment, but clearly taking me off her insurance hadn't been on Celia's mind, because no one has come to my bedside demanding money from me so far. While I'm at the desk signing my discharge papers, I double-check with the clerk just in case.

"There's nothing for me to pay today?"

"No," he confirms. "Your husband's insurance is quite comprehensive."

My mouth drops open, spit lodging in the back of my throat as I almost choke at his words. Husband? I must be more loopy than I thought, because there's no way he actually said that. Right?

"My what?"

"Your husband," he repeats, a dreamy smile on his face as though I was married to Channing Tatum himself. I think he's the loopy one, actually . . . since he's clearly got me mixed up with someone else. I'm about to confirm my name with him when he nods toward the doors. "He's outside to collect you."

I finish up my paperwork with a flourish of my signature and then venture outside, rolling my eyes when I see my chariot awaiting. I stroll up to him as he lounges against the side of his bike, his playful eyes on me.

"Husband?"

"You can call me best friend," One offers with a smirk. "Or Kace, I guess." I get why the clerk was so moony now. He looks like a grungy Ken doll in his dark jeans and leather jacket, pale blond hair pushed away from his face.

"Whatever. Thanks, I guess, *Kace*. I'd rather a white lie than a huge medical bill." I guess it was kind of sweet to commit fraud to ensure I was covered. Maybe my aunt did refuse her insurance after all.

"There's no lie. You're officially a married woman." I don't even realize my mouth is slack until he gently nudges my chin with his helmet, closing it for me.

"Nooooo . . . I'm pretty sure I'm not, actually."

"Whatever you say, spitfire." He holds out the helmet for me to take, but I blink at it, my mind blank. What the hell is going on? "You ready for your answers?" he asks, waving the helmet at me to take, but I still don't. Taking it feels like I'm agreeing to something, and while I do want answers, I'm not sure getting on a bike with my so-called *husband* is the smartest idea. But then again, I apparently woke up married, so what else do I have to lose?

"That feels like a trick question," I grumble, but he continues grinning. My dad's words when I came to ring in my head. *Grab every opportunity with both hands, sweet girl. Everything happens for a reason.*

So, I reach out and take the helmet with both hands. "I can't believe you're expecting me to get on this thing," I say, as he climbs onto his motorbike and holds his hand out for me to get on behind him. "I've literally just left the hospital."

He grimaces. "I know, but I don't actually own a cage."

"Own what?" I ask, sure I heard him wrong. Why would he own a cage?

"A cage," he repeats, gesturing toward one of the many cars parked outside. "Four metal walls, trapped inside? Yeah, not for us. We don't drive cars. I'll be careful, promise."

Maybe I have a concussion. I must, as I find myself grumbling an agreement and climbing onto his bike without asking him who *us* is. If anything, I feel excited—way more than I probably should.

"Hold on tight." I do as he says, letting him guide my arms around his waist. He pats my hands condescendingly, like I'm an elderly relative, which makes me bristle. "Let's go home."

A flutter stirs inside of me at his words—apprehension with a side of wonder. I don't have a home—haven't since my dad died—but for some reason, I'm suddenly hopeful I might be about to find one.

CHAPTER SIX

AXLE

I'm nervous as all fucking hell waiting for her to turn up. I should've gone myself. I wanted to, but that wouldn't have been a good idea. I've barely slept since I got the call saying she was on the move again. She's not a late wanderer, so I sat and watched her tracker like a goddamn psychopath. I wanted to be ready to jump on my bike the second she stopped, to make sure she was fine with my own eyes.

I feel like that'll be a new obsession of mine.

Imagine my surprise when she did stop, in the *hospital*.

It's been headache after fucking headache since then, what with getting the papers done, making sure her aunt was kept away from her, and spending every minute I could with her as she lay unconscious, waiting for her to come round. I'm dead on my feet, but I can't stop now. It's like my brain is hardwired to be manic until she's here. I don't like it. I'm normally calm, rational, and logical.

Not the traits you'd normally associate with a biker, but being president means you can't be storming around without thinking, like the majority of us do. It comes with responsibilities, though they went out the window the moment I realized where she was. Since then, I've been stomping around like a bear with a bad tooth. I'm getting sick of myself; God knows what everyone else is thinking.

"Kace gone to get her?" Vaughn, my VP, calls out on his way over. I nod as he sits opposite me in the booth and drops another beer on the table, pushing it toward me. "You gonna chill the fuck out once she's here?" I take a drag of my beer, ignoring his question, and he scoffs a laugh. "Is it the big change of plan that's got you wired?"

The plan. The plan was always to keep her away from this. It's what Trey had wanted from the moment Isabelle's mom died. She was too young to even remember her life before that, so it was easy to extract her, keep this life separate. He had to step down as president, but he chose that for her.

We changed course once already—when Isabelle became an orphan. The *new* plan was to continue keeping an eye on her, but solo now, while she grew up with blood family and became an adult. Twenty-one was our end point. Now that's all fucked up again.

There was no contingency for if her only blood relative turned out to be an abusive cunt. Her aunt *was* the contingency. Being in a biker gang that runs the kind of shit we do, you always know death may be closer for us than a normal civilian, but knowing doesn't mean it's expected, or a lesser blow when it comes and you do lose someone.

"There's been too many changes to the plan."

"Well, why stress about all that now? Unless the whole fucking club goes down in a hail of gunfire, she'll be alright." Easier said than done.

"Of course she'll be alright." She's Trey's daughter. She's gonna be surrounded by people who loved her dad and who will love her too. But I don't want her to be *alright*. I want her to be settled. Happy.

"Is Kace breaking the news to her?"

"Which bit?" I hope she's not easily overwhelmed.

"You gonna tell her all of it?" His eyebrows rise in surprise, but I shake my head.

"She'll know her dad was a huge part of this MC, and she'll know she's now an ol' lady. Those are the only things she needs to know right now. Anything else isn't important."

"Okay. Clever idea of yours to marry her off," he says, before taking a large swig of his own beer.

"Didn't have many other options. Celia couldn't remain her guardian, could she?" He knows the reason I had Bishop expedite the documents, forged signature and all.

"Plus, it makes her off-limits."

My head snaps up so I can glare at him. "She's off-limits anyway. She's eighteen and Trey's daughter."

"Okay. Try and remember that, Prez."

"Fuck you," I grumble, but he grins back at me.

Vaughn calls to one of the club girls Kace is usually hanging around with over behind the bar. "Brianna, get over here."

She struts over to where I'm nursing my beer, and when he points to my lap, she drops the towel in her hands onto the table and straddles me. Everyone else is ignoring me except Vaughn, but she doesn't care as she grinds against me, not noticing the way my dick remains limp. She turns her face to mine, leaning in to kiss me, but I pull away.

This shit is doing nothing for me, yet she doesn't get the hint, pouting but continuing to roll her ass on my lap when Vaughn leaves, a chuckle following his exit. He knows I don't fuck around with the club girls, so whether he's fucking with me or trying to give me a distraction, he's at least amused himself.

Screwing my eyes shut, I think back to the last time I was hard. Deep brown eyes stared defiantly back at me, a gun held against my chest. I still feel the warmth of her arms through my fucking cut. What I wouldn't give to feel her on my skin, to feel hers. And just like that, I'm hard a-fucking-gain for this girl. It's just because I know I can't have her, can't cross that line with my best friend's daughter. That's why I can't stop thinking of what she'd feel like, what she'd taste like, what she'd sound like—it's the forbidden fruit.

These thoughts shouldn't be filling my mind. She's barely legal, if nothing else, but that's not stopped me from getting hard for her. Brianna, who, come to think of it, is probably not much older than Isabelle, must notice, as she rubs against me like a cat in fucking heat, which only pulls me away from my fantasy and ruins the whole thing. Good. I've got no business getting hard to thoughts of Isabelle.

The door slides open, and my eyes jerk up, focusing on the object of my obsession. She's here. My jaw tenses, and Brianna senses it, looking over her shoulder to see what's grabbed my attention. She tenses, too, but I barely pay any notice. Not now I have *her* eyes on me. They may be full of disgust as she takes in what's going on, but my dick doesn't seem to care. In fact, disregard from her turns me on more than a half-naked woman writhing on my dick, apparently.

She walks in with Kace, straight over to where I'm sitting. While he drops down opposite me, she remains standing, warily eyeing the seat next to him as he slides across the bench and pats the open space.

Her lip curls in disgust. "I'm pretty sure there's a risk of getting pregnant sitting here."

He laughs heartily, throwing his head back, and she rolls her eyes.

"Sit," I say, my tone not brokering any arguments, but she folds her arms and raises a brow.

"You can sit on my lap if you need a barrier," Kace teases, wagging his brows at her. "Let me protect you." I just about suppress my growl.

"Eurgh," she says with a mock shiver. "Stop giving me the ick."

He grins, unashamed, but before she can do anything crazy like take him up on his offer, I throw the towel down onto the empty seat.

"I said sit." She narrows her eyes, but I don't break my glare until she finally fiddles with the material and drops her ass down on the edge. "It won't bite you."

"I'm sorry, I'm having a hard time taking all of this seriously," she says, with a wave of her hand at Brianna on my lap. I'd all but forgotten she was there.

"Fuck off," I say, pushing her to the side. I feel bad being so short with her, especially as I wouldn't usually be, but she climbs off gracefully and hurries back to the bar now she's been dismissed. "Are we *serious* enough for you now?"

"*We* are nothing. *You* are a pig," she counters.

I rest my forearms on the table between us, leaning into her. "*I* am the president of this club, and you will show me respect."

She balks slightly at that information but straightens her shoulders anyway. "I'll show respect to those who earn it and no one else."

"Spitfire, I'm gonna need you to rein it in just a little bit," Kace says gently, placing a hand on her arm. Spitfire?! She looks at him disbelievingly, and he shrugs. "This is a motorcycle club. I know that probably means little to you, but there are rules. I would never hurt a pretty little hair on your head, but I'm not the prez. If the others hear you talking to him like that, they'll demand retribution." She scoffs at his explanation, and I raise a brow at her.

"That's fine. I don't want to stay at this archaic fucking place anyway," she hisses, moving to stand, but I reach across the table, dropping my hand against her before she can get anywhere. I swear there's a spark of electricity that runs through my palm as it lands on the soft skin of her arm, warm under my touch. Is she soft and warm everywhere?

"Where are you gonna go?" It's a low blow, and the flash of realization with the defiance in her eyes makes me feel like shit. "Not being a bitch in front of people is a small price to pay for having somewhere to live."

"You're not listening to me. I don't *want* to live here."

My hand is still on her, even though she's not running right now, and I snatch it back, hating the way my body reacts to the one person it shouldn't. "Tough. Your husband is your guardian. This is where you're staying."

"Stop with the husband shit. The hospital bought it already, didn't they?"

"They bought it 'cause it's true."

She looks from me to Kace, who shrugs his shoulders. "I told you that already."

"Yeah, but—"

"Hey, it's Little T!"

Rider distracts her from her questions, and she turns to look up at him with a frown before recognition flashes across her face.

"My name's Isabelle," she says in confusion.

"I like Little T."

"Fine, *Four*," she replies with an arched brow.

"Four what?"

She shrugs. "That's your nickname."

"For the amount of blow jobs you wanna give—"

My fist shoots out to hit him straight in the dick before his question has even finished. He crumples between us as she watches me, a groan coming through his parted lips, and Kace cackles next to her.

"Rider hit on her already, huh?" Vaughn asks as he toes a fetal Rider out of the way.

"Three," she says as she looks at him. He frowns slightly down at her, but his smile is friendly.

"Hey, Little T. I'm Vaughn."

"Don't call her that." "Don't call me that."

I can feel her eyes on me after we both speak at the same time.

"What does it even mean?" she continues when I keep my gaze on Vaughn, avoiding those eyes.

"Little Trey."

CHAPTER SEVEN

Isabelle

It turns out when I'm feeling overwhelmed and out of my depth after being pulled down the stairs and nearly sexually assaulted, waking up in the hospital, and finally being released only to find out I might possibly be married to someone in an MC who's been following me for years and wants me to live with a bunch of strangers who seem to already know me, the thing to tip me over the edge is the mention of my dead dad's name.

My breaths come quicker as I hurriedly leave the room, leaving them all blinking after me. My chest is tight and my head full of static. I can't be here right now. It's too much. I rush through the parking lot but don't get far before Kace catches up to me.

"Hey, spitfire, where you going?" he asks, his voice light.

"I just need some space," I say, trying to keep my voice even and not show him how much I'm affected.

"Space where?" he asks, stepping in front of me so I have to stop. I look at his chin while I speak, not trusting myself to meet anyone's eyes while the swirl of panic is still growing in my chest.

"I don't know! The woods?" We rode alongside the woods all the way down the road until we pulled into this lot, and they're still opposite us now, just across the road. They look like the perfect place to have a tiny breakdown.

"I dun—" He stops talking as he looks over my shoulder, but then steps out of my way and waves at the guy on the gate to let me pass without issue. Grateful for the time alone, I hurry across the road and lose myself in the trees.

The temperature drops a couple of degrees as I step under the cover of the branches and leaves, and I make my way through until I find a decent space far enough from the edge that I can't see the intimidating enclosure. If I can't see them; they can't see me. Just what I want. But as I stop, the sound of snapping twigs and crunching leaves that was coming from under my feet carries on from behind me.

"You said I could have space!" But it's not Kace's voice that comes from behind me.

"Kace doesn't make the decisions around here."

I start pacing a hole in the mud and debris, not able to stand still for more than a moment or calm my brain. I don't even know what I'm freaking out about. Every thought is flying around at once and I can't grab on to any. "Just calm the fuck down," he says with a sigh, as if I'm acting like a child. I spin to face Axle with a scowl. I'm already irrationally pissed at him for how he was when I arrived, and he's not exactly warming me to him right now.

"Oh, *thanks*, I didn't think of that," I say, sarcasm dripping from every word.

"You're overreacting." I resume my pacing, glaring at him as he stares right back, his pale blue eyes keeping me focused on him.

"Actually, I think I'm *under*reacting, seeing as I feel like I know nothing right now." I count out the list on my fingers. "How have I woken up married? How does everyone know who I am? How do they all know my dad? Why were you all staying away before, watching but not doing anything? Who are you all? Where do I go if I don't stay? What's happening with the police? What about my stuff?" I'm running out of fingers when he interrupts me.

"Pick one." I go to argue but he talks over me. "One, Isabelle."

I really wish he wouldn't say my name like that. It's all too comforting and distracting as his rich tone vibrates through me, and I'm supposed to be stressing over here. I sit myself down where I'm standing with a huff, the moss and leaves softer underneath me than I thought, and he waits while I decide.

Which is the most important right now?

The curiosity might be burning up inside me to know everything about these guys, but the immediate need is somewhere to stay . . . and if I'm safe here, I guess. I can feel myself flagging already with everything going on, and if I need to find somewhere else, then I'd rather do that sooner than later. It's weird to be questioning my safety with them after all these years of accepting intrinsically that they were there for that, but I'm not some naive six-year-old anymore.

There's a difference between believing seven men were protecting you from afar for whatever reason, and agreeing to stay with any of them. Especially after they've already done a kind of shitty job of it.

I lay back, looking up at the canopy as I think. It's beautiful here. We're only a hundred or so feet from a main road, but we could be in the middle of the countryside. The dappled light fights through the leaves and turns the world a million different shades of green.

I let out a breath that feels like it empties my lungs, and he sits next to me, not seeming to care that it's on the ground. I guess presidents of MCs don't mind that kind of shit.

"How does everyone know who I am?" I ask.

"Eesh. Big one to pick," he says, running his hand over his cropped hair. It looks like it's just on the edge between prickly and soft.

"I know you've been following me."

He turns his head to look down at me with a cocked brow. "Yeah, I gathered that."

"I recognize Four and Three." I really should find out their names. If I decide to stay, that is. "And Kace, obviously. Why?"

"Keeping an eye on you," he says, but that doesn't answer my question.

"Why?"

"To make sure you're okay."

"Well, what a great job you did of that." I regret it the second I see him flinch as if I've hit him. I can see his teeth clench as a muscle in the side of his face tenses.

"We didn't know."

Didn't know that I hated it there almost as much as my aunt seemed to hate me? Didn't know Gary was such a complete piece of shit? Shouldn't they have known if they were supposed to make sure I was okay? Although, if my teachers and friends didn't notice the bruises I covered up so well, how could I expect them to?

"Then what was the point?" I ask, but he doesn't answer, his elbows resting on his knees as he stares out into the clearing. We sit there for a long moment, the breeze in the branches and the passing cars that feel so far away the only sounds between us. By the time he acknowledges me again, he has a small smile on his face. I narrow my eyes suspiciously at him.

"You calmed down," he states simply, and it takes me a second to realize he's right. Without even noticing it was happening, he got me talking and thinking without feeling overwhelmed.

"You tricked me," I accuse halfheartedly.

"I focused you."

I blink up at him, knowing he's right as his lips twist as if he's trying to fight a smile. When Kace was too nice and placid, Axle came barreling in and calmed me down by riling me up; giving me something to focus on that wasn't everything threatening to drown me.

He keeps his gaze locked on mine, his eyes searching for something. I don't know what, but I suddenly want to give it to him, and that's terrifying. His eyes start to darken, and my skin tingles. I blink out of my stupor, focusing my gaze back on the safe leaves above.

"So, how do you all know me?" I ask again.

"Because we knew your dad." I'm expecting him to mention him now, so my heart doesn't give the huge lurch it did earlier. Just a painful little jolt. I swallow down my sorrow and wait for him to continue. "He was club president a long time ago." I don't know much about an MC, but even I can tell the president is pretty big news.

"Before I was born?"

"Yeah, and after."

My brows knit together in a frown. "When did he stop being president?"

"When it came down to a choice between attending to the needs of the club or spending time with you."

My chest squeezes painfully, although I don't question the truth of it for a second. That sounds exactly like something my dad would do.

"And when did he leave the club?"

"He didn't."

"Of course he did. I would've known—"

"Would you?" His voice holds no snark or condescension. He's simply asking the question, one we both know the answer to.

Dad died when I was fourteen. I had no way of knowing what he was doing while I was at school or at a friend's house. He made sure that I knew nothing of this, but why?

Why keep this side of him so far removed from me?

I sit up, not brave enough to turn to face Axle. "Who are you?"

He doesn't reply straight away, and I barely dare to breathe as I feel his fingers gently raking through my ponytail. I didn't even think of the fact that there's probably half the forest floor in there, but I hold myself still while he carefully removes it, loving his soft touch. I have the urge to lay back into his lap and let him carry on. Thankfully, his hand falls heavily back to his lap before I can embarrass myself.

"We're the Knights of Mayhem."

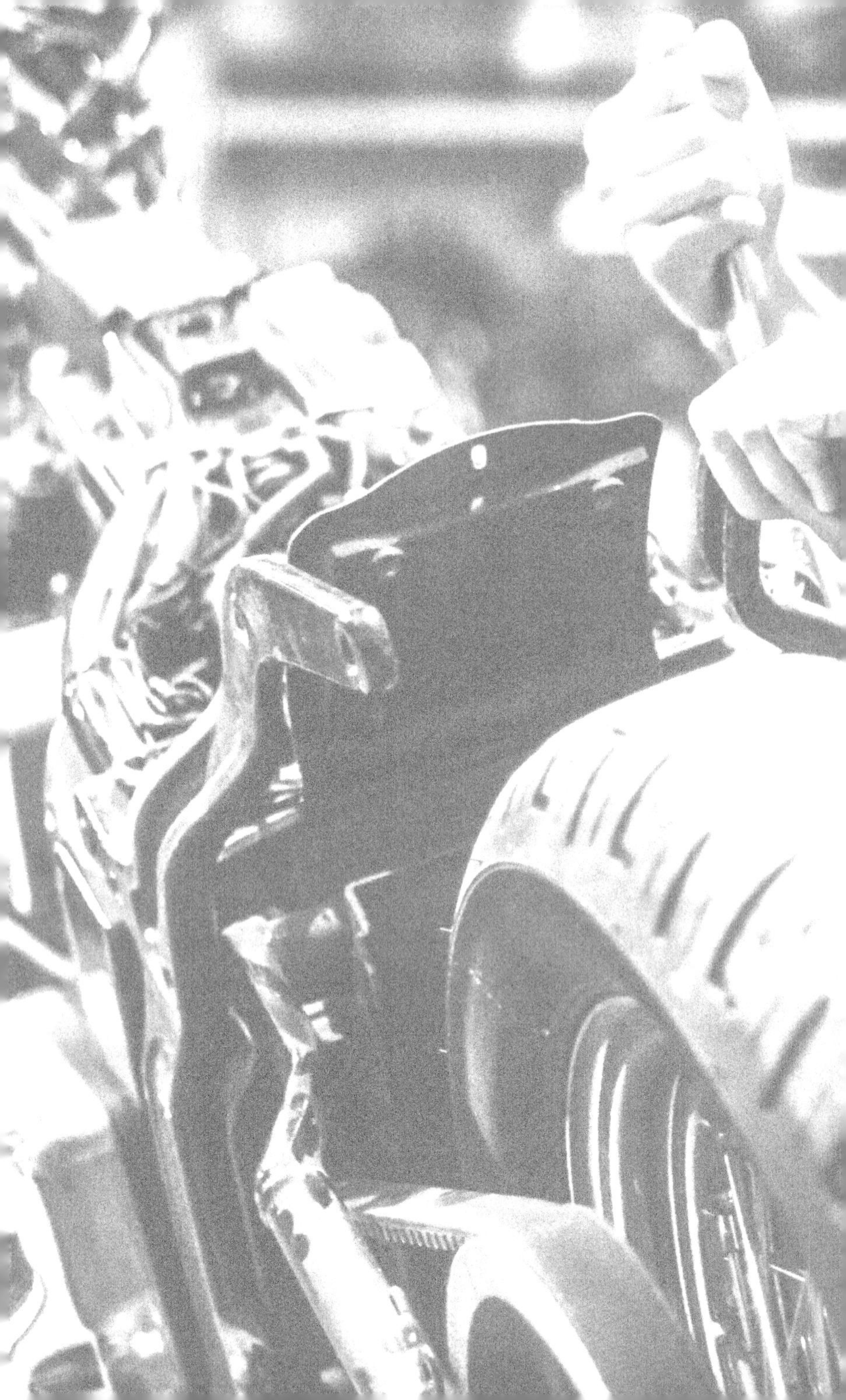

CHAPTER EIGHT

Axle

"Is that supposed to mean something to me?"

Of course she's unimpressed. I watch the side of her face as she looks down at the ground, her hair up in a ponytail on top of her head, unable to shield her from view. Trailing her finger in the debris in front of her crossed legs, I watch her shoulders lift slightly with every breath as she waits for my answer.

"No, probably not. Your dad kept you away from it for a reason."

"Which was?"

I think back to all the conversations Trey and I used to have about it—both of us new fathers and so young—then years later, when we were trying to run a club. How many times I tried to convince him it could be done. How hard I tried to keep him as president. Even being so young, he was made for that role.

"I guess he didn't think it was the best place to raise a kid." Shrugging, I try to keep my tone neutral, but the moment she spins to face me, her eyes questioning, I know I've failed.

"You don't agree?"

"My son is a biker, so obviously not."

"Who?" she asks, tilting her head curiously.

"Kace."

"Kace is your son?" Her eyebrows jump in surprise, and she hums to herself for a beat before turning back to the trees. "Wouldn't have guessed that. You don't look alike." We both have light hair, but our eyes are on opposite ends of the blue spectrum, and facially, we're not similar.

"No. He looks like his mom."

"She a biker too?"

"No." She could be, I guess. I haven't heard from her since she ran when I found her shooting up in front of our six-month-old baby.

She turns to look at me over her shoulder again, curiosity filling her dark eyes, but I offer nothing further, instead taking the opportunity to study her face. She's stunning. She doesn't take after her dad either, thank God. Ain't nothing pretty about Trey. Nah. Her dark, ebony eyes, sharp cheekbones, and round lips are nothing like him. The silver hair definitely is not, but neither is her natural dirty blonde.

She's watching me just as closely as I am her, and she sits there well within my reach, but when her eyes flick to my lips, I break the connection. Hardest fucking thing ever. Way harder than I'd have ever thought. Her eyes flick forward so she's looking into the woods and away from me.

She exhales a long, slow breath, closing her eyes for a moment. I get it. She's overwhelmed. It's a lot to learn, especially what must seem like lies and secrets her dad kept from her when she adored him so much. She lays back on the grass, staring up into the canopy again as if she's in a world of her own. She belongs there, a little platinum-haired imp amongst the green. I expect her to ask a million more questions, about the club and everything she mentioned earlier, but she doesn't.

"What am I supposed to do now?"

She asks it almost rhetorically. She doesn't need or want someone to tell her what to do—she's asking herself out loud. I could give her options—could tell her there's no fucking way she's going anywhere anyway, so it's irrelevant—but I won't.

Instead, I let her sit with her thoughts, offering her silent companionship. I force the president in me to the front. I've never wanted to be the guy that shouts over everyone and dictates; I want them to feel respected and evolve on their own. But it's different with Isabelle. With her, all I want is to wrap her up and take the safe road, keep her shielded from the hardships of life.

Sitting here, pretending to let her make her own decisions, makes me itchy. What if she tries to make the wrong one? I know I can't keep her here, locked away in the clubhouse, but fuck, I really want to. Just 'cause she's so young and part of the family, right?

But she was raised by Trey, and she's no wallflower. She rolls her face to the side and looks up at me. The sunlight peeking through the leaves reflects in her eyes, making them look lighter.

"What was your plan?" I don't know which one she means. When Trey died and we were keeping an eye on her, or now that she's here? She must note the confusion on my face. "When Kace picked me up. What was the plan?"

"To have you stay with us."

"Why?"

"Where else is there?"

She turns her face back, trying to hide her wince, but I catch it and feel like shit. I'm not used to mincing my words. I may try to be logical and inclusive, but I've never *had* to be around here. I can say whatever comes to my mind in front of my guys and anyone at the clubhouse.

With Isabelle, though, it turns out I say the wrong stuff constantly, and I hate that my words hurt her. "I mean, is there anyone else you'd rather stay with?"

"Don't censor yourself. It's not your fault I'm alone." She lets out a sardonic laugh, but it doesn't hide the pain lacing her words.

"You're not. You've got us." My arms itch to pull her against me, offer her the comfort she so desperately needs.

"Do I?" She doesn't sound like she believes that for a second. I should've told her she's here because I want her to be, because she belongs here.

"You wanna stay at the clubhouse?"

"What's the clubhouse?" Her brow creases in confusion, but she doesn't look back at me, focusing up into the canopy.

"The hall you were just in inside the compound."

"People stay there? It's not just a bar?"

"It's a lot more than a bar. Some stay there, some have houses."

"I don't know," she says warily. I get it. I wouldn't want her staying someplace with a bunch of unknown guys either, but I know them. "What about Kace?"

"What about him?" A flash of irritation hits me at her asking about him. I've never once been jealous of my own son, but fuck, I might be right now. I should've gone to get her.

"Where does he stay?"

"At the clubhouse with whatever girl he falls asleep on top of." It's a shitty thing to say, I know that, but I don't care. Kace doesn't care for Isabelle in that way, and I need to make that clear to her before she goes getting any stupid ideas where my son is concerned. She isn't meant for him.

"I assume that'll change now we're married." She laughs humorlessly, clearly not assuming that at all.

"You believe us now?"

"God knows." She rubs at her eyes with her knuckles, then blinks back up into the sunlight with tired eyes.

"Come on, you should rest," I say, before standing and brushing the dirt off my jeans.

"But I have more questions," she says, looking up at me from the ground, where she hasn't moved.

"I'll answer one of the big ones a day," I bargain, knowing I have to give her something but not wanting to spill every secret yet. She looks quizzically at me until I hold a hand out to her. She zeros in on it for a long moment before reaching for it, and I pull her up gently. She sways slightly, wincing as she gets upright. "You okay?"

"I'm fine." I gesture in the direction of the compound, and she starts to walk quietly back. When we reach the edge of the road, she waits, staring across at the compound without blinking. "Am I safe here?"

"Absolutely." She turns her face to look at me, searching. Willing honesty. "For one, we don't do shit to kids or women."

She rolls her eyes at my answer, interrupting me. "I saw how you treated that girl."

Yeah, not my finest moment. "*That girl* does nothing she doesn't want to. Anyway, you're an ol' lady."

"Ol' lady?" she says with a wrinkle of her nose.

"Missus, wife, whatever you wanna call it. You're protected by your husband and your title."

"In return for what?"

"Your loyalty." She scoffs.

"And the other way around?" I don't answer. I couldn't explain how much she means to her husband if I tried right now. "What was two?"

"Two, you're Trey's daughter." Something I need to fucking remember. I respect that fucker way too much to be thinking the thoughts I think when I look at his barely legal daughter. She crosses the road at my words, though. Catching up to her, we walk through the gate, and I nod at the prospect. "Why do you walk away when someone talks about him?"

She stops in her tracks, spinning toward me with a scowl on her face. "I don't want to know about him from *you*, any of you. I want to remember him as mine and not a liar."

She starts to stomp away, but I grab her arm, tugging her flush to my chest. A sharp breath escapes her, her eyes widening at our closeness, and I purposefully don't linger on how good she feels pressed against me.

"He was not a liar. Trey was the best of us and a damn good president, so don't go spouting shit about him in front of us." Her eyes war between annoyance and guilt, but the first wins out when I continue. "We're not bad people."

"No. I'm sure you're lovely law-abiding citizens who respect women," she snarks.

"What would you prefer, going back to your aunt?"

Her mouth twists into a grimace, her hand pressing against my chest to push me away. I loosen my hold, letting her escape as my jaw clenches. I don't know why I keep taking these cheap shots with her. I just want her to agree to stay.

But she's scared—scared she'll have to go back there, scared of what comes next—and I'm an asshole for leaning into that, for preying on her fears. Before I can say anything to explain, to tell her I'm not a threat—that she's safe here, with me—she beats me to it.

"You know that day in the parking lot, with the gun . . ." she says, changing the subject, and I have to fight the grin that threatens to break across my lips at her next words, the fighter never far from the surface. "I know who you are now. I still don't regret it."

CHAPTER NINE

Isabelle

I wait for Axle to fire back with something else, maybe hold the threat of my aunt over my head again, but his lips twist into a barely concealed smile when I tell him I still don't regret holding a gun to his chest. If I was hoping for an argument, I'm clearly not going to get one—not now—as the tension bleeds out of his body. He taps a finger to the side of his chest, and my mouth drops open as I take it in. A patch, sewn into the leather like the one on his back but much smaller. It's of a knight's shield, Knights of Mayhem through the center, with his name curved around the top and president around the bottom.

"And here I was thinking you were observant." Yeah, okay, fair . . . but I've been kind of overwhelmed. "Come on, let's get you settled."

He starts toward the main building, and there's not much to do except follow. I'm not thrilled to be staying with a bunch of strange men, but as Axle keeps reminding me, the alternative isn't exactly promising.

I take a look around the lot—or "compound," as Axle called it—as we walk, but it's pretty uninspiring. There's the huge building in front of us, the clubhouse, and a bunch of outbuildings that look like glorified sheds, plus what must be some kind of garage. The front is open, and there's plenty of engine parts laying around, a few motorcycles inside . . . Other than that, it's the car park and the high metal gate that encloses everything. But it's the parking lot full of bikes that keeps pulling my attention. I've seen motorbikes before, of course, although I rarely saw my knights on theirs through the years. Not enough to notice a pattern, anyway. But now, up close, I can see most of the bikes here are customized—some with names, others with images—and they intrigue me. I don't get to see much as I'm led through, but I'd love to take a closer look sometime.

Axle steps up to the large double doors, pulling one open and holding it for me to step through. I do, and he follows before leading me through the throng again. It's still pretty busy. Clearly not a lot to do at three on a weekday afternoon around here. It makes me wonder what kind of life this would be for a kid, and if that's part of the reason my dad kept me away. This place doesn't exactly scream child friendly.

The room is massive and holds different areas, but they all seem made for adults. A bar with stools lines one side of the room, booths line the opposite wall, and pool tables, well-worn sofas, and small mismatched tables and chairs fill the space between.

I keep my head down, chewing my lip as people call out hi and Axle acknowledges them all with a nod. I follow him to the back corner, where he opens another door that leads to a staircase.

"All of the rooms are up here," he explains as we climb.

"How many are there?"

"Twelve."

"It's got a real commune vibe," I mutter, but he ignores my snarky comment and leads me right to the end of the corridor, past all the other nondescript wooden doors.

"You can have this one."

"Are the others all full?" I ask, not seeing or hearing anyone else up here.

"No. But this room isn't a sharer, and it means no one has to pass yours to get to theirs, so you should be disturbed least."

My brows rise at his thoughtfulness. "Apart from that one," I say, nodding to the only door further along than mine, if only by about two meters, on the opposite side of the hallway.

"That's mine," he tells me, and I have nothing to say to that, especially as everything in me tingles at the thought of being so close to him, so I push the door open instead.

As I walk in, it's like walking into any standard hostel room across the country. There is a double bed with a small table and a chest of drawers next to it, and that completes the whole room. A window next to the bed lets in lots of natural light, brightening the cream bedroom, and another door sits on the corner, so I wander over and look out onto a whole lot of grass.

"There's a bathroom in here, too, so you won't need to share," he says from behind me. I turn to find him closer than I thought, leaning on the second doorframe like a freaking model as he opens it up to show the small toilet, shower, and sink. Then he nods behind me. "The view isn't exactly inspiring, but it's better than overlooking the pit."

I don't turn to look at it again, my eyes flicking up and down his frame completely against my intentions, but he doesn't seem to notice. I swallow and try to focus on anything other than him. "The pit?"

"Yeah. You'll probably see it later. Knox has gone to get your stuff."

"From my aunt's?" My eyes snap to his in alarm, and I chew my lip reflexively. I'm not sure who Knox is, but now that I'm free of her, I find I don't want Celia to know where I am.

"Yeah. Chill. It'll be fine." He reaches out to hold my chin before tugging my lip free with his thumb, and I try to remember how to breathe. "He's just grabbing whatever is in your room, but if anything's missing, we can go back or replace it."

"Okay," I say weakly, and his face hardens as he steps back, dropping his hold on my face.

"I've got some shit to do, but I'll see you at dinner. Weather's good, so it'll be in the pit at seven." He's gone before I can ask him what any of that means.

The air returns to the room following his exit, and I shake my head at my idiocy. I do not have the time to have a stupid crush right now. I've got to figure out my living situation, college, money—oh, and my freaking *husband*. So, this is it. My new space for the foreseeable future, however long that might be. I take in the room once more, and a great sigh escapes me.

Home sweet home.

Seeing as I have nothing to unpack just yet, I make my way to the door. Might as well explore this place and get to know my new surroundings. Maybe then I'll feel more grounded. As I pull the door closed behind me, I wish there was a lock before remembering I have literally nothing in there for anyone to steal anyway. As I make my way down the hallway, I resist the urge to peek into the other rooms, assuming they'll all look the same as mine, and head back down the stairs.

I was kind of hoping to avoid the main room, but it appears as if you have to go through it to get anywhere else. My hope of sliding through unnoticed is thwarted the second I step into the room and someone yells "Little T!" There's a huff immediately after, and I smile at the thought of someone hitting Rider for calling me what I've already requested he not.

"Spitfire, over here!" I relax slightly at the sound of Kace's voice. He's sitting in the same booth as earlier, and as I make my way over to him, I'm surprised to notice a few kids sitting at the tables that were empty only twenty minutes ago. They must be anywhere from five to eleven years old, and it looks as if they're doing homework . . .

I find Kace with a couple of other guys, including Vaughn—Three—who I recognize. His dark hair that matches the full beard is pulled back in a bun, and he sits a little straighter than the others as he smiles at me. I make a point to read his patch now that I notice them. Vaughn, Vice President. Rider is obviously here too. Treasurer. Hmm, I wouldn't have guessed that. He's shorter than most of the others and has a shaved head—he'd be the one you'd assume was a thug. It's funny that he seems to be the joker of the bunch. They all shuffle round as I take the spare space at the end, noticing another guy I've never seen before who ends up opposite me, but I can't read his patch with his arm slung up on the back of the booth. "How's it going?" he asks.

"It's going, I guess. I was just gonna explore a bit."

"Oh, yeah?" Kace says. "There's not much other than here and the pit." He shrugs, but there seemed to be a lot more than that when I walked through the parking lot. Maybe he just doesn't want me exploring it.

"Gonna introduce me to the gorgeous addition?" the new guy asks before I can ask what the pit is. It really sounds like somewhere you'd keep prisoners, but I doubt they'd all be mentioning it so casually—or that we'd be eating dinner there—if that were the case. The new guy looks a little older than me, I'd guess, with jet-black hair and a lip piercing that he uses his tongue to play with as he smirks. He looks like he belongs in a rock band. Kace rolls his eyes, but his smirk lifts into a wide grin as he shakes his head at the guy.

"That's Jag. You'll learn to tolerate him . . . I hope."

"You hope?"

"This face is too pretty to be getting slapped, darling," Jag says, in a smug but friendly tone. He doesn't seem leery, just way overconfident, although I'm sure when you look like that, the girls would inflate your ego big time.

"I beg to differ."

They all chuckle, even Jag, and I relax a little, warming to him instantly. He feels easy to be around, like Kace. Which is a good thing, I guess, because you can tell immediately how close they are. There's a real camaraderie feel running through all the guys I've met so far, and I can't decide whether it's welcoming or isolating, but Kace and Jag especially so.

"Another round?" Rider asks, shuffling off the other end and standing. They all nod, and he looks at me expectantly, his brow raised.

"Just a water, please," I request with a small smile.

"Gonna need to turn you into a proper ol' lady soon, Li—" He reflexively covers his crotch before he finishes the nickname, which makes me laugh despite the reminder of the whole "married" thing.

"Still just water, thanks, Four," I say primly, and he heads over to the bar.

"What are the numbers all about?" Vaughn asks. He takes a long drink of his beer, and my cheeks heat as everyone turns to look at me.

"Do I get one?" Jag asks with a wink, and Kace scoffs.

"Dude, she's an ol' lady!" Something flickers over Jag's easygoing expression, his smile becoming strained for a second before he schools his face.

"They're not a big deal," I mumble, suddenly feeling childish for naming the bikers that followed me around. Thankfully, before they can push the issue, the doors open, pulling their attention from me.

"Hey, how'd it go?" Vaughn calls over my head, and I turn to see a mountain of a man coming toward me. Two. I nearly cower. Even having seen him before, it's pretty scary seeing someone that size barreling toward you. Paired with his blank expression, I almost want to lean back into Kace.

"Fine. I think I got everything." His voice is deep and gravelly, and for some reason, he says the second part of that sentence to me, while I blink up at him in confusion. Eventually, he holds up three huge bags in his one meaty hand, and I recognize them.

"Oh!" I say, jumping up to take them from him. This must be Knox. "Thank you!" He moves them out of my grasp.

"Where do you want them?"

"Erm, I'm at the end of the hall." He nods without saying anything else and then marches off toward the stairs. I'm not sure whether to follow him or not, so I sway awkwardly next to the table.

"You need a hand unpacking? I'm great at sorting underwear drawers," Jag says, wagging his brows at me. Kace leans over the table and punches him in the arm, but I flush anyway, registering how Knox has just *packed* that underwear drawer.

"Thanks, but I think I can manage."

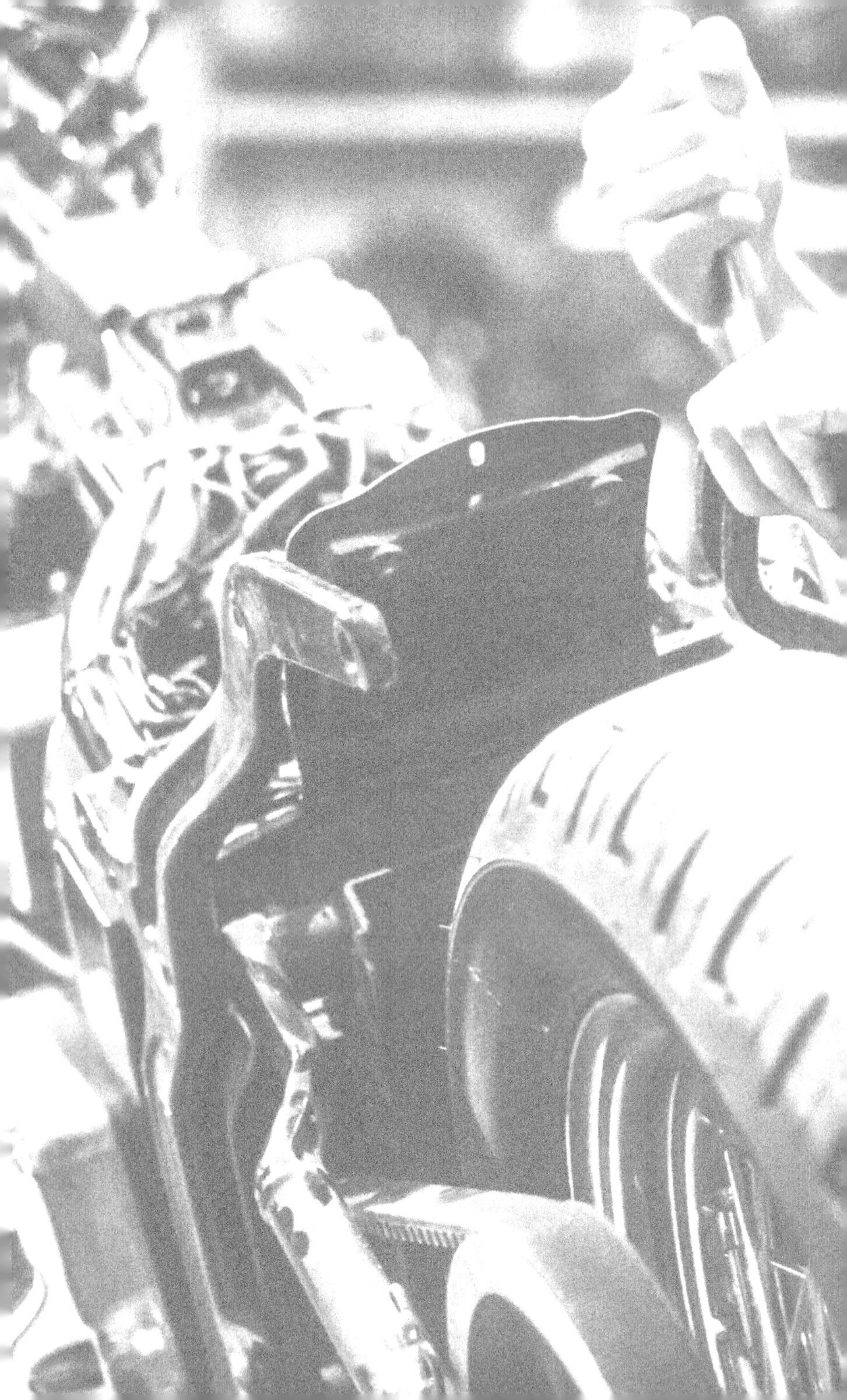

CHAPTER TEN

AXLE

A knock on the metal door pulls my attention from the bike in front of me to the open entrance of the garage. I'd jumped into working on the bike, my favorite way to try to keep myself busy, and hadn't even noticed Knox approaching, but now he fills the doorway.

"You got her stuff?" There's not a mark on him, but that doesn't mean everything went swimmingly. Knox often comes out of confrontations unscathed, regardless of how much blood was shed.

"Yeah. Couple hours or so ago."

I check my watch and realize it's nearly seven. I really did get caught up. "Everything went well?"

"Her aunt threw a fit when I let myself in with Isabelle's key. Threatened to call the cops but didn't when she realized I was only taking Isabelle's stuff. I didn't stick around."

I nod. The piece of shit is still in the hospital, but Celia could've had others with her. Clearly, we know less than nothing about this woman, as we were content that she was raising Isabelle right all that time.

"Where's Isabelle?" I ask. He watches me shrewdly for a minute, and I feel myself wanting to fidget but keep my ass rigid in the chair. I'm the president here. It's just a shame my VPs are such good fucking friends. They'd never disrespect me, but they know me too goddamn well, both him and Vaughn.

"Left her to unpack," is all he says, before leaving quicker than you'd think possible for a guy his size.

Letting out a long sigh, I run my hand over my scalp, the short bristles softening under my hand. I need a haircut. Pushing myself up out of the chair, I lock up the garage and make my way through the main room to the staircase.

The layout is purposeful. Everyone has to go through the main room to get anywhere in the clubhouse, so there's no sneaking in or out of anywhere. Ignoring the calls from various bikers, I climb the stairs and head to the end of the hallway. Her door is closed, and there's no answer when I call her name, so I push the door open.

The room is empty. It doesn't look much different to when I first showed it to Isabelle, except there are three full bags partially hidden under the bed now. She's not unpacked a thing. I'm on my way back to the stairs when I hear Vaughn's booming laugh as he comes through the door at the bottom.

"Do me a favor," he says between full belly laughs. "Don't tell him that part."

I see her blinding smile as they climb the stairs and immediately want to keep that look on her face forever, while slaughtering Vaughn for being the one to earn her smile instead of me.

"Where have you been?" I ask abruptly, and the smile dims, although Vaughn's chuckles continue. Asshole.

"Vaughn took me to the shops."

They stop in front of me, and Vaughn hands me a huge bag before saluting and returning down the stairs. She tries to take it from me, but I head back to her room with it instead. What I want to say is that I would have taken her, but instead, I grumble, "You're allowed to leave. You don't need any of the guys with you or anything to head out."

"I don't have my car." She shrugs and watches me drop the bag onto the bed. Pulling it over to her side, she starts to pull out bedding. I should've told her all the bedding already here was brand new—only for her.

"I'll take you to get it tomorrow."

"Kace is gonna do it."

My teeth grind as I clench my jaw. Of course she'd ask Kace. That makes sense. That was my idea too, after all. Kace—the easygoing kid a similar age to her, and someone I trust. My own son. So why do I hate it so much now?

"You didn't unpack?" I ask, refocusing my mind to the task at hand.

"I wanted to get to the shops before dinner."

Nodding, I glance at my watch, taking note of the time. Dinner can wait while I help her finish making the bed. It feels oddly domestic, doing such a mundane task with her, but she doesn't object. We work in silence to get it all straightened up and then head down.

I lead her through another door off the main room, then down a corridor before pushing the double doors open to show her the backyard. It's completely hidden from the front, which means no one can watch over us from the road. Exactly the way we like it. There's a playground farther out for the kids and grass that goes on forever, but the main draw is the seating area.

It's an enormous sunken pit with comfy seating, fire pits, an outdoor kitchen, and a huge dining table. It really needs to be extended at the rate these bikers procreate, but we'll get to it. Most people who are coming are already seated, and I expect to see Isabelle next to me, but when I turn, she's still by the door we just exited. I retrace my steps and stop in front of her.

"You okay?" Tight eyes flit to mine, but she doesn't answer. I get that it's overwhelming walking out to everyone, but there's really no way to ease her into biker life—she's had the easiest transition I could give considering the circumstances. "People-watching?" Her eyes soften and she gives a small shrug, so I go with it, returning to stand next to her and looking out at the pit. "What are you thinking?"

"I think anything I made up would pale in comparison to the real stories here." That's probably true. She's silent for a moment but doesn't make a move toward the crowd, so I stay next to her. "There are a lot of kids," she adds after a moment.

"Yeah. The compound is still a work in progress, but it's a space for the families of bikers, not just bikers. Having someone to come home to makes you a better person and less reckless. Helps in many ways."

She doesn't reply, and when I turn my head from the view to look down at her, she's already looking up at me, a question in her eyes. She doesn't ask, though, instead whispering, "I kind of feel like I'm drowning." She blinks, as if she's just realized what she's said, and hurriedly steps forward to head to the table.

"I'll save you every time," I say softly—half to Trey and half to myself, because she's too far away to hear now. She takes the seat Jag pulls out for her between him and Kace, and I take a free one across the table, next to Vaughn.

Food is served and dug into by everyone, and the conversation quiets as we fill our faces. It slowly builds again as everyone starts to finish, and I try to join in with whatever

Bishop is telling Knox about, but my attention is across the table from me.

When I pick up the word *jailbait* from Jag, I zone Bish out completely.

"I'm eighteen, you know," Isabelle says defiantly. Eighteen. Fucking hell. I really wish she'd stop reminding me. Or maybe she should remind me more.

"Just testing out some nicknames," he says with a laugh. "You seem to love them so much."

"Upset you don't rate high enough to have one?" Kace interjects, and Isabelle looks smug, turning to Jag with Kace at her back, his arm thrown casually over her chair. I fucking hate it. I shouldn't. What I should be doing is encouraging them—not thinking about how many bones I could break in my own son's arm.

"Share with the group," Vaughn calls across to her in challenge, and she narrows her eyes at him as if they have an inside joke. I want to choke the secret out of him. I'm glad she's forming friendships, I really am . . . so long as every fucker here knows that's all they are. "What's Rider got four of?"

"It's not four things," she explains slowly. "He's number four."

He doesn't look surprised at all, and I know he knows this whole story already; he's just coaxing it out of her in front of everyone, and I'm the idiot left hanging on her every word, but I can't bring myself to not care.

"So I'm number one?" Vaughn brushes his shoulder arrogantly, even though she's called him three before, and she laughs.

"You wish," she says with a chuckle, throwing him a playful wink that has my hands fisting at my sides.

"So Rider is four, I'm three . . ." He gestures in a "go on" motion before picking at the food left in front of him.

"Knox is Two," she says slowly, looking warily over at him, but he salutes with his bottle and swigs.

"You can't have numbered everyone here already, 'cause I don't have one," Jag complains, and she pats his hand patronizingly.

"You've never followed me around." She shrugs, as if the answer is obvious, and maybe it is, as a chorus of realization sounds around us, but I'm stunned.

While I may trust everyone here with *my* life, trusting them with her is vastly different. They don't have the same loyalty to her that they do with each other. Even as Trey's daughter, she didn't grow up around here, cementing her place with them yet. And guys like Jag she might've noticed more. That means she got me when I relented, but mainly the six guys I hand-picked for the job. She told me she realized she was being followed, but does she know all seven of us that I put on her tail?

"You're Five," she says almost apologetically to Bishop. "And the guy with the blond mohawk?" Cyrus. He's actually not here tonight, he's on a run. "Six."

That leaves me and Kace.

It's ridiculous how much I want to be number one. I'm thirty-seven years old, for fuck's sake, and I want to be ranked number one by an eighteen-year-old . . . An eighteen-year-old who was fathered by my deceased best friend. An eighteen-year-old I've watched grow up.

I go to push away from the table, wanting out of this conversation, but I'm not quick enough, and she's spoken again before I have.

"Lucky me, getting to marry number one." She rolls her eyes good-naturedly, but I see red. I'm surprised I'm still sitting here calmly, because inside, I am anything but. Kace is number one.

That means I'm number seven.

"Oof, so Prez is number seven?" Jag confirms, as the group dissolves into laughter. Fucking assholes. "You're lucky he's so chill," he splutters, though right now chill is the last thing I feel.

"Chill?" She scoffs, eyeing me in astonishment. Normally, yes, I am—just not where she's concerned—so it's hardly surprising she doesn't believe it.

"Prez is crazy chill," Rider continues, "but like savage at the same time. He has this way of sorting out arguments and making you all think you've won it."

Isabelle cocks a brow at me and I cock one right back.

"Loyal and caring, but savagely protective... and scary as shit when he needs to be," Jag finishes, then takes a swig of his beer as Vaughn claps me on the shoulder and I roll my eyes.

"That's quite the mix," Isabelle says, her tone laced with curiosity as she continues to hold my gaze. My lips twitch, lifting into a slow smirk.

"Enough of the ass-kissing. You're making me nauseous."

The conversation continues, but Isabelle doesn't look away for a long moment, rolling her lips between her teeth. Finally, she breaks the spell between us and turns her attention back to the guys.

Good thing she did, because I couldn't, stuck in the trance of her gaze. The temptation to take her for myself and watch as other emotions cross her eyes—happiness, safety, lust—is steadily growing, and fuck me if I can't slow it down.

CHAPTER ELEVEN

ISABELLE

Thankfully, the conversation moves past the whole number thing without anyone asking *how* they're ranked. I've no idea what they're assuming, but they seem satisfied, for now.

It takes me longer than is respectful to pull my eyes away from Axle, but he's like a magnet, drawing me in constantly, and I find I love seeing him like this—relaxed and surrounded by people he obviously loves.

Seeing them all like this, it feels like I'm having dinner with one big family rather than infiltrating an MC. If I never see the other side of them, the side you assume when you hear about bikers, I'll be happy. Although, imagining a savage Axle does things to me I'm not willing to admit.

Kace and Jag are comforting. It almost feels like they could be my brothers, even though I've known them for probably less than twelve hours ... oh, and one of them is my *husband*, apparently. They mirror each other so well, and there's no doubt they're best friends. They probably grew up together.

Before this dinner, I couldn't even imagine kids being in a place like this, but seeing the way they've transformed the outside space and how happy all of the children running around look, it makes sense. They seem free and confident, even with the eyes of the bikers on them, and they're not afraid to run up and politely interrupt conversations to settle an argument or get a hug.

There's also way more women here than I thought. Everyone seems to get together for dinner and so there are plenty of other ladies now sitting around the table. I haven't met any of them yet, and for some reason, they make me more nervous. The guys I was forced to meet before I could think too much about it, but the women—I find I want them to like me, although none of them have introduced themselves yet.

As everyone jokes around me, my stomach clenches, causing a slight ache. Is this what I could've had? Growing up, my time with my dad was amazing, but it was always just me and him. Did we miss out on all of this?

A family?

Instead of finding love and home here, I'm their leftover burden after my aunt made it clear she didn't want me anymore. Sure, they're all friendly enough, but do they even want me here, infiltrating their family unit when my own kept me away from them all this time? Is it some weird sense of obligation?

A wave of impostor syndrome stills me, my breaths growing heavy as panic sends adrenaline crashing through my body. The urge to get out of here—to lock myself away—is strong, and I rush to take it. As I push my chair back, Kace turns to me, his head cocked, eyes assessing.

"I think I'm gonna head to my room. It's been a big day."

His face softens into a boyish grin, and he nods, shoving his chair back and standing. "Of course. I'll walk you up."

I say a generic goodnight while Kace explains where he's going to Jag before throwing his arm around my shoulders and tugging me toward the clubhouse. Scattered wolf whistles come from behind us. I'd bet any money it's only Jag and Rider winding us up, but even knowing that still does nothing to settle my growing anxiety.

If anything, my throat seems to be getting smaller, my hands becoming clammy as their echoes follow us. Kace must feel the tension increase in my shoulders, as he gives me a light squeeze, pressing his lips to the top of my head before murmuring, "Ignore them, they're basically kids."

He's not wrong—they are acting childish right now—but is their reaction to be expected? The fact that I am actually married to the man taking me to my room makes sweat break out along my brow. I'm in this place with all of these strangers... what if he expects more than I'm willing to give?

A huge ball grows in my throat, and I cough, trying to dislodge it, but it won't go. I push at my breastbone with my palm, rubbing, applying more pressure than necessary, but nothing. My head starts to throb as I blink against my blurring vision.

"Spitfire," Kace says sweetly, stopping when we get into the hallway and spinning me by my shoulders until we're facing each other. Concern is etched into his face, which only makes me feel worse. "Are you okay?"

I can barely hear him as the blood rushes to my ears, drowning out noise with the cacophony of my heartbeat and the buzzing of panic. Closing my eyes, I try to ground myself, to settle this horrible wave that's taking control of my body. Before I can take a breath, something hard presses into my stomach, lifting me off the ground, and suddenly, my world is flipped upside down—literally.

A gasp escapes me as my eyes fly open, locking on to a broad back covered in leather, that insignia staring back at me from the wrong way up. Vertigo hits me hard, and it's all I can do to focus on breathing normally. How do you do that again? *In, out. In, out. You did the in. Now actually release the breath, Isabelle!*

I exhale and then inhale again, and the scents of fresh soil after a rainstorm and gasoline fills my senses, making me heady but helping the breaths come easier. When I'm set upright and two strong hands settle on my hips, holding me steady as I straighten up, I finally feel like I can remember how to breathe again.

"You wanna explain to me why I'm seven?" he asks, and my eyes fly open. I can't believe he's asking me this right now. Can't he see I'm in the middle of a breakdown? I push against his chest, and his hands drop from my waist, although he barely moves.

"Really? You think now is the time to heal your wounded ego?"

"I could've asked in front of everyone else," he says with a shrug, and it's only then I realize we're alone. My eyes flicker over the room but don't find Kace, who must have run off. *Traitor.*

"Except you wouldn't want to be embarrassed now, would you?" I ask, as if it means something way more than it does, but I need to do something to get back in control. His eyes narrow, and he steps closer, eliminating any space between us as my chest grows tight and my breathing shallow for a whole different reason.

"Why would I be embarrassed?"

Smirking at him, I take a step back, hiding my reaction to him with faux confidence. I fold my arms over my chest, but my lips stay firmly closed. He watches me for a moment before a smile spreads across his face, brightening his icy blue eyes, although it's clear he tries to contain it. I wish he'd let it go.

"Feeling better?" he asks. I blink at the change in subject, and it takes me a second to realize what he's talking about. He's distracted me from my freak-out. Again.

I want to snark back at him, fire back with something derisive, but my brain won't compute. All I can think is that he left everyone else to calm me down the way only he seems to know how. I still haven't replied by the time he's at the door, because I'm worried if I open my mouth, I'll ask him to stay.

"Goodnight, Isabelle."

Sleep isn't coming easily, and I toss and turn for what feels like hours. Axle was right—you can't hear anything from the pit over this side, so it's not that keeping me up. My body is shattered, and even though I'm wearing my own pajamas in a comfortable bed with fresh sheets, I still can't drift off.

I didn't have a problem sleeping in the hospital, but now that I'm here, surrounded by men I just met today with no lock to keep anyone out, I'm struggling to relax. Every time I close my eyes, I see Gary. The way his face looked when he loomed over me, his hands at my waistband, the alcohol on his breath. Putting a stop to the images flashing through my sleepy brain, I wrench my tired eyes open again and let out a sigh as they sting against the need to be closed. It also doesn't help that I'm wearing about fifteen different layers as some kind of protective armor, but it makes me feel better.

I still as footsteps sound in the hall, and my breath catches in my throat as they stop outside. A soft knock on my door makes my heart lurch, and I consider ignoring it but decide it's better to face head on.

What if they assume I'm asleep and I suddenly hear them opening the door or something?

Padding on soft feet across the room, I open it tentatively, holding my breath when I find Axle there. Then I regret facing it because my face must look a tired mess, and for some reason, that's not how I want him to see me—as if that's important right now.

"Sorry, did I wake you?" he says with a frown. "The light was on."

"No, you're good. What's up?"

"Why are you still up?"

"I'm not tired," I say, but a huge yawn overtakes the end of the sentence, branding me a liar, even if my heavy eyes didn't give me away.

"You need rest." He's right. I've had a hell of a couple of days and am completely drained, but it's not like I'm not trying. I cross my arms defensively and look at the floor between us. I don't know if he can sense I'm reluctant to say what I'm about to, but he waits me out either way.

In the end, I have to force the words out. "Every time I close my eyes, I see him." I catch the way his hands clench, but he's relaxing them when my eyes flick to his fists.

"You don't need to worry." Well . . . how reassuring.

"Easy for you to say," I scoff.

"You're right. I'm not a young girl in a strange place with men milling around." So he does get it. I nod lightly, still avoiding his eyes. I hate feeling this vulnerable. And yet he makes me want to be vulnerable with him. "What would help? What's going to make you feel safe?" His questions surprise me, but not as much as the answer that I have to bite my tongue to keep inside.

You.

Why, I have no clue. I couldn't explain if you begged me to. But I'm certainly not telling him that. So instead, I say the only other name that would.

"Where's Kace?" I ask, watching curiously as his body grows taut and tension radiates from him.

"He's busy," he says abruptly, and I feel like an idiot. I shouldn't need anyone with me to sleep, for God's sake, especially not someone I only met properly for the first time *today*.

"Okay, no worries." I'm about to push the door closed when he speaks.

"You think I'd hurt you?"

"No." My answer is again immediate, but spoken this time, and his shoulders drop minutely.

"I'll stay," he says simply.

"You don't—"

"I'll stay," he repeats, leaving no room for arguments.

I give him a small nod, confusion filling me as he turns and leaves despite his words, heading to his own room. It doesn't have time to settle, though, as he's quickly back in the hall, an armchair in his arms. I step back as he carries it through to my room and places it in the corner.

"Is it cold in here? Why are you bundled up?" he asks as he settles into the chair, pulling his phone out.

"I'm not cold," I tell him truthfully, then close the door and move awkwardly toward the bed. When I face him again, he's still frowning, so I continue. May as well get all the crazy out at once. "I wanted some more layers . . . of protection."

The anger that had simmered comes back full throttle, and he squeezes his phone in his hand as he swallows. "You can go and change," is all he says. So I do.

I go into the bathroom and shed the extra clothes I'd put on as some kind of textile forcefield until I'm just in my pajamas. Honestly, thank God, because I may have boiled to death if I'd actually managed to fall asleep in all of that.

Wearing just my cami and shorts, I rejoin him in the bedroom and crawl into bed. He flicks the light off, and I can just about see his features in the dull glow coming from his phone screen. His face is still set into hard lines, and I feel guilty for offloading my insecurities to him. I'm sure he's got way better things to do than babysit me.

But I like having him here, even if it's in companionable silence. He makes me feel safe, and like someone is looking out for me. Plus, watching his profile isn't exactly a hardship. The way his brow furrows at whatever he's reading, the clench of his jaw, the way he's angrily tense in the chair—it all screams *masculine* to me, and it might be making sleep harder to come by, my skin sensitive against the sheets as my body warms of its own volition.

"Go to sleep," he murmurs softly in the dark when I fidget again, and I flush at my thoughts being interrupted by his deep voice.

"I can feel your angry energy."

He huffs a surprised laugh. "I'm not angry." Well, he's definitely *something*. I think he's gone back to his phone and startle slightly when his voice comes through the blackness again. "Do you still feel like you're drowning?"

Maybe there's something about being shadowed in darkness that makes me brave, or maybe it's easier to share with him in the dark, because I answer honestly, not wanting to lie to him. "Yeah. But in warm water. It's almost comforting how overwhelming it is." I don't know if he knows I can see him, but the way his face softens hearing it makes my whole body relax. "I don't need anyone to save me."

I don't need to be rescued by anyone.

His gaze settles on me, and I know he realizes I heard him promise he always would. He looks for so long I wonder if he can actually see me. It feels as if he's staring straight into my soul, but it's so dark in here, surely he can't.

"Go to sleep, Isabelle," he eventually says, before dropping his attention back to his phone, and I shiver at the way my name sounds coming from his mouth. Rolling over, I settle into the plush bedding, and I don't know if it's the comfort of letting my insecurities be voiced or the reassurance of Axle being in this room with me, but sleep finally comes.

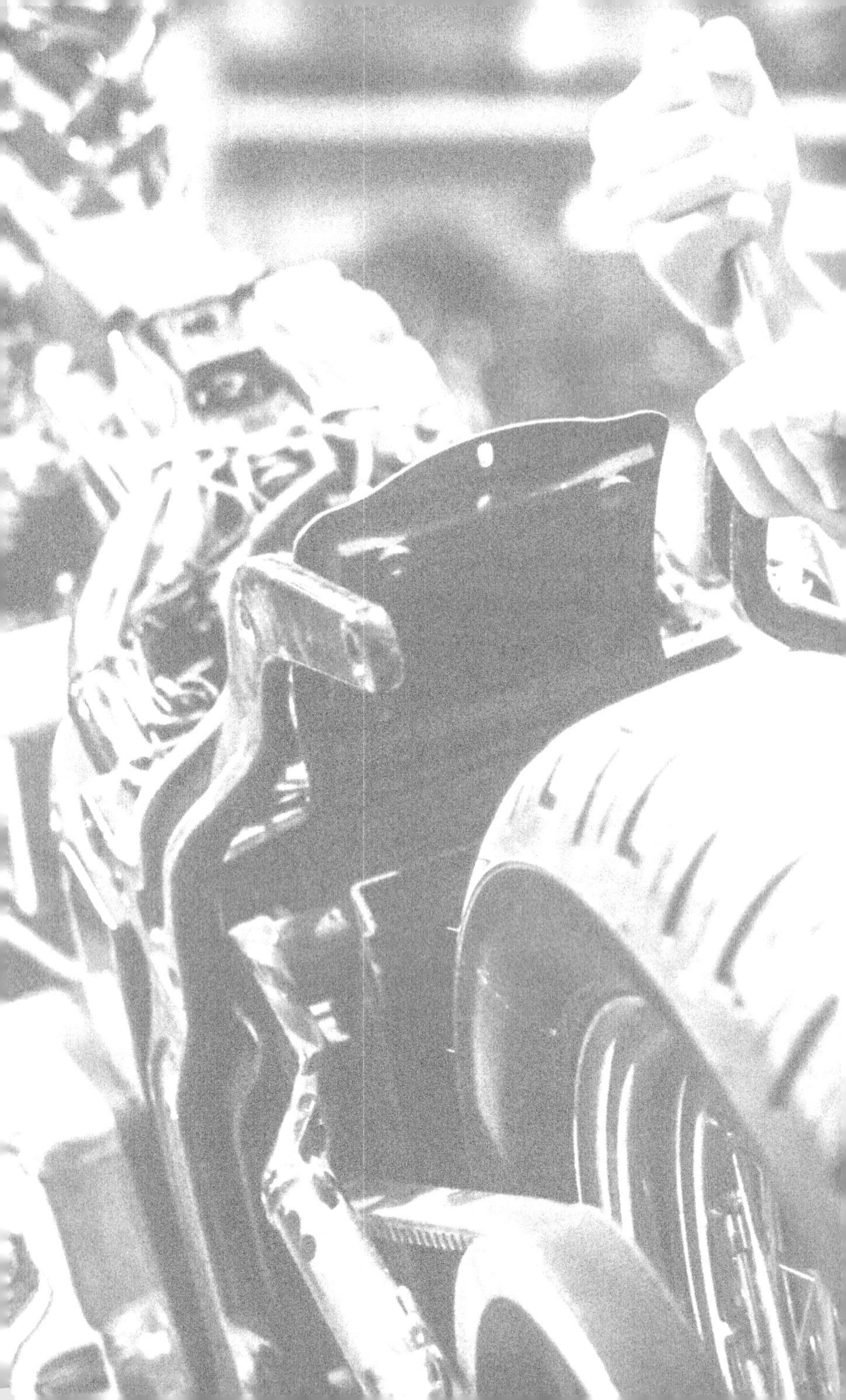

CHAPTER TWELVE

Axle

I pretend to be occupied by my phone until her breathing evens out and then I watch her outright, matching my breaths to hers. The urge to climb in next to her—to curl around her and feel her against my chest, her head tucked under my chin and her gentle breaths on my neck—is overwhelming.

To wake her up with a gasp and a moan.

Fuck.

Readjusting myself, I curse under my breath. The reason I'm even in her room, watching over her, is because she's worried about some sicko coming in when she's unaware. Yet, like an old perv, I'm sitting here remembering the way the silk of her pajamas clung to her skin. Trey would kick my fucking ass, but I also can't deny there's something about watching her sleep that leaves a contentment within me. She says she doesn't need me to save her, but she needs me *now*, and I'll take it. I'll save her anyway, even if she won't ask. Even if she doesn't want me to.

She's always been important—if only because she's my best friend's daughter—but I was busy with other shit. Busy running the club Trey left to me. It was his responsibility to care for her. We had guys watching them both, of course, over the years. A president stepping down while still alive is almost unheard of, making him a hot target for rivals, but I didn't need to be involved.

When Trey died, I could barely bring myself to remember he left a living, breathing human behind, let alone look over her. She might not look like him, but she's the best of him in every other way. I put my best guys on her out of respect and left it at that.

Except one day, we got the alert she was off, and I was closest by a mile. She was fine that day, but my world has never been the same since. She was captivating. Exquisite, confident, independent, enchanting . . .

She was also *seventeen*.

After that, I tried to stay away. I might be the president of a motorcycle club, but I'm not a cradle snatcher. I only went when it was necessary, when there was no other choice, but I found myself getting more attached each time—constantly watching the tracker Trey had secretly installed in her phone for us like a madman whenever I had a minute. Waiting for updates so regularly the guys must think I'm a psychopath, but I kept the instances when I saw her in person to a minimum. And every time I did, it was like a punch to the gut.

The depth of her eyes when she's gazing into the distance. The shrewd expression she gets when people-watching. The crinkle of her nose when she laughs, which is way too rare. It's all intoxicating, and way too often comes to my head when I'm balls-deep in some faceless stranger.

I was convincing myself it was just her looks, and it was working. I was almost glad she turned out to be a bimbo back at the bar, until she shocked the fuck out of me in the parking lot. I think my heart flipped in my chest at that moment, and now... I'm *fucked*. She's all I think about—the first thing I think of in the morning because she's the last thing I see in my mind at night, with my fist around my dick, visions of her riding me plaguing my dreams.

Why did her aunt have to be a complete and utter piece of shit? Why has she ended up here, across the hall and taunting me? I've tried, tried like hell to be a decent fucking human when it comes to her. I want to say she deserves more than this, but this club is pretty fucking great. She'll never be as protected, as loved, as part of a family as she will be with them. With us.

With *me*.

My phone vibrates in my hand, jolting me out of my internal battle as two messages come through at once.

Knox: Where are you, boss?

Kace: I'm coming up.

I hear footsteps, followed by a knock at my bedroom door opposite, so I stand and make my way to Isabelle's door. Opening it quietly, I step out, then pull it closed behind me. Kace does a double take over his shoulder at me exiting her room.

"What are you doing in there?" He's not mad, just curious, which is fair, but I don't feel like explaining myself to him.

"What's going on?" I ask instead, watching as he looks back to the door behind me. He doesn't answer for a beat, his eyes assessing as he flicks back to my gaze, but thankfully lets the whole thing go.

"Luke just got back from a drop. They asked him for more next time, and for that next time to be next week."

"That's not how shit works. They don't get to demand that." One of the main reasons we even run drugs through our county is so we know exactly what's here and how much. The dealers don't get to decide they want more product or more drops on a whim, and they certainly don't ask the runners.

"*I* know that," he says pointedly.

"But Luke doesn't," I finish for him. He's not new, but it's the first drop he's run himself, and they've clearly capitalized. "He agree?"

Kace nods with a grimace.

"Fuck." I can't let this go much further. The guys he met with will have already communicated back to their boss, and it needs shutting down right now, which means I have to break my promise to Isabelle. "Fuck," I say again, scrubbing a hand over my head. Kace looks quizzically back at the door.

"You wanna put Rider on the door? Or Knox?" Kace asks, and I immediately hate the idea. While I trust them implicitly, a guard standing outside isn't what she wanted. She hasn't asked for much in this situation, and so far has rolled with the punches pretty well, considering. I just want to give her this one thing, but I can't. Kace reads the indecisiveness on my face correctly. "They've watched her before."

"That's different."

"Different to what? Before she moved in? Cause you were pretty fucking obsessed even when she didn't live here." He chuckles lightly.

"I wasn't obsessed," I spit, not feeling the same humor at the situation. "She's important."

"To you."

"To the club. To Trey," I say with a glare. "I'm putting you on her. Look after her. No one else gets near this room tonight, and you stay awake and present until she's up. Got it?" He nods, though his eyes glimmer with unspent humor. "There's a chair in there. And there's no lock on this door. Go get her a decent one tomorrow—one with a key."

"Yes, Prez," he says with a twist of his lips, and I know he's not finished. As he takes his place in the ajar door and I make my way down the corridor, I pretend I don't hear his last words, though I don't doubt he sees my flinch. "I'd love nothing more than to comfort *my wife*."

Little fucker.

CHAPTER THIRTEEN

Isabelle

Peeling my eyes open, I blink against the brightness, relishing in peaceful contentment for the first time in days. The sun is working its way into the sky. Being roused by warm sunlight is my favorite way to wake up, guaranteeing a good mood.

A stuttered snore makes me jump, ruining the relaxed atmosphere I have going on as heavy grunts echo through the room. Memories from last night filter back, and I remember Axle was here when I fell asleep.

Rolling over with a smile, I see Kace laying on his back, his arm thrown over his face. *What's he doing here?* A wave of disappointment washes over me when I realize Axle isn't here now. Not that I feel unsafe with Kace—surprisingly, there's an easy comfort about having him sprawled out on top of my comforter. But there's an ache, too, that he isn't someone else—something I quickly shove deep down inside. Acknowledging it is something I'm not willing to do right now. Fantasizing in the dark is different to thinking about it in the cold light of day.

Another grumbling snore brings my attention back to the man lying in front of me. I shove at Kace's arm, mainly as a reflex, but also because snoring has to be one of the most infuriating sounds in the world. He wakes with a jolt, his eyes wide before his head rolls to the side and he sees it's just me, then the sleepiness hoods them again.

"Morning spitfire," he mumbles into my pillow.

"What are you doing here?"

"Keeping you safe," he says casually, his eyes dropping shut again before he finishes, and my heart flips in my chest. It's been a while since someone has so openly done that for me, and I love how he's not made it a big deal. Did he ask Axle to swap with him? My earlier disappointment quickly sours, turning to guilt. I should be grateful Kace is so willing to look out for me.

"You sure snore a lot for a guard dog," I say, covering the emotions swirling inside. He stretches with an obnoxious yawn before turning onto his side to face me with more alert eyes.

"How you doin'?"

"Slept well," I tell him simply, and although he doesn't call me out, we both know he meant more than that.

"You bought new bed sheets."

"God knows what I would've found on the others," I say with a wrinkle of my nose as he smiles.

"So, are you staying?"

"I didn't know I had a choice." He gives me a look that I'm guessing roughly translates to *cut the shit,* and I try not to smirk. "For now, I guess. School's not too far, and there's nowhere else to rush to. This has to be better than living on the streets. Although, now I'm not unconscious, *I* don't need a guardian, and *we* need an annulment."

"You can take that up with my dad." He sighs, then rolls from the bed with a grunt. Why on earth would his dad care?

"Are you not old enough to make decisions?" I taunt him, but he smirks lazily. When he smiles like that, he reminds me of Axle, and I kind of hate it. They might not look alike, but he's definitely inherited some characteristics. "How old are you anyway?"

"Twenty."

"How old is your dad?" I ask, trying to keep my tone casual. The question is totally innocent—I'm definitely not wanting to do mental mathematics to see what the age gap is between us.

"Thirty-seven." My face must show my surprise, because he rolls his eyes. "I know, I know. He had me young, and he looks younger than he is."

Well, yeah, he does. While he doesn't have the same boyish charm that Kace and Jag have, he damn well looks good for his age. Kace shakes his head at me, his nose wrinkled at my reaction, and I can't help but tease him.

"Jealous?"

"Oh, please. I'm sure I can go three times more rounds than papa dearest." The cheeky smirk on his face quickly lifts into a wide grin when a flush creeps over my cheeks. It's not him that has me blushing. Kace is already firmly in the "brother" category—whether we're married or not—but the image of Axle that pops into my head unbidden, *going a round,* has me wanting to squirm.

"Charming. You can leave now," I say with an overly haughty tone, and he chuckles but does make his way from next to the bed to the door.

"What are you gonna do today?"

I stretch as I think about the answer to that. "I should probably sort out school."

"You were signed off for the week, there's nothing to sort." I sit up with a questioning look on my face, because I really was not expecting it to have even been thought about. "Dad called them. You're all good. They're emailing you anything you miss."

"Axle did?" I ask disbelievingly. Seems like the president of a motorcycle club would have more important things to do, but Kace shrugs like it's totally normal.

"He's big on education."

"Is that in the bikers code?" I snipe, and I'm not even sure why.

"You're judgy, huh," Kace says, a statement rather than a question, but I offer an answer anyway, bristling under his assessment of me.

"No." I'm not normally, but I seem to find anything to judge these guys on, Axle especially, and I'm not sure why. "I just don't know much about this whole thing."

"Ask away," he says, hands wide in front of him. I appreciate it because I do have a lot of questions, but for some reason, I remember Axle promising me an answer a day and don't want to take the excuse to speak to him away. It's pitiful really. Instead, I groan and flop back on the bed.

"This is a lot first thing in the morning. Do people not feed their wives around here?"

It shows how comfortable Kace makes me that I'm able to even joke about being freaking *married* to him, but here we are. I hear a small chuckle from him but don't take my eyes from the ceiling.

"Sure. But I'm gonna wake Jag up. He makes the best pancakes. Meet you downstairs."

It takes me about half an hour to get up and ready for the day. Knox did pretty well with the collection of my stuff yesterday. Not that I have a lot of belongings anyway, but he managed to get pretty much all of it. I shower with my own body wash, do my normal skincare routine, and brush my teeth with my own toothpaste. It's nice.

For just a moment, everything feels almost normal—like my whole life hasn't been picked up and moved across town.

I leave my hair—now clean—down, dress in another pair of denim shorts and an oversized tee that I tuck in, and slip some Vans on before I head out. I pull the door shut behind me, cringing at having to leave my things unlocked.

It's not that they're massively valuable, just that I hate to think anyone can wander into what I've designated as my space. Shaking that thought away, I make my way downstairs and spot Kace in his usual booth as soon as I push through the doors.

It's bustling down here, and I realize that yesterday the kids were probably at school and the adults at work. I don't know why I expected them all to hang around here all day, but clearly the rowdiness starts once school is out. I join Kace at his favorite booth and sit where he's patting the seat next to him before Jag joins us. There's a huge plate of pancakes that looks like it could feed thirty, not just us three, sitting on the table between us with bottles of syrup and Nutella alongside.

"How domesticated," I joke, as Jag slides me a plate and they both dig in.

"It's literally the only thing I can cook, so make the most of it," Jag says with a grin.

"No fruit or anything, though. Sorry, spitfire."

"What, 'cause I'm a girl, I must want fruit instead of Nutella? Or are you saying I should be watching my figure?" Raising a brow just to wind him up, I purse my lips as I wait for his answer, but before he can open his mouth, a hand comes from behind, smacking him clean around the head. The act has me jumping, my heart barely settling into a normal rhythm before another body joins us.

"No son of mine is that stupid," Axle grumbles, motioning for Jag to slide along as Kace huffs.

"I didn't say that!" he whines, glaring at me while I grin mischievously at him, chuckling when he nails me in the ribs lightly with his elbow.

"No bacon?" Axle asks as he helps himself to three pancakes at once.

"Pancakes only, people," Jag huffs, scowling at us. All three of them eat in silence, and I don't blame them. The pancakes are delicious—but the domesticated family vibe and the memory of who I used to eat pancakes with has my throat restricting after my first bite. I chop at my food and push it around my plate, but I'm not fooling anyone.

"You don't like it? Sally's in the kitchen, she can make you something else," Axle offers gruffly. I don't know who Sally is, but she shouldn't have to cook for me.

"You don't like my specialty?" Jag seems affronted, as if I've personally offended him by not enjoying pancakes, and I shake my head.

"I love pancakes, I'm just not that hungry."

Jag and Kace seem happy with that, but Axle continues to watch me shrewdly. That doesn't help at all. Having his icy eyes on me makes my stomach flip, and with the tension already lining it, I start to feel quite nauseous.

I push my plate away and swing out of the booth. "I'm gonna pop out," I blurt out, for some reason unable to meet Axle's eyes, though I can feel them burning holes into my skin, even when he speaks.

"Where are you going?"

"For a walk. I'm allowed out, remember?"

He nods tightly but wipes his mouth before standing up. "I'll walk you out." Oh yippee. The other two mumble goodbyes around their full mouths and I practically run out of the clubhouse, feeling him behind me.

I don't know if it's because I was vulnerable with him yesterday, or because of damn Kace giving me the non-PG image of him, but I feel itchy and unnerved around Axle this morning. It needs to stop.

I'm about to head straight to the gate when he calls behind me.

"No question today?"

I stop and spin, not having one to hand. Instead, I ask the first one that comes to mind.

"Is Axle your real name?"

It's probably a waste of a question, but oh well. His eyebrows rise as if he wasn't expecting me to ask it, which isn't surprising seeing as *I* didn't know I was going to ask it ten seconds ago.

"No." I think he's going to stop there, but just as I'm turning away, he carries on. "Bikers have road names. Nicknames, essentially."

"And Axle is yours?" He nods. "Kace?" He looks slightly displeased as he shakes his head, but I have no idea about what, so I press on. "Not everyone has one?"

"They're earned. Some have been here long enough to earn it; others haven't. Some people fit their nicknames quicker than others."

"Okay," I say softly, content with that answer, although I have to push just a little further. "So what's your real name?" His lips twitch with a ghost of a smile, but he doesn't answer, asking his own question instead.

"What's your favorite drink?"

My eyes widen in surprise.

"Huh?"

"You're learning about us, we're learning about you," he says, but it seems kind of irrelevant to me.

"Peach iced tea."

He nods in satisfaction, and I warm under that gaze. Finally turning away from him, I feel his eyes on me the whole time I make my way to the gate.

I really wish I had my car here, or at least the sketchbook I keep inside it, but it's still sitting at my aunt's, as far as I know. As I pass through the gate with a nod from the guy on patrol, I suddenly stop and spin back to face him.

"I don't suppose you've got some paper back there, and a pencil, maybe?" I ask the guy at the gate, a wry smile on my face.

He looks at me as if I've just asked him to pull a skeleton out of his pocket, but he dutifully goes inside to check. He makes a lot of noise rifling through a very small space, but when he pops back up, he's brandishing a stack of plain paper and a pencil.

"Thanks," I grin, way too happy with this discovery, and he blinks at me. After taking it from him, I practically skip across the road and into the woods, where I can disappear from the world.

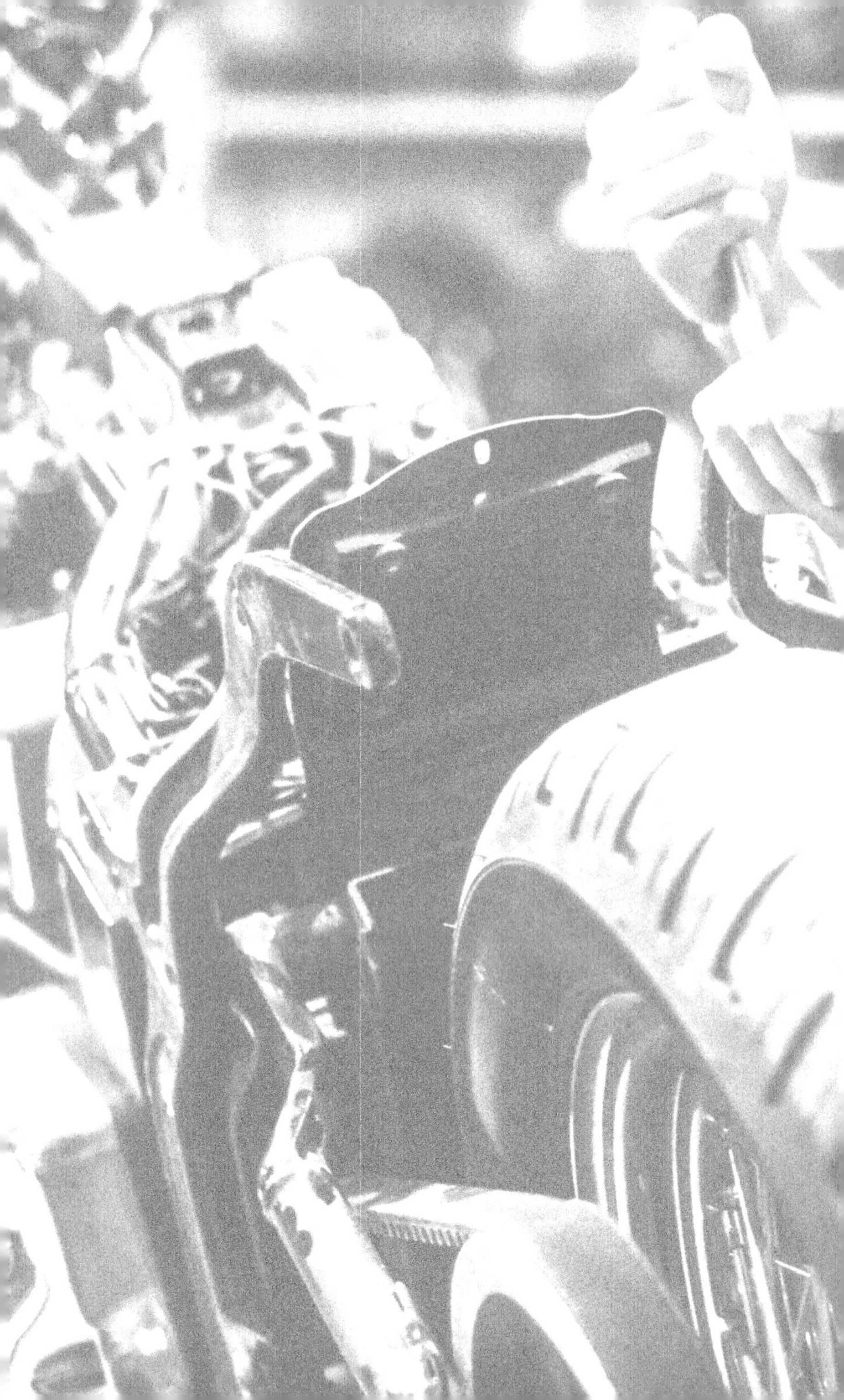

CHAPTER FOURTEEN

AXLE

I hate when she runs away. I hate when I have to leave her. I hate that I couldn't be there when she woke up this morning.

Did she wake looking for me? Was she happy Kace was there instead?

I watch her go, her hips swinging in those tiny shorts as she rushes to the gate before stopping to speak to the prospect. He hands her something, then she happily heads over the road to the woods. Once she's inside and I can no longer see the glint of her silver hair, I make my way to the garage. I've barely pulled the tools I need out when Kace is at the open roller door, leaning on the jamb.

"She wants an annulment," he says casually, while my jaw tightens with his announcement.

"What did you say to that?"

"That she'd have to speak to you." Wonder how that went down. "You're gonna have to tell her."

"I doubt it'd change what she wants," I admit. "Are you getting her car today?"

"I was gonna ride her over," Kace says with a shrug, "but she doesn't seem in a huge rush."

"I'm going into town soon, so I'll see if she wants taking then." He nods, before leaving as quickly as he arrived. It seems it's a revolving door this morning, because Knox appears, making his way over to me instead of hovering at the door. He doesn't speak until he gets to me and keeps his voice low.

"He's awake. He woke up just after she left yesterday."

My eyes narrow at the mention of the guy who dared to lay his hands on Isabelle, and the fact it's taken a whole day to find out this information.

"And?"

"Nothing. The police haven't been allowed in to question him yet. The chief says it's not likely for another day or two."

"Can we get in there first?"

"Probably, but we'd have to be waiting."

"Then that's what we'll do."

Knox and I ride over to the hospital, park our bikes, and wait in the cafeteria on the floor the piece of shit is on. We sit there for fucking hours, fully prepared to wait for the end of visiting hours when Celia finally leaves his side, but on our third round of coffees, she walks past the cafeteria with her phone and a pack of cigarettes in her hand. Knox and I stand in sync and make our way to his room once she's out of sight, where I slip inside and he waits on the other side of the door.

"Fucking finally," Gary grumbles as he hears the door. "I'm in agony—"

His words cut off when I step into his room and he realizes I'm definitely not a nurse, his face paling. "I'll press the call button," he warns, but I shrug.

"Go ahead. I don't need much time."

"For what?"

"To warn you that if you even think about coming near Isabelle again, I will make sure the full hell of everything I have and everyone I know comes down on you."

"She pushed me down the stairs," he hisses, suddenly brave with his outrage. I don't know if this is true or not, but it's irrelevant. We've seen the video evidence of him hitting and pursuing her. I hope it is true, though.

"You're a disgusting excuse for a human who's lucky he's still breathing. She didn't get the job done, but if you cause any more grief for her, you'll regret it for every second left of your very, very short life."

His mouth opens and closes, but nothing else comes out before the door is rapped, and by the time the nurse is entering, I'm there to hold the door open and greet her as I leave.

"Done?" Knox asks as he walks beside me to the elevator.

"We'll see." I sure hope so, for Isabelle's sake. We're on our way from the front doors to our bikes when the chief of police himself intercepts us.

"What are you doing here, Axle?" he says with a sigh. He's not on our payroll, but he's a half-decent man and knows when to pick his battles. We keep our shit to ourselves, and he leaves us be, for the most part. We're careful about the drugs, and it's better for the town to only have the clean, controlled shit that we move rather than any of the dodgy crap that's floating around, even if he doesn't like having any at all.

"Just visiting," I reply casually as I climb onto my bike.

"You shouldn't have done that."

"I'm not the one making bad decisions here." He looks up as if he can see Gary through the walls, then nods reluctantly before I peel out of the lot.

"Has Isabelle come back?" I ask the prospect on the gate as I stop halfway through.

"No, Prez."

Once we're parked, instead of following Knox back into the clubhouse, I turn and head over the road, following my hunch from earlier. It's been hours, but I don't know where else to look for her. I slow my footsteps as I step from the grass to the mossy floor, scanning the trees for her, but it's not until the road is hidden behind me that I see her up ahead.

She's sitting cross-legged on the floor, her hair covering her face as she hunches over something in her lap. As I step toward her, a twig snaps underfoot, and for some reason, I hide behind the nearest trunk, watching her scan the area.

She looks around for only a moment before focusing back on whatever has taken her attention. I watch her from my hiding spot as she tucks her hair behind her ear, gifting me her profile as she chews her lip between her teeth in concentration. Her arms move as she continues on with whatever's in her lap before stilling as she straightens, gazing up at the sky, or what little sky she can see through the trees.

She looks ethereal, head thrown back as the sunlight bathes her. I want to stroke the planes of her face that the light highlights, touch her plump bottom lip that's freed as she parts her mouth slightly. Too soon, she's facing down again, and her hair falls, obscuring my new favorite view.

As much as I want to stay here watching her so unguarded and relaxed forever, I walk toward her carefully until I can see that it's a drawing in her lap, something she's currently working on.

"You draw?"

CHAPTER FIFTEEN

ISABELLE

I jump as I swing toward his voice, holding my pencil like a tiny weapon. Axle smirks as he takes it in, and I lower it to the paper in my lap.

"How long have you been there?" Was it him who made the sound before? Was he watching me? Why does that thought send heat spiraling through me instead of creeping me out? He doesn't answer anyway, stepping closer and peering at the sketch I'm pretty much done with. I want to hide it for some reason, not wanting him to judge it. It's only done with a crappy old pencil the guy at the gate found.

"It's beautiful," he says simply. I look back down at it and try to view it from someone else's perspective. I guess I managed to get the light pretty spot on, even if the graphite doesn't smudge like my favorite ones do. I wish I had some color to bring out all the different shades of green above me, but the shades of gray are still effective. "He used to draw too, you know."

I feel my body tense, and as usual, irrational anger hits me at the mention of my father. I don't know where this surge of emotion comes from every damn time one of them mentions his name, but anger is preferable to the tsunami of sadness that threatened to take me under yesterday. Combative emotions I can wear like armor. I'd much rather be furious than vulnerable.

I stand abruptly and brush the debris off my ass, clasping the pencil and paper in my other hand. Good mood evaporated. I go to step past him, but he moves so he's in the way and I'm forced to look up at him.

"You can talk about him," he continues, his face an open book. "I'll tell you about him, if you want."

How dare he? Offering me pity information about my own father? A father I thought was mine, but they try and lay some kind of claim to? It only makes me angrier.

"I don't need to know anything about my own father from *you*." I go to walk around him, but he stills me with his dismissive tone.

"If you say so."

"What's that supposed to mean?"

"There was plenty he would've told you, Isabelle, if he'd had the chance. We talked about when he was going to, but now . . . he can't."

My walls are breaking, and I hate it. I look away from him, too many emotions swirling inside me, emotions that I don't want him to be able to see, but his hand comes up and tilts my face back to his with a finger against my jaw. His touch sends sparks across my skin.

"Don't hide from me."

I shake my face out of his hold because he makes me want to spill everything inside, and his jaw tightens.

"I *don't* need to know anything about my own father from *you*," I repeat slowly while looking into his eyes, and then I walk away.

The truth is, I'd love to hear stories about my dad from people who knew him. I've wanted nothing more than to share my love for him since he passed, but my aunt wasn't the right person. But now . . . knowing there's this whole other life he was living has me feeling betrayed. I couldn't bear to find out they knew him better than I ever did.

He doesn't catch up to me as I stalk my way through the gate, nearly bumping into Kace on his way out of the clubhouse.

"Woah, where's the fire?" He chuckles, holding me by my shoulders. "Did you get your car?"

I frown in confusion. Kace was supposed to take me.

"I'm going into town. I'll take you," Axle says from behind me, and I fight the urge to roll my eyes, not wanting Kace to pick up on the tension brewing between me and his dad. Kace drops his hands, letting me turn slightly so Axle is in both our lines of sight.

"I thought you were taking me?" I ask Kace, knowing my voice comes across as whiny, but I don't care. Being with Kace is easy. His dad, on the other hand? Whatever is between Axle and me is full of tension and confusion that I'm not ready to deal with right now.

"Sorry, spitfire, I would've earlier, but I've got something to get done before dinner."

I didn't realize it was getting that late. "No worries, we'll go tomorrow. Don't want to miss dinner." I'm about to head past him and go straight to my room when Axle grabs my arm and holds me still, his hand burning a print in my skin.

"Get on the bike, Isabelle," he grits out through clenched teeth, his eyes drilling holes into me. Kace grins at us both, shaking his head as he passes me and mounts his bike with a salute.

"Those things are death traps," I complain, but Axle ignores me and follows after Kace as if knowing I'll follow him. Which, of course, I do, if only because I'll be happy to have my car and some freedom back . . . and only that.

I've never seen Axle's bike up close, but it's gorgeous. The body blends seamlessly between colors, orange to red to deep purple. It kind of reminds me of a sunset, right before the sky goes completely dark.

He takes the pencil and paper from me when I make no move to get on the bike, puts them in a pouch on the side, and tries to swap them for his helmet.

"What are you going to wear?" I ask instead of taking it, and he sighs, placing it on my head for me. He clips it under my chin before sweeping a lock of hair that's got trapped over my face to the side, his finger grazing over my cheekbone.

I shiver at the surprisingly tender contact, and his eyes harden as I flush red. God, it's embarrassing how my body fully simps over him. We get it, he's attractive, but do I have to act as if everything he does is like a shortcut to my libido?

He climbs onto his bike before holding out his hand, which I take as I straddle the seat behind him. I didn't really think about how close I'd be to him when I accepted this lift and now am vehemently wishing I didn't. He puts my hands on the side of his jacket, and I leave them there loosely until he revs, forcing me to grip tighter. He turns his face to the side so I can hear him when he speaks.

"Hold on and lean with me."

The words make sense, but as instructions, they do not. He doesn't give me a chance to ask what he means, maneuvering slowly through the compound until we pass the gate where he pushes the engine harder, and then we're flying down the main road, way faster than Kace or even Vaughn went. My heart lurches at the change, and I wrap my arms around him tightly, and his stomach tenses underneath me.

Thankfully, I don't have the brain space to focus on how hard his abs feel even through his layers too much, because it's mainly taken up with a mix of terror that I'm about to be thrown off the bike and across the asphalt, and the pure thrill of speeding through the open air. It's so different from being in a car. I can feel the cooling air on my skin leaving goosebumps, the warm body in front of me I'm anchoring to, and the ends of my hair whipping around as we move. I love it. And when we hit a corner and he leans in to the way the bike tilts, I follow suit.

I feel ten pounds lighter when we stop in town, and by the time Axle has helped me off the bike and taken the helmet off, I'm grinning widely. His eyebrows raise as he takes in my happy expression, and his smile is slow.

"You like?"

"Yeah, I like," I agree. A long moment passes as we look at each other, without anger or irritation for once, and my chest starts to flutter as I realize how close I'm standing to him, with only the helmet between us. When my eyes flick to his lips unbidden, I swallow, and he takes a step back. "How come we're here?" I ask, turning to look at the stores for something to do to hide my embarrassment. "My car's at my aunt's."

"Yeah, I know," he says behind me. "I need to drop in at the shop and then I can tail you back." I nod in understanding as he climbs off and heads for the end of the row.

I haven't been to this side of town in forever—certainly not recently enough to remember, although I'm sure the stores have been revamped. For something to do, I wander over to the window of the one closest to where he parked the bike and peer through the glass instead of going in. It's a boutique full of pretty, floaty dresses that wouldn't look out of place at a fancy garden soiree. Not exactly my style, but they look gorgeous.

The next one along sells handmade gifts—jewelry, personalized cards, crafts, things like that. Their window display contains different versions of graduation gifts, including a shadow box with a 3D graduation cap inside. It's cute, somewhere you could lose some time browsing.

Moving along past the restaurant that smells delicious and makes my stomach grumble, I reach the storefront Axle disappeared into. This one doesn't have a window display like the others, allowing you to see into the open white space beyond the glass. It's pretty empty, except for a couple of bikes right there in the middle of the shop floor.

The bright white walls are laid out like a gallery, the bikes the main exhibition with a wide mix of different art styles lining the walls. From graffiti to abstract colors to black and white sketches, but it's all stunning. As I peer further into the store, I catch Axle's eye and notice him watching me take it all in. The guy next to him is looking my way too, and the thought they may have been talking about me hits me hard. He has the oddest look on his face as he looks at me, and I just know he knows who I am, knew my dad, and it makes me feel way too *seen*. I turn away, even though I'd love nothing more than to go inside and see every piece, and make my way back to the bike. I don't get that far, though, because when I turn, I spot another bike parked up directly in front of the store. It's gorgeous and it's come straight from the wall of the gallery, having just seen the same image through the window. I admire the way the blues blend seamlessly into black with purple highlights, the background to the night sky painted onto the body of the bike. It somehow looks even better wrapped around the metal than it did in the gallery, seeming more beautiful and appreciated out here against the rough.

I don't know whose bike this is, and even though I want to trail my fingers over the metal, I'm sure whoever it is won't appreciate my fingerprints all over their art, so I drag myself away, but as I turn I see Axle watching me from the doorway. He doesn't say anything as he walks to his bike, puts the helmet back on me when I join him, and then climbs on, holding his hand out for me to take my space behind him, so I don't say anything either.

My relief at seeing my aunt's car not there must come off me in waves, and we manage to collect my car with no drama. Then Axle follows me back to the clubhouse, as promised.

He disappears when we get back, but it's definitely dinnertime by now, so I head out alone and scan the seats that have already been taken. I don't see Kace anywhere. In fact, I don't see anyone I've said two words to. Not Jag, not Vaughn . . . nobody. I'm making a beeline for the empty section to avoid any awkward small talk when someone bumps into my shoulder from behind.

The girl that was straddling Axle's lap the first day I arrived stops in front of me. My first instinct is to hate her, but I'm above hating a woman for a man's actions. At least, I want to be. Not that I have any right to be annoyed with her, especially as she's about to be the first woman I've interacted with here. I assume it was my focus on snagging the empty seats that made us collide, until her lips tip into a smirk.

"Oops! Sorry, girl," she drawls without an ounce of apology in her tone. "You need somewhere to sit?"

"Come on, spitfire," Kace calls as he passes me, heading toward the table.

"I guess not," I say to her.

"Another time, then. I'd love to fill you in," she says in a super sweet voice, but the way her eyes narrow have me asking.

"On what?"

She shrugs, twirling a lock of honey-blonde hair around her finger. "The guys 'round here. How to get in their good books." She winks, and I cringe. As if I'd give a fuck about that, even if it wasn't obvious she meant by being on your back. "Although, remind me not to mention daddy dearest."

My stomach sours at what *must* be lies. She couldn't possibly know that stuff about him. She can't be much older than me, and he's been gone for four years. "You're lying," I hiss, stepping toward her, but she bats her lashes in mock confusion.

"Why would I do that? Trey—"

"Don't you dare say his name!"

"Everything okay?" Kace asks as he comes to see why I haven't joined him.

"Of course," she says. She smiles widely and plants her hand on his arm, and he just fucking *leaves it there*.

"What's going on?" Axle asks behind me, which just pisses me off. Why does he always disappear, only to pop up again at the most inconvenient time? I don't turn to look at him, speaking to Kace instead.

"I'm not feeling too great. I'm gonna head up."

"What's wrong?" The question is asked from both in front of and behind me, but again, I ignore Axle.

"Just a headache." I smile reassuringly at Kace and turn, heading back inside without looking at Axle. I'm nearly back to my room without interruption, but Kace calls behind me as I reach the top of the stairs.

"Hey! You'll need this." He hands me a key as I look quizzically at him. "It's for your room."

I still for a moment, gaping at him as gratitude, surprise, and guilt war inside me. Gratitude that he recognized what I needed and got it for me. Surprise he's even paying enough attention to notice. Guilt for spending the day thinking about his father. I know our marriage isn't exactly normal, but it still seems like a shitty thing to do, especially when he's being so sweet.

Life would be a lot easier if I could see my husband in the same way I see his dad.

CHAPTER SIXTEEN

ISABELLE

The soft buzzing of my phone as it works its way along the bedside table brings me out of sleep. I blink my eyes open slowly and squint against the bright light as I fish for it, unplugging it from its charger and holding it up to see what's waking me. It's a number I don't recognize, so I plan to ignore it, but it rings off and starts up again before I've even managed to put it down.

"Hello?" I greet sleepily after answering.

"Hi, Isabelle?" a gruff voice barks from the other end, making me jump and focus a bit more.

"Speaking."

"It's Chief Norris from the County Police Department. I just wanted to remind you we're still waiting for your statement."

Dammit. I'd completely forgotten I promised to go back in for that. Honestly, I've put everything to do with that whole event to the back of my mind recently. It's been too full of other things. *Like Axle,* the voice inside my head whispers. She can mind her own business.

"Isabelle?" he prompts from the other end of the line.

"Oh, yes, sorry. I can come in today?" It's the absolute last thing I want to do, but I've blurted it out before thinking it through, and he's eagerly agreeing to meet me in an hour. Hooray. I'm surprised when the time reads 10:30 a.m., because I'm normally an early riser, but I stayed up late last night sketching and completely lost track of time.

My creativity is really thriving at the moment, and I'm not one to say no to some inspiration. Last night it came from the shop Axle stopped at, and I ended up sketching out a whole design for one side of a bike. I've never thought to do it before, but when inspiration hits, you've got to go with it.

I have a quick shower and throw my hair up into a ponytail, then choose a lightweight shirt-and-shorts two-piece set. I leave the shirt undone and pair it with a bandeau crop. The weather looks gorgeous, and I'm making the most of it. I slip into my trusty Vans and brush my teeth before making my way out. I'm just locking the door when another opens behind me, and the skin prickles along the back of my neck.

Axle doesn't say anything, but he doesn't move either, and when I can't pretend to still be locking the door, I turn slowly to face him. There's only about two feet between us, and I can see the way his chest rises and falls steadily under the white T-shirt he's wearing under his leather vest. His gorgeous face is blank of emotion. He just stands against his door, watching me, which makes me want to fidget.

"Kace got me a lock," I say pointlessly, gesturing over my shoulder with the key.

"Is that so?"

"Yeah. I guess he wanted me to feel safe."

"And do you?"

Like a coward, I break eye contact and shrug lightly, but he doesn't let me off the hook, remaining silent himself.

So, without looking back up at him, I say the only thing I can think of to say next.

"He said to speak to you about the annulment..."

"So I heard," he murmurs. "What's the rush?"

He finally moves, striding toward the stairs as if knowing I'll follow him, which I do, panting as I try to keep up with his long steps.

"The rush is that I don't want to be married to someone I barely know."

"Not even someone who wants to keep you safe?"

I scoff at that, as if it's that simple, and he stops, turning on the step he's on a few below me. We're practically eye-level like this, and it makes me feel braver. Not that I need any encouragement to argue with Axle.

"Kace and I don't need to be married."

His unaffected expression wanes, and my stomach swirls at the way his eyes soften with sympathy.

"Your aunt was your next of kin and refused to allow you on her insurance or approve medical intervention on your behalf. The only way out was for you to be married. You wanted to wake up untreated, with nothing for the pain, still propped up in the waiting room?"

I blink at him as I take in this information, even if I'd assumed most of it anyway. His icy blue eyes show nothing but sincerity, so I'm pretty sure he's not lying, and I'm shocked at the level my aunt would stoop to. Did she really not care for me at all?

Something must show on my face, because in the next moment, his whole demeanor changes. His shoulders lower and his hands flex, and for a second, I think he might reach out for me. I panic.

I know what to do with angry, bossy, and even asshole Axle, because he pisses me off, which reinforces my armor. What I don't know is to act around a gentle Axle, especially when my whole body is urging me to go to him, to let him make me feel better. That can't happen. I flick my eyes away from him and swallow the lump in my throat.

"Well, he's a decent guy, then, and I'm incredibly grateful for what you all did, but I don't need or want a husband anymore. Especially not a biker." I don't know why I add the last bit. I might not know much about what being a biker means, but I can tell Kace is the decent guy he seems to be.

Maybe I just want to push Axle and I back to warring. I step around him and push through the doors at the bottom, expecting to see Kace or Jag, but neither are to be found instantly.

Although what Axle said about my aunt has me thinking and distracted. I guess the paramedics that came for Gary couldn't just leave me out cold at the bottom of the stairs, but what would've happened had she had her way? Would they really not have treated me?

Best case scenario, I would've woken up to a hefty medical bill that I have no way of paying. What was the worst-case scenario? That they would've checked I was still breathing, then wheeled me out? Would she really have let that happen? I have no idea, and honestly, it doesn't even matter anymore.

My aunt is officially the worst, and it seems like Kace may have actually saved me—or at the very least, saved me a whole chunk of cash. And what happens after the annulment I keep asking for? I get the protection of my husband, right? I trust that Kace is a good guy, but does the protection he offers me in a place where I'm surrounded by strangers stop? Will he not care after? Will I have to leave?

I have barely any money in my account. My aunt used to transfer a set amount each month for me to not have to ask her every time I needed something, but that's bound to stop now, and it wasn't enough to get any savings to begin with. I scraped together the pile of notes in my dresser from cash I had lying around in pockets. I have this car, but even though it was a gift, I wouldn't put it past her to have kept it in her name and to have it collected any second. Again, I'm sure it was only provided so I didn't have to ask her for lifts to school.

Shaking my head, I decide not to worry about it right now. Plenty of time for that after.

I look around blindly, willing someone I know to appear, but instead, I catch the eye of a lady behind the bar. She's got thick black waves to her waist and smiles warmly as she beckons me over, so I go. I've seen her around at dinner before but not spoken to her yet.

"Finally," she huffs when I reach her, the bar between us as she dries a glass. "We can never introduce ourselves with the guys around you constantly. How are you doing?"

"Erm, I'm good thanks," I say shyly. I don't know why I'm suddenly shy and why it seems more important to make a good impression with this woman than I cared about any of the guys I've met so far. Maybe it's because of Brianna yesterday—I don't want them all to end up being bitches. "I'm Isabelle," I say with a small wave that makes me blush immediately. I'm such a dork. The lady chuckles sweetly though.

"I know, girl. I'm Ashton."

"Are you a biker?" That must be a stupid question, because she looks at me as if I'm five years old.

"Nah. The club is pretty respectful, but they're still bikers, and it's still a men's club."

"Respectful?" As much as I like Axle and our question of the day sessions, it's nice to hear from another female's perspective.

"Yeah, hella. Even if you're a club girl, you don't do something you don't want to."

"Club girl?" I ask, confusion creasing my brow, and she smiles at me.

"Remind me to introduce you to some people. But essentially, you've got club girls—the ones who tend to work here. There's me, Brianna, Sally, and some others who do the cooking, bar work, cleaning, that shit." I must have a frown on my face, because she rolls her eyes lightheartedly. "Don't worry, we're not being taken advantage of. They're well-paid positions that we applied for. It just so happens that we're surrounded by fit as fuck bikers at the same time."

"So you don't . . ." I'm not really sure how to finish the sentence without causing offense, but Ashton doesn't seem to take any, a wicked smile showing her teeth.

"Oh, no, we definitely do. But it's all consensual." My stomach sours at the thought of Brianna with Axle, because of course that's my first thought, but thankfully, Ashton continues. "Then there's the ol' ladies. They're claimed by one specific biker and are normally followed around by a gaggle of kids." She leans forward and lowers her voice conspiratorially. "My favorite ol' ladies are Sable and Rose, but don't tell anyone. I'll introduce you to them soon."

"That'd be great," I say, and I mean it. I'd love to have some girlfriends here. "I gotta go, but I'll see you around." She waves me off with her rag and goes back to her task. I'm feeling happier as I get behind the wheel of my car and make my way to the station.

I make my way into the station and ask for the chief, waiting in the lifeless waiting room as they call up. He greets me kindly and leads me to a small room that looks exactly how they do on the television, though thankfully, I'm not in handcuffs.

"Thanks for coming in, Isabelle," he says, and I nod, nerves getting the best of me now that I'm thinking of the detective shows I've seen before. Are they going to try and trip me up? Am I going to say something I regret? Is staying with the bikers something he'll question me about? I didn't even think about asking someone to come with me, so used to doing things alone, but now I feel like an idiot. Should I have a lawyer?! My thoughts go to Axle and how calm he would be in this situation, how he'd probably rile me up to focus my panic and take control.

"Isabelle?" I blink at the chief as he waits expectantly for a response.

"Sorry, could you say that again?"

"Of course. I was just letting you know Gary has decided not to press charges." My eyebrows jump. "He's said that you both got carried away and didn't think of how dangerous the place was, but that it was no one's fault."

Carried away? My stomach sours at the thought of people thinking I was willingly doing anything with him—that we'd just been in some kind of lustful haze—and I might throw up right here on the table in front of me. The chief obviously notices my reaction, because he speaks softly.

"Your version of events may of course be different, and we are here today for you to discuss those if you wish to do so."

But I don't want to. I don't want to tell this stranger in front of me about how he held me down, had his hands all over me, my jeans undone. How I was terrified and felt sick and panicked. How I *did* push him. I might not have thought he'd fall, but I don't regret it, even if he did take me with him.

I don't want to tell the strange man in front of me, and I don't want to have to tell the many strangers after him. I'm not an idiot. I know that if I have a different version, then it'll be more interviews and maybe even court. Am I prepared to tell this story over and over while he makes out I was a slut desperate for her aunt's partner, and then wait and see if the world believes me or him? Absolutely not.

"My version is the same as his." His brows twitch, although he schools his impression quickly.

"Are you sure? My officers mentioned you said he'd attacked you when you were in the hospital." Shit. I forgot about my conversation with them.

"I'm sure." I nod decisively. "I guess I was confused." He smiles sadly at me, something akin to pity in his eyes. Or is it disappointment? I squirm uncomfortably on the hard chair.

"In that case, there's not much more to talk about here." He slides a card across the table and taps it twice before he leaves it in front of me. "You call me if you think of anything else, okay?"

I nod again but can't bring myself to meet his eyes, more disappointed in myself than he could ever be.

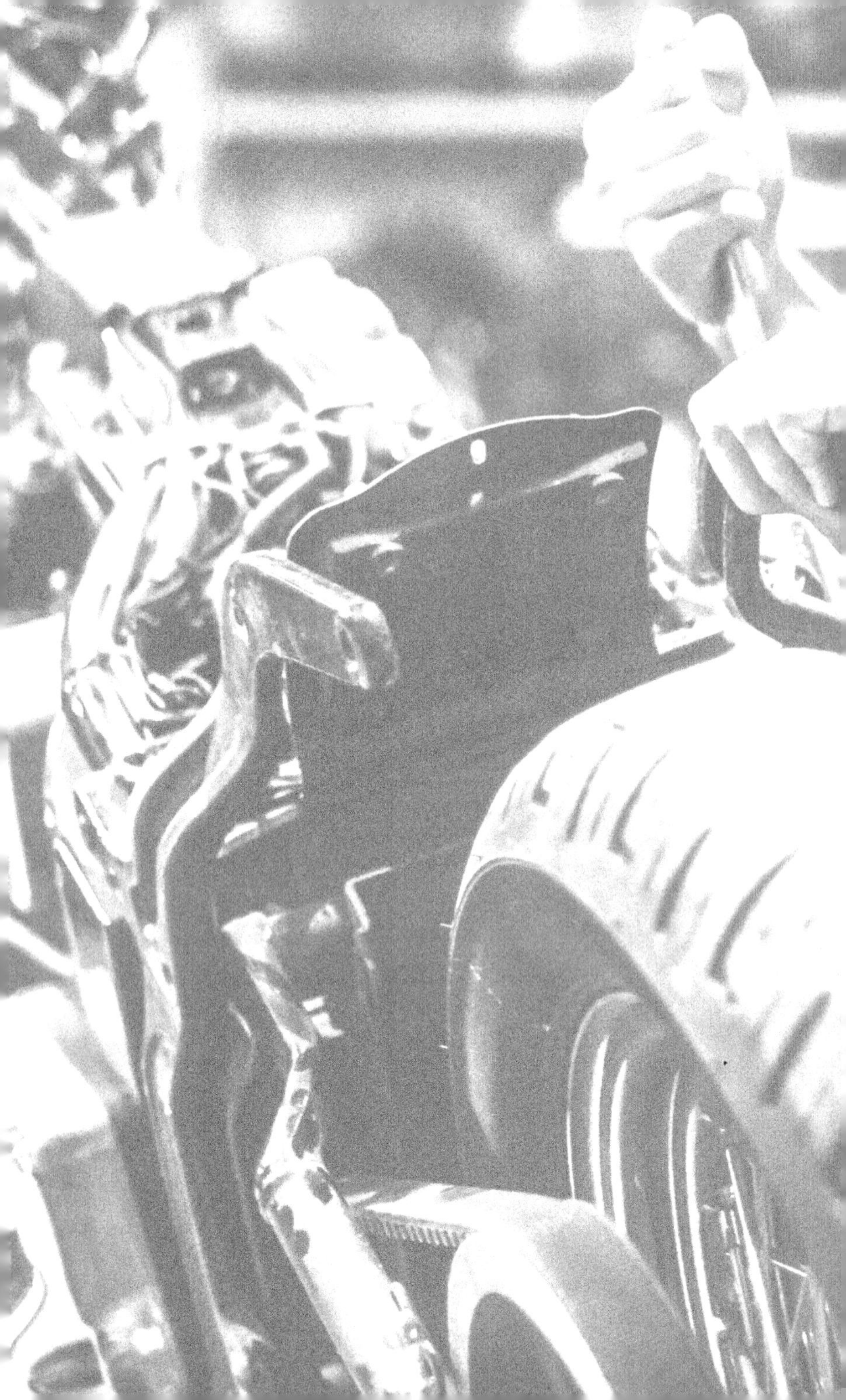

CHAPTER SEVENTEEN

Axle

When Kace asks me if I've seen Isabelle, I don't even think to use her tracker. I assume she went to her favorite spot among the trees this morning to draw. I also don't even entertain the idea of telling him where that is. I like being the only one who knows—the only one who can find her in her oasis of peace.

But when I stroll over the road and under the canopy, I realize how over-cocky I've been. She's not there, and when I finally check the tracker, she's at one of the last places I'd want her to go alone.

My bike has barely stopped when I'm kicking the stand out and bolting for the door in front of me. It bounces off the wall as I stride through, and I see Isabelle off to the side, standing with the chief. She looks so fucking young here—so naive and vulnerable—surrounded by the harshness of the police station and the worldly police chief. So much soft golden skin on show against his dark blue uniform. They both start and look toward me at the abrupt intrusion.

"Don't say another word," I bark, eyes fixed on Isabelle. She frowns in confusion, but the chief steps forward to meet me.

"Axle," he placates. "You don't need to overreact about this."

"There's no overreacting when it comes to her," I tell him, and he nods in acceptance. He thinks he knows why—Isabelle being Trey's daughter—but he really has no idea. It's not the fact that she's the former president's blood that has mine pumping three times too fast in my ears, nor why I raced here as if the bats of fucking hell were on my tail.

"Axle—"

"I don't want to hear a word from you," I grit, sparing Isabelle the briefest glance to keep my control. I'm sure she's confused as to why I'm so angry, and honestly, so am I. This is so unlike me, but the split second of not knowing where she was—then realizing I'd assumed too much and she'd kept something from me—was torture. That she could've made her situation worse by not asking for my—*our*—help. The relief at seeing her is being drowned out by everything else. "Is she free to go?" I ask the chief, and he nods.

"Call me if you need anything further, Isabelle."

She opens her mouth, ready to respond and placate him, but that's not how this is supposed to work. She needs anything, she comes to me.

"Go back to the compound, Isabelle. Now," I add when I know she's about to argue. She's no doubt cursing me with every imaginative name she can think of inside her head, but she does as I say anyway, leaving the precinct as I turn back to the chief. "You don't speak to her without me again—not one of you. You don't even fucking ask her how she's doing without running it past me first."

I don't give him time to argue or agree, instead turning round and getting outside just as Isabelle slams her car door. I follow her home, and when she turns into the compound, I stall outside, messaging Knox. Then I watch her stomp inside the clubhouse before I carry on down the road.

I park up in the same spot I did last time and take the same route through the halls. This time, I don't care if the aunt is there—let her call security. There's nothing subtle about me today. I'm so angry, and I want answers that I should've asked Isabelle for, but if anyone deserves to see my rage, it's him. Why is she being questioned again? I swing through the hospital-room door, expecting to see the rat-faced bastard still wired up in his bed, but there's nothing.

No wires, no aunt, and certainly no man. In fact, the bed is fresh and made up. I'm about to search the fucking bathroom when someone enters behind me. The nurse jumps when he sees me in here, clearly expecting the room to be empty, as it was when I found it.

"Where's the guy in here gone?" I ask before he can question me, and I must be giving off the right pissed-off vibes because he opens and closes his mouth a few times before deciding to just come out with it.

"The patient in this room has left."

"What? He was comatose forty-eight hours ago." Right? He'd only woken up the day before yesterday. The nurse's face purses as if that fact displeases him as much as me.

"Due to patient confidentiality—"

I take two steps toward the door and the nurse, and he takes two steps back, quivering, hands raised protectively in front of him.

"The patient decided to discharge themself!" he says quickly.

For fuck's sake. He's running. I pass the nurse and leave, then find Knox outside, leaning on his bike next to mine. Every person that passes gapes at the mountain of a man, but he doesn't give a fuck.

"You still got that key?" I ask, climbing on my bike as he nods.

It takes longer to get to the house than it did the hospital, and when we pull up on the drive, it looks as if it's a waste of time. There's no car outside and no sign of life when we let ourselves in. It's silent inside, and we confirm the bottom floor is empty before heading upstairs, searching one side of the house each. The first room I get to is just a bathroom—unsurprisingly empty—and then a spare room. There's just a double bed and some storage furniture. Everything else is bare. I meet Knox back out at the stairs.

"Nothing?"

"Nope. Their room looks untouched, so if they've run, they haven't taken anything."

"And Isabelle's?"

"You searched hers," he says, with a nod to the door I just came out of. That bland, sparse room was hers? No drawings, no photos?

"Did you take all her stuff to the compound?" Maybe he already emptied it out.

"There wasn't really anything to take," he says solemnly, his eyes looking around the space.

This space, this room—nothing about it screams home for her. Did she ever feel at home here, with these people? A new sense of determination fuels my blood. The need to make her comfortable with us. To give her a home she can be proud of. One that she can stay in forever.

CHAPTER EIGHTEEN

Isabelle

It's been a rough morning. When I get back from the police station, Kace finds me on the stairs heading to my room. After dealing with Axle acting like an asshole caveman back at the station, feeling sorry for myself in bed feels like the best option, but when Kace asks if I want to head out with them for the afternoon, I can't think of any good reason not to. So, fuck it. Why not?

I have no idea what to expect, but a chill bar where they all play pool, darts, and chat over some beers is not it. I don't see Ashton, which is a shame, but Jag is here somewhere. I'm pretty sure a healthy chunk of the people here aren't twenty-one yet, and I certainly am not, but no one bats an eyelid at us all ordering drinks. Kace puts a beer in front of me, but when my face screws up at the first sip, he chuckles and heads back to the bar.

"You and Kace look like you're getting on well." I groan as Brianna slides onto the stool next to me, her sickly sweet voice too close. I turn slowly to look at her, already knowing she's only here to piss me off.

"I guess."

"Oh, come on, don't be such a stuck-up bitch," she says with a roll of her eyes, as if *I'm* the unreasonable one here. "We should be friends."

"Why?" Forgetting the fact she insinuated she fucked my dad when she was underage, I can't think of a single thing we would have in common.

"Well, we're practically in-laws, right?"

I frown at how she's worked that out until my brain slowly catches up with me. If I'm with Kace, to be my in-law, she'd have to be with his direct relative . . . like his dad.

"You and Axle?" I ask, not bothering to hide the disbelief and disdain in my voice.

She smirks as her eyes dance. "It's not official, except in the bedroom."

I feel sick for the second time today, and when Kace comes back with a colored cocktail, I take it from him eagerly, downing half in an instant.

"Woah," he says with a chuckle, and I smile gratefully at him.

"Thanks for that. I needed it."

"What's up, Brianna?" he asks easily.

"Isabelle and I are just bonding," she replies, and he seems mollified by her lie. We are *not* bonding. I'm currently wondering if you can drown a person in half a cosmopolitan.

"Isabelle! Is that you?!" Startling at the familiar voice I'm not expecting to hear, especially here, I pull in a breath before turning to face Betsy. Her eyes widen in shock as she flicks her gaze around the bar, taking in my company for the evening. "I thought it was. What are you doing here?"

"Hey. Just hanging out, what about you?"

"I'm with Shannon and Taylor." She waves over to another table, where I can see two other girls from our school. "Who are your friends?"

"I'm Kace, her husband," he says, stretching a hand out to her with a wide grin as her mouth falls open. I dig an elbow into his ribs, and he huffs out a laugh, pulling his hand back and turning back to the others.

"He's joking," I say.

"I'm Brianna, her stepmom," Brianna so kindly offers, which sends a spike of heat through my blood. I grit my teeth as Betsy blinks at us all.

"I'll come say hi," I say quickly, jumping off my stool and pushing her toward the others. They're all fake smiles when I join them, but all three are still eyeing up the group I've just left as if they're not sure whether to run or join them.

"Isabelle, babe!" Taylor croons. "Where have you been?" Of course, to them, I've just been off school for a week or so.

They have no idea my life has changed irrevocably in those days, not that I'm about to tell them any of that.

"I haven't been very well," I offer weakly, but they don't seem to care either way, nodding distractedly.

"Dan's been asking about you," Betsy offers, but as usual, that means nothing to me. I don't think I've ever given her a reason to think otherwise. "Actually, he's going to this barbecue we're planning on popping in to once we've finished these," she adds, before she grabs my glass and takes a sip of my drink. "You wanna join us?"

"I dunno," I start, but as I look back at the bikers I came with, I see Kace leaning down so Brianna can say something into his ear, then he leans back and lets out a full belly laugh. I see Jag playfully shoving the shoulder of one of the other guys while a group of girls I can only hope to speak to giggles, and suddenly, I feel like I'm clinging on to the outside, looking in. I don't belong with them. They were a group long before me, and they'll continue to be so after. Not that I fit in with my school friends either, but for now, they seem like the lesser of two evils. "Let me grab another drink before we go."

"That's the spirit!" Shannon beams as she picks up her purse from the table between us. "But it's my round." I won't say no to that, and when she comes back with not only drinks for us all but a round of shots too, I don't say no to those either. The alcohol warms my throat and numbs my mind beautifully, so I struggle to remember why I avoid these girls. It's definitely a *me* issue, like most things.

When we've all drained the last of the drinks on our table, we make our way to the door. I decide I should probably tell Kace I'm leaving, but when I find him in the crowd, he's frowning at Jag, both their postures tight as they whisper between themselves. I'm not about to get in the middle of that, so I happily take the excuse and follow the girls out to the taxi, and no one stops me. They chatter excitedly about the guys that are going to be at the barbecue, and I'm starting to think it's a bigger event than I assumed.

This is confirmed the minute we clamber out of the taxi and push through a side gate of the massive house we've arrived at. The backyard is bigger than the whole freaking compound and seems to go forever, which is useful because there are a *lot* of people here. Some I recognize from school, and many I don't, but I try not to panic at the mass of strangers and instead make a beeline for the drinks table. It's overflowing with options, but I grab whatever's closest to me and wince as the tang of grapefruit hits my tongue.

"Well, well, well," a voice drawls from behind me. "If it isn't the missing Isabelle." I smile politely as I turn to find Dan grinning at me. There's nothing actually wrong with him, and I guess it's not his fault Betsy's been trying to force him on me for months.

"Hey. I heard you might be here." The alcohol has my tongue looser than usual, and his eyes light up at my words.

"Heard or hoped?" he asks. I want to grimace but keep my face neutral.

I could easily flirt, have some fun chatting to a guy and get some attention, but I don't want to. There's only one guy my brain is letting me focus on at the moment, and irritatingly, it's his face that comes to mind as Dan continues to talk, but I don't catch what he's said. Because on the other side of the yard, in front of the gate I just came through, stands Knox. That was quick.

He doesn't say anything, although he'd have to yell for me to hear anything this far away, and he doesn't look like the type of guy who likes to make a scene. Instead, he just stands there with his arms crossed across his massive chest. I don't know how many other people have noticed him, but his disappointment coats the space between us.

He's disappointed in me? Why do I hate that so much?

"Sorry," I say, cutting Dan off midsentence, though God only knows what he was talking about. "I'll be right back."

I make my way over to where Knox stands, but as soon as I get within shouting distance, he presses the gate, holding it open. I don't know what it is about him, but I immediately feel like an admonished child. I step through the gate—steeling myself for what, I'm not sure—but all that's waiting is his bike and an Uber. He steps through the gate behind me and holds open the car door for me, still remaining silently disappointed.

It's way worse than if he'd shouted at me.

Although I'm not sure what I'm supposed to feel guilty about. I'm eighteen years old, and I came to a barbecue with my friends. But somehow, Knox makes me feel like I've betrayed him. Betrayed *them*. For leaving Kace and the others? How did he even find me?

I climb into the car, and he closes the door, then walks off into the darkness. As the car pulls away and onto the road, I hear the rumble of an engine, then spin in my seat and see the headlight of Knox's bike behind us. Of course—they don't ride in cages if they can avoid it. When we get back to the compound, he's there to open the Uber door and waits for me to step out, which I finally do, begrudgingly. He still hasn't said a word, and I feel the weight of his disappointment on my shoulders. Why I should care at all, I'm not sure, but for some reason, I find I do. I go to head straight for the clubhouse, but his voice stops me. "Prez wants to see you. Garage." He nods his head in the direction of one of the sheds.

I grit my teeth together and stand straighter before marching to the garage. Apparently, there's no worry of Axle's disappointment. I storm through the open door, and Axle doesn't even look up from the bike he's doing God knows what to, although Vaughn does as Knox steps in behind me.

"Take her to her room," he orders, without even sparing me a glance. Indignation rises in my chest at the dismissal.

"I'm not a child."

"That's funny, 'cause just when I think you're too old for this shit, you show me how much of a fucking *child* you actually are," he drawls, so casually putting me down, although I can see the anger simmering below the surface as his knuckles whiten around the wrench he's holding. The alcohol paired with his easy belittling of me boils my blood, and suddenly, I'm not feeling guilty anymore—only combative.

"Brianna's my age," I tell him, tilting my head and narrowing my eyes. "Did you know that? You always fuck children?"

The temperature in the room drops in an instant, and his glare turns deadly as he finally rakes it over me, his jaw clenched. His pupils are dilated, and my bones lock in place, the urge to run strong, but I can't.

"Everyone out," he growls as he stands, and I'm more than happy to follow that command, if only my body would cooperate. After what feels like minutes, my legs do move, and I start toward the open door, but a hand wraps around my wrist, the grip tight but not painful. "Not you."

"I'm not a biker," I remind him as the other two exit the garage, paying us no mind. He drops my arm and steps back with a raised brow. "You can't tell me what to do."

"As if you'd do what you were told if you were." I bow facetiously, moving back until I'm stepping over the threshold when his steely voice locks me in place once more. "Step one foot out that gate alone and you'll regret it."

"Well, I regret stepping in it, so maybe it'll cancel it out," I say lightly, not bothering to inform him I have no intention of going out again tonight anyway.

"You had freedom, and you abused it, so now you don't."

I spin back around when it sounds like he means for a lot longer than just tonight. "For seeing my friends?"

"For getting drunk in an unsafe environment."

"Oh, so now you're so worried about protecting me?" It's a low blow, I know it is, but it's out before I can tell my mouth that. His eyes harden and I hate it.

"I didn't manage it before, but fuck if I'll fail again." My brain tickles at the way he says *I* and not *we*.

"You don't think you're going a little over the top?"

"I don't care."

I barely even feel that drunk anymore, the trip back and this little chat sobering me up nicely. "How do you know it was unsafe?"

"Isabelle, you can barely stand and you've been with a group of random school-aged guys."

Okay, so maybe I'm not quite that sober. And in my defense, I hadn't expected there to be so many people there, especially guys I didn't know, but obviously I don't say that. I roll my eyes at him instead, like that'll calm him down.

"Would you have fucked one of them?" he asks quietly.

His question takes me by surprise, and for some reason, my stomach grows heavy at his crass language. I'm almost positive he wouldn't be asking if he wasn't pissed at me or I wasn't drunk, and that winds me up. If he wants to know, I want him to ask. But why does he want to know? Would he be jealous? Would he feel how I feel when I think about him and Brianna?

"How is that any of your business?"

"You're married," he reminds me sternly. So he doesn't give a fuck for any reason other than I'm tied to his son. He's not jealous. He's protective of Kace's reputation. Why does that make me want to *make* him jealous? I'm blaming the alcohol.

"You're right. I am."

"Had you forgotten?"

"No, I'm just registering what that means. Guess I don't need to step outside the gates for a mindless fuck after all."

"Careful," he warns, but isn't that what he should want? Why would he be warning me against sleeping with Kace if he wasn't jealous?

"Oh, sorry, does the president get to watch or something? I'll be sure to put on a show." I wink then turn and leave him standing like a statue, every muscle tense, but he doesn't call out to me. I have absolutely no intention of going to Kace right now anyway, and when Ashton waves me over to the bar as I enter the clubhouse, I make my way over.

"Hey girl," she calls as I get closer, but Kace calls for me from the other side before I get there. She waves me off with a smile, and I turn to him instead.

"Hey! Glad you're back. My dad ripped me a new one for letting you leave."

"Yeah, I just got the same," I grumble. "Where are you going?"

"He wants to see me again."

My chest soars at that information. Has Axle just called Kace so I can't go and find him? But I wouldn't have. We have actually become friends, and I wouldn't use him like that. Not that I have to let Axle know.

My stomach takes this moment to rumble loudly and remind me I've not consumed anything other than cocktails all day, but the last thing I want to do right now is remain upright and try to socialize down here.

"Go grab some food before you pass out," Kace says with a grin as he heads off. I could definitely eat, but I'm sure Sally or whoever is cooking today is already busy prepping for dinner, and I don't want to add to their workload.

I let myself into my room and throw my key and phone onto the bed, toe off my shoes, and use the bathroom. I'm trying to decide whether to change or just rest in my clothes when there's a knock at my door.

I open it to see an awkward-looking prospect holding a plate with a sandwich and chips on it. I grin at him in thanks as I take the food, assuming Kace asked them to bring it up on his way to the office.

"Prez told me to bring this up," he mumbles, as we both just stand there.

"Oh. Thanks," I say quickly. He nods and rushes away as I close the door, locking it again. I take my food to my bed and practically inhale the sandwich, moaning at the strong taste of the cheese and fresh salad as I mull over this latest development.

Axle claims it's all about me and Kace, but he calls Kace away when it looks like I might make a move and then sends me up a food delivery. Maybe jealousy is the way forward. Although toward *what*, I'm not sure.

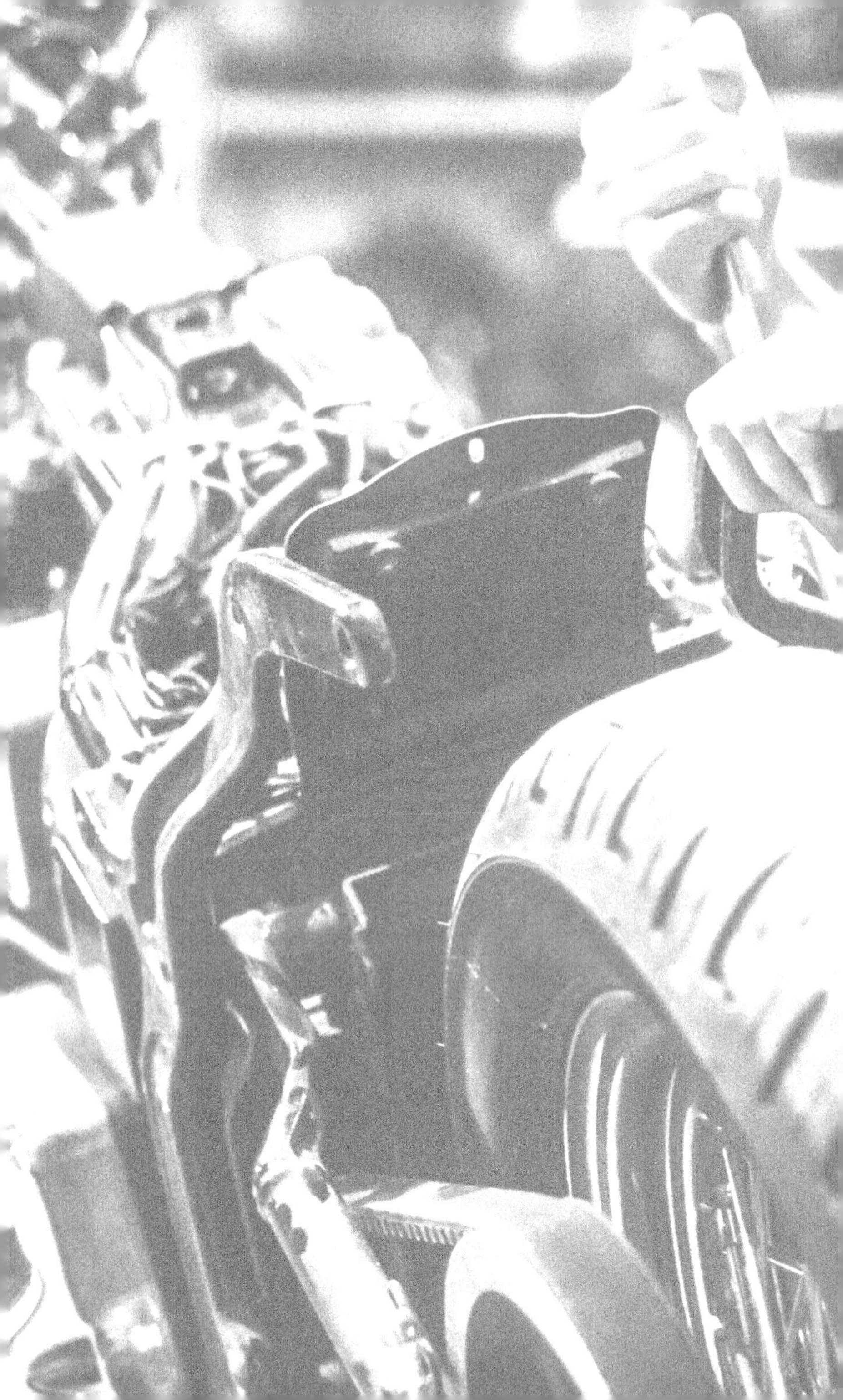

CHAPTER NINETEEN

Axle

She's going to drive me certifiably crazy. I guarantee it. Kace laughed his fucking head off when I told him what was running through my mind yesterday. He wouldn't have gone through with it, but I don't want Isabelle throwing herself at *anyone*.

She didn't come back down for dinner, so I hope she ate everything I sent up to soak up some of that alcohol. I should've sent Kace up with it, but fuck giving her the chance to make good on her word and convince him of anything. He's the only one I need to worry about—I'm sure she respects him too much to be messing with other guys, even if the marriage is a sham.

I'm an early riser on a good day—you can't really relax and sleep in when you're in charge of an MC—but today I'm up with the sun, too fidgety to try and sleep any longer.

Isabelle's due to go back to school today, and I need to talk to her about the *not going out alone* situation. She probably thinks I said it in the heat of the moment. I did not. From now on, she goes nowhere without one of us by her side.

The guys may have thought babysitting duties would ease now that she's here, but they'd be wrong too.

When I get my shit together and get downstairs, she's already sitting with Jag, although Kace is nowhere to be seen, which is rare for those two. They've been practically inseparable since they were young—a friendship I'm sure Isabelle would've slotted just as easily into eighteen years ago as she does now.

"Morning, Prez," Jag calls as I head over to their booth. Isabelle flinches but doesn't turn, so I slide in next to her.

"Mornin'. What are you up to today?" I ask him, and he shrugs with his mouth full.

"Nothing out of the ordinary."

"Great. You can go with Isabelle."

"You were being serious?" she asks, and I feel her eyes on the side of my face.

"Completely. You don't go through that gate without someone with you."

"I don't need babysitting."

Jag looks between us like it's a tennis match as I turn to face her with a cocked brow.

"I think you proved you do." She clenches her jaw.

"What about—" She cuts herself off with a glance toward Jag, and I wait for her to finish, but she doesn't. I'm pretty sure she wants to ask about the woods, but for some reason, she holds out asking in front of Jag. Maybe I'm not the only one who wants me to be the only one able to find her there.

"Well, I need to be leaving, so you ready, Jag?" she asks, and he nods as he drains his glass. "Are you riding with me?"

"Fuck no. We don't ride in cages. You're on the back, babe."

My eyes shoot up from my plate to him, glaring at the nickname for her that so easily slipped out. He tries to hide a smirk, but I'm not playing.

Stuffing down my objections, I grit out, "Get a second helmet," and he nods before going to grab one. Isabelle fidgets, waiting, seeing as she can't leave the booth with me blocking her in. I turn to face her, so close I can see the warm brown flecks in her dark eyes. "The woods is the only place you can go on your own. Don't make me regret it."

Her eyes widen slightly before she sucks that plump bottom lip between her teeth with a nod. God, what I wouldn't give to get a taste of that lip myself. Before I can talk myself out of it, I'm lifting my hand and tugging on her chin with my thumb so it pops free. She stills completely as I return my hand back to my side and nearly jumps out of her skin when Jag's voice comes from behind me, guilt clouding her gaze.

"Come on, then. Ready to spend your day with your number zero?"

"Zero?"

"I'm not even on the scale, baby. I set the bar." I'm pleased to see Isabelle roll her eyes playfully at his cockiness, and I suppress a growl in my chest before she turns to me.

"Excuse me, Seven," she says sweetly, and Jag barks a laugh where he waits.

Yep, she will definitely the death of me.

***

Every spare minute I have, I check her tracker to make sure she's where she's supposed to be. Not that Jag would be stupid enough to let her walk off again. I made sure they all knew the consequences of it happening a second time when they got back without her yesterday. I don't think many of them had seen me so enraged. They certainly weren't used to it.

But she stays where she's supposed to be all day, and I watch her arrive home on the back of Jag's bike from my position in the garage. Jealousy flares at her arms being wrapped around him but settles as soon as she climbs off and makes her way over to the garage. To me. She doesn't come in, standing in the large open doorway instead so the sun is behind her as she watches me watch her.

"Good day?" I ask, and she shrugs as if it doesn't matter.

"It was fine. Everyone cooed over Jag," she answers dismissively before changing the subject and asking her own question. "How come I didn't hear your bikes over the years?"

"You would've sometimes, but the sound of one bike is different to the sound of five or ten." Plus, I used to tell them all to park a street or two away so she wouldn't notice them roaring up to her, but I guess that was kind of pointless in the end. She doesn't seem overly satisfied with my half answer but nods anyway.

"Music or films?" I ask, and her eyebrows jump slightly, but she doesn't need too much time to think on it.

"Films," she says before making her way inside the clubhouse. She returns outside a couple of minutes later with her pad and pencils and heads over to the woods, smiling at the prospect on the gate, and that's the last I see of her until we sit down in the pit for dinner. Then I make up for barely seeing her all day by watching her every move like a fucking stalker. Knox has to repeat what he says to me on more than one occasion because she has my undivided attention where she sits.

Which is how I know there's something up with her.

She smiles politely and answers questions, sitting with a group of the club girls tonight, but she doesn't jump to join in. I thought she'd been getting used to everyone—she certainly seemed more involved over the past few days—but tonight she's more detached than she was the first night here. I check with Jag that nothing noteworthy happened at school, apart from the looks he got for following her around all day, but there's nothing.

The next day, I send Vaughn and instruct him to drop her off and hang outside in case she's feeling suffocated, but she still comes home withdrawn. She asks me about the prospects and I find out she loves the beach, even living inland, but she still spends the rest of the afternoon in the woods and comes back for dinner, where, once again, she's barely present.

On Wednesday, Kace goes with her, and it's still not enough to cheer her up. When she comes back and once again leaves for the woods, my curiosity is at a boiling point. Yes, I'd rather she just told me what was wrong, but I'm not deluded enough to think that she's there yet, even if I ever saw her for more than a couple hours every evening at dinner. It feels like she's taking steps back from feeling at home here, and I hate it. I want her to *want* to be here, not just tolerating it, but I have no idea what to do about it.

After watching her clear the tree line, I head back inside and make my way up to her room. I don't even know what I'm looking for, but there must be something. Something to explain why her mood has dropped so suddenly, and why it seems like she's keeping herself locked away even more than before.

Her door lock came with a spare key that I wasn't about to let anyone else have, so I pull it out and let myself into the room. Once I'm there, surrounded by her scent and her things, my sense returns. Even when she's not physically here, she can calm me. It's a little late, but I finally realize what a bad idea this is. This is *her* space, where she feels safe, and I shouldn't be here without her knowing.

Turning to leave, I pause when I see the wall separating her space from the hallway. Pinned up on the empty space are six A4 sheets of paper, each one a different section of the tree canopy that she's currently probably lying under.

Once again, her talent astounds me. Some are black and white and some are color, but each one is incredible, showing the leaves and the way the light spills through as if it were a photograph. Leaving her room untouched and locking the door behind me, I realize it might not be about forcing her to tell me what's wrong, but about making moves to make her feel as welcome and comfortable here as possible anyway. I head downstairs to find Kace and give him his task for tomorrow.

With my eyes on the door, I'm half listening to the conversation washing over me when she finally enters. She's running later than most, and everyone else is already seated. I don't even notice Brianna storming off until she's passing Isabelle.

Brianna must say something to her, because in the next moment, they're turning toward each other. I can't hear a word they're saying, but Isabelle is even tenser than when she first came out, which is all I need to get up and make my way over there.

I'm not sure anyone's even noticed, not paying as much attention to this girl as I do. I'm clearly not quick enough, though, because when I'm about twenty feet away, Isabelle cocks her fist back and slams it into Brianna's face. I almost want to laugh, but as Brianna spits something back to Isabelle and she winds up for a second hit, I reach out and grab her fist. She spins to glare at me.

"Alright, that's enough." She rolls her eyes, and when I let her hand go, she lunges for Brianna again. Grabbing her around the waist, I take her inside where she continues to flail around like a madwoman until I put her down once we're alone. My hands crave to stay on her waist as I steady her, but she takes a step back, pent-up anger making her restless. "What is wrong with you?" I ask her.

"Me?! She—"

"She what?"

She folds her arms and clamps her lips together, clearly not about to tell me anything. "Can I go now?"

"No. You can tell me why you're so fucking angry right now."

"Why aren't you angrier? She's saying shit about my dad, and her being your *fuckbuddy* shouldn't excuse that. Unless you don't actually give a shit what she says?" Her brows rise, and she's on a roll, not stopping for an answer. "Maybe you weren't really that close. Did you want him gone? Did you want his president's seat? I bet it was real convenient for you when he dropped dead."

She steps closer as she rants, the emotion in her voice getting stronger with each step, and I have to hold myself back from closing the small distance between us and cutting her words off by occupying her mouth. It's getting harder every fucking day. Whether it's the urge to make her happy, hear about her day, or get my hands on her, the need runs through me like a constant hum. Right now, it's a pulsing current.

"You can't say this shit to me," I remind her, thankful everyone else is outside.

"But she's allowed to say it to me?"

"No, she . . ." I don't know what to say because I haven't known what was going on. Brianna will be dealt with, and honestly, I'm not even mad Isabelle smacked her. It's hot as fuck seeing her cement her place in the pecking order here—a right of passage. She looks away from me as her eyes sparkle, and I know it's so she doesn't get emotional when she tells me the truth. I hate that she hides from me that way, but I don't blame her.

Cupping her cheek, I bring her face back to mine, but her eyes flutter closed, still keeping all of her vulnerability to herself. We're so close I can see the way her lashes rest on her cheeks, her lips parted, and her face tilted ever so slightly into my palm.

"I don't know how to *not* be angry," she says softly. "I'm trying to live for him, but I hate the thought of life without him." She finally opens her eyes, and I see the truth, the grief, the struggle shining in them. "I hate thinking he had his proper life without me." I feel so fucking hopeless in this moment, when I want to be able to fix it for her more than I've ever wanted anything, but it's impossible. I can't fix everything, but I'll always give her what I can.

"Come with me." I take my hand away from her face, and she doesn't ask questions, just follows me to my bike and lets me put my helmet on her head. Then she climbs on behind me and we ride to my spot.

My version of her woods.

She's quiet as I park up, help her off the bike, and sit on the small patch of grass overlooking the city. It's hidden off a quiet road and is barely big enough for two before the cliff drops off into the sky. The sun's already on its way down, so she'll only get about fifteen minutes of the color changing, but that's enough. She wordlessly sits next to me, her crossed legs so close to mine I can feel the heat of her body, and I look over at her.

"If you'd have punched Brianna half an hour earlier, you would've gotten to see the whole thing."

Her lips twist, but she doesn't let the smile free. The sky is streaked with deep orange, and it's not long before it fades into pinks and reds before the dark overtakes completely. She remains facing out, gazing into the black, even when there's nothing to see but the city lights dotted around. "What is there to be angry about if you still get to experience these?" I ask.

"You've been angry at many things this week," she reminds me. "Like when I went to the police station." My eyes narrow again just remembering the moment I realized she was at the police station.

"They shouldn't question you alone."

"I'm an adult. Plus, they weren't questioning me, they wanted to give me the chance to say my side and let me know no charges were being brought against me." That I didn't know.

"Either way, you shouldn't have had to do it alone." If I got my way, she'd never do anything alone ever again. "What did you say?"

"Is this your way of asking me what happened?" I shrug lightly, not wanting to pressure her. "Well, I told them that his version of events and mine were the same."

My head whips round to face her. "You what? There's no way that's true."

"How would you know?"

"There's no fucking way what he was doing to you on those stairs was consensual, and no fucking way he'd have admitted to it."

"How do you know about that?"

I grind my teeth together at the memory, and her eyes widen before dropping to the ground quickly.

"You saw the video footage? How?"

"You don't need to be scared to face him," I say, and she scoffs.

"Scared? Of what? Him? That he's out? Roaming around wherever the fuck he wants? Or maybe that I have no way to support myself, nowhere to stay? That day in, day out, I go to a school I fucking hate with people I hate even more to make my dad proud. My dad, who isn't even alive anymore and has a whole group of people who knew him longer and probably way better than I ever had the chance to. I *am* scared. Scared that I'm going to be by myself forever."

She's radiating tension when she finishes, staring out at the view, and I just let her sit there. I want to tell her she's wrong—she'll never be alone again. I want to fix every single one of the things that are scaring her.

"You're not by yourself," is all I can bring myself to say.

"Oh, *please*. You can barely stand to be around me. Kace is forced to because of some weird sense of obligation relating to some fictional marriage—which I've never seen the certificate for, by the way—and the girls have taken an instant dislike to me."

Why does she suddenly think this? She seemed to be settling in at the weekend.

"What did Brianna say to you?"

She doesn't reply, fiddling with her hands as she looks down at her lap. I'm not sure what I'm expecting her to say, but it's not what comes out of her mouth.

"Do you fuck her?" she asks.

No, of course I fucking don't. I should tell her. I want to tell her. But the fact that she's even asking the question scares the shit out of me.

"That's none of your business."

"I guess I'm the only idiot baring their soul tonight, huh?"

She sighs as she stands, and I immediately regret it, but what's the point in telling her the truth? It doesn't pass me by that I asked her a very similar question last night.

"Isabelle—"

"Can we go? If you wanna stay here, I'm more than happy to walk back."

CHAPTER TWENTY

Isabelle

As soon as we roll through the gates and pull up to the clubhouse, I jump off the back of his bike and shove the helmet into his waiting arms. I'm trying to rush inside, but he grabs my arm, holding my hands against the helmet between us.

"You haven't been asking your questions."

What's the point of learning about this place I don't belong?

"You don't answer my questions," is what I say instead before rushing inside. I don't want to think about how he keeps Brianna as a secret or how much I love clinging to him as we ride through the dark or how safe he makes me feel. I just want to go and wallow in my own space.

Of course, I can't resist looking back at him one more time as I near the stairs, but it's a mistake. He's already sidling up to Brianna, and I know I have no chance of hiding the betrayal I stupidly feel all over my face as he catches my eye, my own narrowing in response before I turn and rush up the stairs.

I fucking detest that girl.

I hate her for fitting in so well here. For what she insinuates about my dad, and for the way she has some kind of claim on Axle. Why *her*? Obviously, he fucks around—he's the president of a motorcycle club and is hot as fuck. It'd be weirder if he wasn't a player.

But why did it have to be her? Why did he have to stop for her instead of coming after me? Why does he have to act like whatever is between them is some big, private deal?

He could've just brushed it off if he couldn't deny it, but no.

Does she sleep in his room? Did he leave me with Kace the other night because he was desperate for her touch like I'm desperate for his? That thought stops me in my tracks. Because it's true. Somewhere along the way, I've started to crave Axle's touch. Whether he's sweeping the hair from my face when he places his helmet on my head, or pinching my chin to force my eyes to his, or even when he's restraining me. His hands always leave an imprint I can't forget, like they're branding my soul. To think of him having that same effect on Brianna makes me feel nauseous.

It's pure jealousy that has me checking the hallway when I reach my door and creeping into his room instead of mine. I just need to know for sure. If I find something of hers in here, then I can accept he's sleeping with her. Because without his admission, I can hang on to the one-percent hope that she's lying, however dumb that makes me.

I know that he can do what he likes, fuck who he wants, and it won't mean anything if I do find something. To him.

It'll mean everything to me.

The room is a mirror image of mine, except the bed is bigger, everything is darker, and it smells like him. I've barely reached his bedside drawer when the floorboards creak under someone's weight outside, and I freeze.

What the fuck am I doing?! What if it's him? What if it's her?

Whoever it is stops outside, which gives me enough time to rush into the bathroom, but I'm hesitant to shut the door fully behind me. Will he remember he left it open? Is it even him? Why is he waiting outside?

I'm freaking out in the dark bathroom when his bedroom door creaks open before clicking shut again. Footsteps sound, then nothing. Or nothing for me to hear, but the blood is rushing so hard in my ears it's probably drowning anything else out. I can't stand here in the middle of the bathroom waiting to be found. I open the airing cupboard door as slowly as I can, but my heart drops when I see how little room there is in there.

Pressing my back against the shelves, I pull the door in, but with my body in the way, it won't close fully. My heart pounds erratically, its beat painful against my chest, and when the bathroom light flicks on, I shrink into myself, hoping I'm hidden enough not to be found.

I see him in slices through the wooden door as he saunters into the room, running a hand down his face. He looks tired. And stressed. Did he and Brianna have an argument? Thank fuck he didn't bring her back here, because I definitely wouldn't be able to hide out and listen to those two.

I squeeze my eyes shut as he pulls his shirt over his head and begins to unbutton his jeans. God, I feel like such a pervert. I should get out of here, but how? If the glass fogs up enough and he turns the other way, I might be able to make a run for it. The water turns on, and I can't help myself. The curiosity is too much.

My eyes open of their own accord and widen when I see Axle completely naked, his body glistening as the shower streams above him. This man is a god. There's no other explanation for how he could be carved that way. His wide shoulders are well defined, with pecs I actually want to lick. His usual uniform of white T-shirt and cut shows his size but doesn't do his honed physique any justice at all.

My clit throbs as I take in his abs, trailing my eyes down to that prominent V, and when I see his hand wrapped around his already hard dick, my jaw hangs slack, and drool may actually slip from my mouth. *Oh my God.* I'm on fire. That's the only way I can explain how I'm so hot all over, my skin lit up with nerves.

His eyes are closed as he leisurely strokes himself from base to tip and back again, his dick standing proudly, and all I want to do is snake my hand between my legs and match his rhythm. I need to get out of here before I come just from watching him.

I shouldn't even *be* watching him.

His hand picks up speed, and he turns his back to me, resting one arm against the tiles as his other picks up speed. I gape as I take in the huge tattoo that covers the expanse of skin—one that matches the back of his jacket perfectly. It's stunning, and I want to explore every inch up close as it moves, the muscles underneath flexing as he works himself.

How is watching someone else masturbate so hot?

I genuinely can't keep still, my breath coming in pants and my body fidgeting, my thighs rubbing together as they grow slick.

Suddenly, he stops. He turns the water off without finishing and wraps a towel around his waist, then steps out and fishes around in his vanity. I have no idea what he's doing, but when he stands up again, the last thing I expect is for him to pull the closet door open.

Actually, that's a lie. The last thing I expect is for him to be holding a gun as he does so.

I'm not sure who's more surprised—him or me.

I stare up at him with wide eyes as he narrows his. He looks down, and I know he can see the way my chest is heaving. Will he think it's from anything other than fear? My eyes close and my head turns as I brace myself for what's coming next. He'll probably cuss me out for being a pervert, throw me out of here right now. He'll tell everyone—Kace, Jag, Knox—that I snuck into his room like a psychopath to watch him shower.

"Staying for the show?" he asks cockily.

"I wasn't—" Except I was, and it sounds like he knows it.

"Wasn't what?"

I slowly open my eyes again and peer up at him, his lips tipped into a knowing smirk. "I got busted in your room and had to hide. I didn't know you'd do *that*."

"You look flushed."

"You've got a gun pointed at me," I point out, seeing as he hasn't lowered it. That's the *only* reason.

"Does that make us even?"

"Can I go now?" I ask, looking over his shoulder at my one chance of escape. He chuckles under his breath, his eyes raking over every inch of me, and if my skin weren't already on fire, I'm pretty sure that look alone would be enough to scorch me.

"No. You wanted to be here so bad. Why?"

There's absolutely no way in hell I'm telling him that I was looking for signs of Brianna, so I roll my lips between my teeth as I try to think of another excuse—one that's believable and doesn't make me seem like a complete weirdo.

"I'll give you a choice, Isabelle," he continues, when nothing comes to my mind quick enough. His voice is a deep rumble that raises goosebumps along my arms. "You can tell me what you were doing in my room—the truth, Isabelle—or you can show me exactly what watching me did for you."

My eyes widen, my pulse beating frantically against my neck as my hands grow clammy. "What?"

"Tell me why you're snooping in my bathroom, or put your hand down your pants and show me just how wet your pussy is right now."

A shudder runs through my whole body at his words. He's never spoken to me in this way—no one has—and knowing he has this filthy side is intoxicating.

"It's not," I lie. Badly. He watches the way my throat bobs, shrugging as if it doesn't matter either way, but his shoulders are tense. He's more worked up about this than he's making out.

Is he mad? Is this to embarrass me?

My feet try to move, ready to step past him, but they don't. My breaths grow shallow as my heart pounds, my body frozen in place. Why is he doing this? I don't think for a second he would actually shoot me, so why? What does he want me to do here? Admit I'm a snooping psycho? Except he's still hard, his towel tented, hiding absolutely nothing. Does he *like* this?

"Words, Isabelle, or a show. What will it be?"

Swallowing hard, I clench my teeth and find enough brazenness to stare him down for a long minute before making a decision. I'm unsure as to what option would be preferable to him, but there's no way I'm admitting why I was snooping in his room like a goddamn creeper. He's given me a choice, and I'm taking it.

I peel my eyes from his, untie my shorts, and slide a hand beneath the waistband. Axle's eyes never leave my face, his pupils dilating until the black has almost completely overtaken the icy blue. A shiver takes over me at his expression, a gasp slipping through my lips as my fingers graze over my throbbing clit, seeking the juices that have lubricated me.

There's no hiding my arousal when I pull my fingers free. They glisten under the light, and when his eyes finally leave my face, his tongue swipes across his lower lip, dampening the skin as a flush creeps over my neck, staining my cheeks.

"Happy?" I ask with an edge, but he smirks, finally allowing some reaction on his stone face.

"Almost. Make yourself come."

My mouth drops open, my brain shortcutting at his demand. "That wasn't the deal."

"I've changed my mind." He shrugs, his tone so nonchalant that it's hard to believe he's talking about me playing with myself.

"I didn't see you come," I quip, though how I keep my voice level I don't know. This is hardly a normal conversation to be having with anyone, let alone the man that is technically my father-in-law.

"But you would've, right? Given the chance? You would've stayed and watched as I continued to slide my fist up and down my dick, watched as my cum hit the shower wall, wondering how it would feel landing on your skin, right?" He steps closer, lowering the gun and blocking me in as he leans in toward me, his lips closing over my ear. I bite my tongue, keeping the moan that wants to escape at the light touch of him inside. "This is me, Isabelle, doing what you didn't get the chance to. I want to see it."

His words are true and we both know it, but does that mean I give in to him now? Do I stand here and come like he asks, like a freaking good girl? It's not like it'll take long after his shower show. Although, it's my husband's father, so I guess that makes me not a good girl . . .

But would it turn him on the way watching him did for me? Would it make him nearly lose control? Because I want that. My eyes lower at the thought as they get heavy, but I keep my gaze on him. Leaning back against the shelves behind me, I suck my lower lip between my teeth as my hand returns to the front of my shorts and slides its way in. The way he watches me, the way he speaks to me, gives me the bravery I need to do this.

I shock even myself with how wet I am. My fingers slide easily from my swollen nub to between my legs. I shallowly pump a finger, but I'm suddenly so needy—for more, and for him. I need to come, desperately. His words and his proximity have me so close to the edge I'm practically whimpering. Axle is tense, every muscle in his body locked, and his jaw is tight as he clenches his teeth. Seeing him so close to snapping lights the fire impossibly higher, and I swirl my fingers around my clit, my hips rocking as my whole body seeks more.

"Are you close already, Isabelle?" His voice is huskier than I've ever heard it, and it makes me shudder. "Are you going to show me how pretty you look when you come?"

My mouth opens, but it's only a small moan before I trap my lip again.

"I need to hear you, Isabelle. Is it my name you're gonna scream as your pussy strangles your fingers? Are you imagining my dick inside you instead?"

I will myself to not give in to him—to not give him the satisfaction of knowing he's right—but his name is a chant in my head, over and over, and his words are all it takes to send me over the edge. My body tenses as I throw my head back on a silent scream, my muscles locking as pleasure rocks through me. It takes over my senses and my body as wave after wave pulses from where my fingers tease the last of my release out, to the tips of my toes that are curled in my shoes. When it finally ends, I slump against the shelves, chest heaving.

When I find the strength to open my eyes, his are ablaze, burning a path over my face. His gaze is red hot and too intense. I don't know what to do now, but when he takes a step back it's like a bucket of ice water over me as I take that as my cue to leave. I've been dismissed, and embarrassment and rejection flood through me.

I rush from his room to mine without even thinking of checking if anyone is out here, but thankfully, it's clear. Fumbling with my lock, I push the door, slam it closed behind me, then throw myself onto the bed and scream into my comforter.

What the fuck did I just do? Why did I even go there in the first place, what good was going to come from it? I've just gone fifty steps too far with the worst person I could've picked. How do I have so much regret when my body is still tingling from the quickest, hottest orgasm of my life?

Rolling onto my back, I groan, rubbing my eyes with my knuckles. I need to just sleep this terrible decision away. Sitting up, I start to tear my clothes off but pause when I notice the new paint job.

The wall opposite my bed—the one that holds the door—is now completely white. Not refreshed in cream, but a freshly painted stark white. There's a stack of things in the corner, and when I investigate, I find paints in every shade of green imaginable. From sage to forest to emerald, with a couple of blues and yellows and neutral shades too. Next to that bag are my drawings, stacked in a small pile with a note on top.

This is the perfect canvas for a proper mural. Kace

My heart sinks, a pit of overwhelming guilt and shame brewing inside me. Well, fuck. I am officially the worst person on the planet.

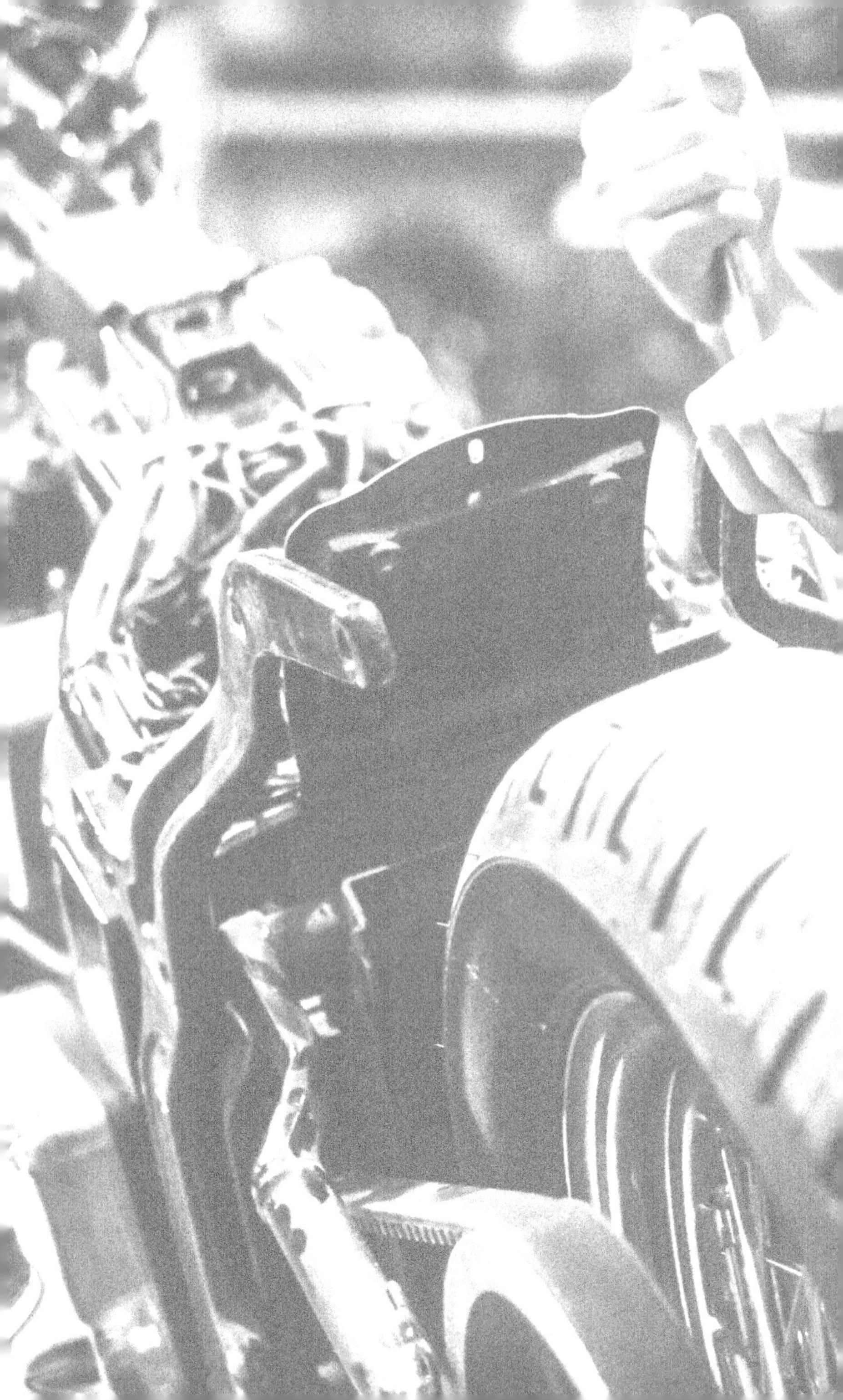

CHAPTER TWENTY ONE

Axle

She fucking wants me. That's what made me snap. The way her pupils were blown in lust, the way her chest heaved as she panted. I've been fighting the attraction between us, but seeing the pure desire pouring off her was enough to push me over the edge. I just couldn't touch her. I know my limits, even if I'm already so far over the line.

I'm convincing myself that she put herself in this position—that she inserted herself into my space and crossed that line first—but deep down, I know that's fucking bullshit. I took the opportunity with both hands and ran with it. The worst thing is that I want so much more.

If I didn't physically take a step back, I was likely to put my hands on her, and I know there's no going back from that. Once I've touched her—felt the soft skin of her thighs—there'd be nothing that could drag me away.

It's criminal that I couldn't see what she was doing—couldn't see the way her lips glistened, or how her cunt greedily took her fingers—but I was fucking transfixed on her face and didn't want to miss a second.

Isabelle is beautiful; there's no denying that. I spend way too much time watching her, committing her face to memory. But I wasn't prepared for the visceral reaction I had watching her come. I don't think—no, I know—that I've never seen anything as hot as that, and I want to watch her fall apart over and over.

It's absolutely futile to even try to not fist my throbbing cock the second I hear the door close behind her. I try to think of someone else—anyone else—but all faces merge to Isabelle's, and just like I did earlier, I give in way too easily. I picture the tiny shorts she was wearing today, imagine pulling them down so her pert ass is bared to me. Bending her over and grabbing a fistful of that silver hair. Leaning a forearm on the tile, I stroke roughly, my hand jerking up and down my shaft with no finesse as I come in no time at all.

I barely sleep, my body taut with the knowledge that she's mere steps away and willing to come for me. The only way I keep away from her is by reminding myself that I'm supposed to be the adult here—the responsible one. I'm supposed to be making her feel safe and giving her a place to belong. I'm definitely not supposed to be taking advantage of a girl who's barely legal.

Instead of remembering the way she moaned as she rocked against her own hand, I wonder why she was in here in the first place. Finding her in my closet had my thoughts spinning, but now I'm curious. I mean, she chose to masturbate in front of me instead of telling me why. There's nothing in here she could find that would interest her. I don't keep the door locked because no one apart from her would ever dare snoop in my space, but that doesn't mean I'd keep anything important just laying around. But what would she be looking for? I can't even pretend that I really mind her being here, especially not with the outcome, and my mind quickly wanders.

The conversation we had on the hill runs around my head as it has done regularly since that night. All I want is to make her realize she's not alone and never has to be again. How can she not see how well she fits in here? I thought she was—she seemed to be—until this week. Maybe the main issue isn't here, maybe it's where she spends the majority of her day. She did admit to hating school, only going to try to make Trey proud, but that's stupid. She must know that she amazed him on a daily basis and still would, whether she has a degree to her name or not. If Trey saw how miserable and withdrawn she'd been this week, he'd hate it as much as I do. Thinking about how her face had lit up as she looked into the paint shop, I make a decision.

"Who went with Isabelle?" I ask Kace in the morning as I join him and Jag in the main room. Isabelle's normally left by now, and I don't see her around here anywhere.

"She's not come down yet." I just walked right by her. I'm about to turn around and go back up but Vaughn catches me on the way.

"What's up, Prez?" he calls as I look up at the stairs. "Looking for Isabelle?"

I don't know why I bother to hide it, but I do. "Why would I be looking for her?"

"As if," he says with a laugh. "She's all you're ever looking for." I glare at him, but he holds his hands up with a smirk. "Not saying it's a bad thing, man, chill out."

"Then what are you saying?" I'm so fucking defensive and I know it, but that's because I know I'm acting like an idiot. What business have I got to be even entertaining whatever this is I feel with Isabelle? She's eighteen. Younger than my own son. And the fact that other people can see how whipped I am for her just pisses me off.

"I'm saying that this isn't good for you." I frown at the light way he's delivered that bullshit line.

"Isabelle would be the best thing to ever happen to me," I argue.

"I'm sure she would. I'm not saying *she's* what isn't good for you. It's you. You're fucking it up for yourself. This whole act of not wanting her. Just admit it and fucking come out with it. You'll be able to focus, and she can start to properly settle in."

I run a hand down my face. He's clearly got the gist of the situation, so there's no point denying it. "It's my fault."

"Yeah, that's what I'm telling you," he says with a cocky chuckle. "You're a snappy asshole with her, which pisses her off. It's not her fault you're fighting whatever you two have."

"I can't have her."

"Says who?"

"Me," I snap back at him.

"Then own that decision. Give her up." My face must flash with the rage that fills me at that suggestion, because his brows rise, and he chuckles again. "Yeah, that's what I thought. Sort it out."

But I can't. I can't take an eighteen-year-old—my best friend's daughter—no matter how much my whole soul begs for me to. I've already gone way further than I ever should've, and Vaughn's right, that's on me. I just hope I haven't fucked it up too much.

"Did you stop me for anything other than shitty life advice?"

He chuckles. "As a matter of fact, I did. Knox is waiting in your office."

Waiting for me to lead the way, he follows me out of the main room and into my office, where we find Knox.

"What's up?" I ask him, sitting behind my desk as they take the two seats in front.

"The drop is sorted and Luke's been informed. He'll be doing the next one. He's been encouraged to step up and hold his own." I nod at that information, sure he'll do just that. It's gonna be a decider—how he handles the first drop after the clients demanded changes that didn't come. He messed up, now it's a good chance for him to prove himself. He didn't really wanna be here in the first place so this is his second chance to show he does now, that he's worthy. "The sale of the diner is going through. Should be finalized next week."

We've been looking for more businesses to acquire to assist with the volume of money we can clean, and I noticed how busy the diner was when I was hanging out waiting for Kace to relieve me of Isabelle duties at the beginning of the month. It's a legitimate business that can keep itself afloat, and with cash constantly flowing through it. Perfect for our portfolio.

"Let me know when it's all done and dusted."

"Anything you wanna update us on?" Vaughn asks with a cock of his brow, and I know he's aiming to mess me around, but now he comes to mention it, there is.

"Actually, I'm gonna have Isabelle intern at the studio."

Their foreheads crease in surprise at the news, but surprisingly, it's Knox that speaks. "You gonna tell her the full story?"

Fuck no. I'm still not ready to risk that, as fucking cowardly as that makes me.

"No. That shit stays the same. But she hates school, and she's so close to graduating I'm sure we can work out a way for her to complete her credits while still leaving time to work."

"You could just let her know. Then she wouldn't need school at all." I grit my teeth at Knox's insistence. He's never normally vocal, so I don't know what his problem is with this. He knows the fucking plan.

"She's months away from graduating. She doesn't need to throw it away completely."

He stares me down, showing me he very much disagrees with my reasoning, which is probably because he knows it's bullshit, but he doesn't outright tell me that. I don't break eye contact, wondering if he'll decide to call me out like my friend or shut up for his president.

In the end, it's Vaughn that breaks the stalemate.

"Satch knew Trey better than most, probably only second to you. You think she's ready for that?"

"I think she's ready for a new challenge. Plus, it might be good for her to hear about him."

"She's not been thrilled to learn so far."

I shrug, saying nothing further on the matter. The truth is, I don't fucking *know* the best choice to make for her, or how to make it better for sure. I've just got to keep trying, and this is the way I'm choosing to do it.

"Speaking of Trey—if you see Brianna, I'm looking for her."

"Jag's little shadow? Why?"

"Something to do with Isabelle decking her the other night?" Knox asks, and if I'm not mistaken, I'm sure there's pride in his voice, although his face is as blank as ever while Vaughn looks smug too.

"Something like that, yeah."

As we come out to the main room, Isabelle has appeared from her room and is sitting with Jag and Kace. We make our way over to their booth, but she spots us coming, stands up, and walks back toward the stairs to the rooms without sparing us another glance. Vaughn and Knox continue onto the booth, but I veer right and follow her. All thoughts of letting her go vanish when she tries to get away from me, the urge to keep her close stronger than my morals.

She has her hand on the door when I catch up to her.

"Are you avoiding me?"

She stills and sets her shoulders, letting her hand drop away from her escape route before turning around to face me, although she won't meet my gaze.

"No."

"Isabelle." She looks up at me with big eyes as I growl her name but then flicks her gaze to where Kace laughs behind me. "What's wrong?"

"Nothing."

"Don't lie to me." She pulls her lip between her teeth and her eyes wander to the noisy booth again, and it dawns on me. "You feel guilty." My tone is full of surprise, although it shouldn't be, as her eyes snap back to me, incredulous.

"Yeah, of course I do. You don't?"

"Why?" I know I bite it out as she starts just a little, but does she have *feelings* for him? Before she can answer me, Brianna's irritating voice comes from behind us.

"Axle! Were you looking for me?" Isabelle raises a brow, then turns and pushes through the door as Brianna appears at my side. She lays a hand on my arm, and I stare down at it until she thinks better of it and removes it.

"I *was* looking for you. I want you to quit the crap with Isabelle."

"What do you mean?" She pouts as she looks up at me through her fluttering eyelashes.

"You know what I mean. I don't want any more of your pathetic bitchy comments toward her, and if I hear you've said one more thing about our former president, then you'll know about it." The corners of her mouth are downturned now, but at least she's not making that stupid duck face. "Do you understand me?"

"Yes, of course." I nod and push through the door, then take the steps two at a time to find Isabelle. I rap my knuckles on the door to give her warning before opening it myself. She's sitting to the side of it, her legs crossed in front of her, a pencil twirling in her fingers as she studies the freshly painted white wall.

"You didn't answer my question," I say.

"Oh, sorry, I thought you were busy with Brianna now." I ignore the churlish comment, because if she thinks I'd rather spend a second with Brianna over her, she's deluded.

"Why are you feeling guilty about Kace?"

"He's supposed to be my husband, is he not?" she asks flippantly, starting to sketch straight onto the wall.

"You didn't care about that when you were coming for his dad."

Her head whips up to me as her mouth falls open, her eyes dark like coal. "It wasn't like that! It was a mistake."

I narrow my eyes at her comment, which I'm pretty sure is just to wind me up, but what if she's decided she does prefer him? "Why do you suddenly care for him?" I ask her.

"Because I don't want to disrespect him. He's a great guy! He lies with me all night to make me feel safe and buys a lock for my door . . . He tries to cheer me up when I'm sad and saves me pancakes when Jag makes them. He even did this for me." She waves her hand at the wall. "He's *good* for me." She sounds like she's trying to convince herself more than me, but still, I need to hear it definitively from her.

"So what, you have feelings for him now?"

"No! I don't, but I should. If there's anyone I should have feelings for right now, it's him."

"But?" She looks down to her lap, where she's fiddling with the pencil again. "*But*, Isabelle?"

She shrugs. "There's no but." She's lying, I know she is. "I *want* to want a guy like him."

"What does 'a guy like him' mean? A guy who knows what you need before you do? Who knows where you feel safe? A guy who would want you to be able to have your own slice of the forest in your bedroom?"

"Exactly." She stands up and walks farther into the room, putting physical space between us as she chews her lip, looking as if a million thoughts are running through her head. She deserves that kind of a guy, and Kace definitely could be, but not for her. Even if I can't have her, I can't watch her try and be with my son. Who am I kidding? I can't watch her with anyone. Her teeth still, her lip popping free as her eyes narrow in suspicion and she looks back at me. "Except he doesn't know . . ." she says slowly, shaking her head lightly, ". . . that I draw the forest. That I go there and feel safe there. You do."

I feel like a fucking deer in headlights as she comes to her realization, her eyes searching mine for the truth. I can't lie to her, but I still try to steer her away. "Kace painted the wall."

"Maybe. But it wasn't his idea." She frowns slightly, but I can't get into this with her. She doesn't get it—doesn't understand that this isn't as simple as two people who want each other. "Did you tell him about the woods?"

"No." It's true, I didn't. For some reason, that's still some sacred, secret place I'm determined to keep just between us.

"Why did you ask him to do it?"

Because I'm racking my brains for anything to make you happy, and I will do whatever I can to make that happen. "That's not important right now."

She scoffs as she folds her arms, looking at me with disbelief, but when I keep my face hard, impenetrable even from her, she relents. "Then what's so important?"

"School. You hate it." She looks away as I remind her of the conversation we had yesterday.

"Don't most people?"

"Maybe, but why are you still going?"

"Why wouldn't I?"

"Isabelle, answer the fucking questions." Her mouth tightens as her eyes narrow, but she answers, which I actually don't expect—or deserve, after snapping at her.

"I guess it's what people do."

"Not everyone," I tell her truthfully.

"Well, what do bikers do all day?" I'm not sure if she's just trying to change the subject, but her voice softens when she adds, "Question of the day."

"Whatever is needed," I answer, but as usual, I want to give her more, so I continue. "The main guard have roles within the club, but most have jobs within the businesses we run."

"Who's the main guard?" She's had her question on MC life for the day, but I can't get myself to end the conversation, especially when she'll probably go back to avoiding me after.

"Knox, Vaughn, Rider, Bishop, Kace, Satch, and Cyrus." Her eyes light up with recognition. She's met them all by now—except maybe Cyrus, who is gone ninety percent of the time—and knows they're all her watchers. She can even find their official roles on their patches if she wants, although she doesn't ask me any more about what their roles entail. She never asks about that side of the club. Instead, she gives me an answer I wasn't expecting.

"I just want to do life right," she says, as if it's that easy.

"The right way for who? For you?"

"For him."

I frown, wondering when Trey ever would've mentioned college. "You think he'd expect you to be doing something that makes you miserable because it's expected?"

"I don't know, and I can't ask him," she bites out, putting up her defenses like usual whenever he's talked about.

"Isabelle, you don't need to be trying to make him proud. He was proud of you just for existing. You were his whole world." And that makes two of us. She blinks and turns to look out of the window, hiding her feelings, but I hate the space she's putting between us, physically and otherwise. I take the steps to eliminate it, stopping behind her as she tenses, sensing me at her back. I could easily lean down, inhale the scent of her hair, wrap my arms around her and pull her back into me.

"Why didn't you tell me about school?" I ask.

"Why would you care?"

"I care."

She shrugs her shoulders lightly.

"Share it with me. Please."

She visibly softens with my gentler tone, turning to face me again, tilting her head back so she can look at me, and I wish I could always be this way with her. My hands twitch with the urge to touch her, but I don't trust myself. Not now I know how beautifully she comes. Half an hour ago, I was explaining to Vaughn why I can't have her, and now, with the way she gazes so vulnerably up at me, all I want is to take everything.

She's still not talking, so I turn and say, "Come with me."

CHAPTER TWENTY TWO

Isabelle

I'm not expecting Axle to take me back to the paint shop, and I'm definitely not expecting him to introduce me to the guy working there and tell us both I'm interning. But the second Satch—the guy running the place—nods his agreement, I feel the weight of the world lift from my shoulders. I don't know how it's going to work with school, but I trust Axle to have my best interests at heart and to sort the details for me. The hope of being able to do something that might actually make me happy makes my heart swell.

Axle leaves quickly, having me stay with Satch and the guys who work there, but I don't mind. He was right—I was avoiding him. I still can't believe what happened last night, and every time I look at him, I'm transported back to when he was dripping water in front of me, his muscles slick and taut. I could do without thinking of that every second of the day if I want to be at all productive.

The second the door closes behind Axle, Satch turns to face me.

"Trey's daughter, huh?" I open my mouth to reply but nothing comes out and I close it again. "We worked together," Satch says, saving me from thinking of a response.

"Here?" That makes sense if Axle said Dad drew too, but I never saw any evidence of that.

"We tattooed." He says it gruffly, as if it's not important, but it seems like it is.

"You don't anymore?" He shakes his head, and I want to ask so much more but I keep it inside. For once, I actually want to hear about my dad from someone else, but I also don't want to piss my new boss off.

Satch gives me a tour of the space, and the front gallery is only the beginning. This place is like a TARDIS behind the small storefront. There's a whole other studio behind with every artistic medium I could imagine—paints of every kind, pencils in every color, as well as iPads and big screens to see the work up close. Pretty sure I've died and gone to heaven.

Behind this is a garage that currently has only two bikes parked up inside but looks like it could fit twenty. This is where the aerosols are kept, and where the designs are transferred onto the final medium—motorbikes. This place is legit the most sophisticated body shop I've ever seen, and apparently people come from all over the world to have their bikes customized by the guys here. It's amazing, and I'm enraptured from the minute Satch starts speaking.

I spend the rest of the week and all weekend at the shop by my own choice, and leave every day with a massive smile on my face. I slowly get to know a few of the guys that work there, but basically camp out in the studio and draw to my heart's content while Satch throws random little stories about my dad into the conversation. They seemed really close, but in a different way to Axle's friendship with him. I think Satch saw my dad as a son, and his grief seems as compounded as mine. It helps me feel . . . less alone.

It's so therapeutic to not think too hard about life, to just sketch, draw, or paint whatever pattern comes to my mind, and to listen and absorb information. I'm not trying to fit the designs to anything, I'm simply quieting my mind and flexing my creativity—that had been missing for so long before coming to the compound—by getting it onto a page as I learn so much more about my father.

Seeing what's inside my mind become a physical entity has always been my favorite part of art. When my dad passed away, I was adrift—still am—so instead of trying to figure out what I wanted to do, I just did what was expected of me as a teenager. I wanted to still make him proud, but I didn't know how or what that would entail. I think he'd love that I'm here. I get to do my favorite thing, which is design and draw all day, as well as fawn all over the other artists' work, which is seriously stunning. Plus, I find out the night sky bike is Satch's, so how could he not be the coolest, when he rides around on that thing? I never would've thought people would be in the market for something like this or that artists would choose this medium, but clearly, I've been living under a rock.

Another of my favorite things is how Axle has taken to dropping me off and picking me up from the shop. Satch and the guys count as my babysitters, I guess, so the others don't have to spend their days with me now, and it's always Axle who's waiting for me in the morning and who comes into the shop five minutes before closing.

We haven't mentioned that night again and nothing further has happened between us, but when he collects me and searches my face to make sure I'm okay, my heart melts. When he grips my thigh to warn me he's going to start the bike, my skin burns. When I wrap my arms around him for the ride and feel his muscles flex against me, I feel safe. And then I get back and see Kace has saved me a seat for dinner, and the guilt floods me all over again.

On Monday, I have to go back to school, but Axle has somehow worked his magic so I only have to attend for two mornings and one afternoon a week. The rest of the time is mine, and I spend it mostly at the shop before spending a couple hours on my mural in the evenings. It's really coming together. I eat dinner with everyone, catching up with Kace and Jag as well as Ashton and Sally, who are fast becoming my favorite club girls. Then I end up sketching after dinner.

You'd think after spending my days creating that I'd be tapped out, but it never stops, like I'm drawing from a bottomless well, although an embarrassingly high percentage of the sketches revolve around Axle. Every day I ask him a question, and every day he answers before asking me one about myself. I steer clear of the subject of Brianna, but he tells me all about how you patch in, as well as all of the businesses they run. Makes sense how he got the bartender to kick me out that first day now. My day seems to brighten when I search Axle out, and his own questions remain just as pointless as the first. Or so I thought, but when Ashton shows me the new iced tea maker for the bar, I know whose doing it is. The man who right now is leaning against his bike, looking like temptation in a leather jacket.

As I get closer, he straightens and places my helmet on for me when I stop in front of him. I don't even bother to try and do it myself now. I like that he focuses on keeping me safe, and I love the way he moves the hair from my face with gentle fingers. These little things make me feel so close to him, it's scary how attached I've grown. We ride to the shop, and he holds the door open for me.

"Hey, Little T." Axle grunts his disapproval at the nickname, but Satch is pretty much the only person I don't want to throat punch for reminding me of my dad. Maybe because he himself reminds me of him. He's so relaxed and comforting. "How's it going, Prez?"

"Good. How's it going here?" I roll my eyes at his *so subtle* way of asking if I'm behaving. Satch grins at it too.

"All good here." Axle nods and leaves without another word.

"How come you're not president?" I blurt out. His patch says Secretary, and I've been wondering what makes Axle the top guy when he's clearly not the oldest, but Satch laughs so hard and for so long he starts coughing like he might choke up a lung. "Is it that ridiculous?" I ask.

"Yeah, darlin', it is."

"I guess you need to be more high-strung for that role, huh?"

"What makes you say that?" he asks, still chuckling.

"Well, Axle is always so growly and tense." That's not completely true. I've seen a gentle side of Axle that makes my knees weak and my hands clammy, but it's few and far between. He mainly scowls and grunts like an angry caveman.

"I think you're the only one who gets that side of him."

I scrunch my nose at the thought I get the less-than version. "What side does everyone else get?"

Satch lets out a long breath. "Axle is normally the most laid-back guy to be around. And he's president 'cause he's got all the traits needed, ones I definitely don't have." I get the feeling he wants to move on from the conversation, but I like hearing about the real Axle from him.

"Which are?"

"Loyalty. Compassion. Brutality." He says them so quickly it's like he's got them memorized.

"Is Axle better than my dad was?" It's a stupid question. Childish. It shouldn't be a competition. I just can't bear the thought of them being glad when my dad stepped down. I want them all to think he was incredible, like I do.

Satch coughs to clear his throat before he replies. "Your dad was among the best of us all. It only made sense that Axle, his best friend, would take up the mantle after he left. He was the only real choice, the only one who could even be compared." I want to rub at my chest where it aches, but the feeling of anger or panic doesn't accompany it when Satch speaks of him. It kind of feels nice, in a tough way. "And if there's one thing anyone can say about Trey, it's that he embodied those traits." I feel the pride straightening my shoulders, easing the ache in my sternum. "You recognize those words?"

I frown at Satch's question. "Should I?"

"I would think so. They're on his gravestone."

"No they're not." I've committed every word on that stone to memory, and there's no way I've missed those ones.

"'Course they are. When was the last time you went down to The Wyre?" He chuckles lightly as if I'd just forgotten, but that's impossible. I know where my dad's gravestone is, and it's not somewhere called "The Wyre." And it definitely doesn't have any of those words on it. He's looking at me curiously, but the phone rings before he can say anything else.

With my heartbeat suddenly three times as fast as usual, I slip out back to the bathroom and search the internet for The Wyre. My blood runs cold as I skim through the first couple of entries, complete with photos. Ordering an Uber, I sneak out through the garage while Satch is still chatting away to a customer.

I stare unblinking at the stone, willing the tears not to fall. He's been here this entire time and I didn't know it. Why did they even have the other one? Just to keep me away? Was it some sick way to keep him for themselves? It doesn't make sense, and sadness threatens to crush my chest. The still air is broken by the rustle of his clothes as he sits next to me.

I should've known it wouldn't be long. I feel the warmth of his body so close to mine as a chill settles within me.

"It was all I had," I tell him, without looking away from the spot my dad's name is etched into the marble. "His grave—his headstone—it was what I clung to for five years. It was all that kept me alive, but he wasn't even there. You tried to take him from me in life, and I guess you succeeded in his death, huh?" He doesn't answer, and I turn to face him, my vision blurring just a little as I capture his pale blue eyes, but I still don't let the tears fall. "I want to hate you for it."

Lifting his hand, his intentions are clear, but I can't handle it. I twist my face out of his grasp, and he lets his hand fall back to the ground.

"He was there," he finally says, but his offering enrages me.

"I don't want your spiritual bullshit."

"No, I mean he was *there*. He is. He was for you, always." He looks serious, but I don't get what he means. My dad can't be there *and* here, in this fancy-ass grave surrounded by all the other fallen bikers.

"I don't understand."

"He's not *here*, Isabelle. He's *there*." I let the words sink in, let the anxiety at having lost my dad for the second time recede. "No one else knows. It's protocol that MC members are buried here."

"Why are you telling me?"

"Because I can't see you hurting, Isabelle. I physically can't. If I can fix something for you, I will." He sounds so sincere that I believe every word. "He was always yours. Always your father first, president and club brother second." I want to look at him, to see the sincerity I know will be in his eyes, but I'm too raw, too emotional. We let his words sit between us as I look back to the etching of my favorite man's name.

"Will it stop hurting?"

"No," he tells me brutally, but I appreciate his honesty. I don't need him to mollycoddle me, no matter how close I am to breaking. I'd always rather feel the truth than be shielded by lies and be disappointed. "Not completely. He was everything to you."

"So this is it?" This aching pain when I think of him, this sense of something missing—it will last forever? How are people supposed to survive, to live like this?

"You need to remember what he wanted for you. Yes, he'd be sad to not see you grow up, but he would be so happy you're still here. He'd want you to join in and live and make choices that make you happy. You being okay was all that mattered to him."

I know that's true—I know he wouldn't care what I'm doing as long as I'm happy, that's always how he was—but it's hard to remember when sadness wants to drown me.

"I'm not okay. Not with him not being here."

"None of us are. But he's not." And that's the crux of it, isn't it? He's not here. And I can never change that.

"If he knew I'd been so sad for so long, he'd be fuming," I half whisper, knowing it to be true. Axle huffs a laugh next to me that makes me look at him with a sad smile.

"Exactly."

When I don't turn away, he brings his hand up, but I pull away again before he can touch me. "Please don't."

His jaw tenses, and he lowers his hand again.

"You're mad," I say.

"At myself. For going too far the other night."

He thinks he went too far? That this is some kind of punishment? Does he regret it?

"It's not because of that." I can feel him searching my face, but I can't look at him. "It's all right here"—I gesture to my chest—"and I'm trying to keep it in, and if you hold me it'll spill out and I don't know if it'll ever stop." I don't even know if I'm making sense, but his thumb and finger pinch my chin anyway, bringing my eyes up to his as my vision blurs. His gaze is so intense that it cocoons me, and I forget we're sitting in the middle of a cemetery—it's just me and him.

"I've got you," he whispers, oh so softly, and the first tear falls. He watches it roll down my cheek until it hits the corner of my mouth, then he leans in and presses a feather-light kiss to the edge of my lips, tasting it. His gentleness is my undoing, and the flood gates open as the emotions I've spent three weeks—probably more like five years—hiding bubble to the surface and crash through me.

The next thing I know, I'm surrounded by him, his arms strong around me and my nose pressed to his neck, his scent invading my senses. I let him hold me as I fall apart, hoping I can put myself back together again after.

He doesn't move until I'm ready and doesn't speak when I slowly pull away. He doesn't say a word while he wipes my face free of tears, or while he's driving me back to the shop. He doesn't mention it when he drops me off either, watching me go in silently, and I'm grateful for it, because I don't know what I'd say back.

Satch's face is the first thing I see when I step back inside and guilt floods me.

"I'm really—"

"Don't be," he says quickly. "Just don't do it again." I nod, suitably admonished, and he runs a hand down his face with a sigh. "I don't have kids, Little T. Never wanted 'em. Your dad was the closest thing to a son I ever had."

I open my mouth to say something, anything. Maybe that he doesn't need to tell me this, maybe to try again to say I'm sorry, but he holds a hand up and I clamp my mouth shut.

"I taught him how to tattoo when he was a prospect. We ran the shop together. I was, or hope I was, his confidant when he got your mom pregnant, when he was asked to be president, when he chose to step down. Losing him gave me infinitely more pain than I ever thought my biker heart could stand."

I swallow down the lump in my throat, my eyes burning with the need to cry, but this isn't about me.

"I couldn't tattoo again. Seeing the Knights of Mayhem tattoos on everyone—inked by Trey or inked by me—it still hurts. So I set this shop up instead. I needed a creative outlet, my soul demands it. But it was fresh. And then you came along."

Now a tear does slip free, but I wipe it away quickly.

"Axle asked me, and he knows all of this, so if he's asking, he's got to have a plan, right? He's got to think it's for the best. I just didn't realize he meant the best for *you*."

"I can quit," I stutter, even though it's the last thing I want to do.

"No, Little T. It turns out it's the best for us both. So you've got to stick around to help me heal, okay? Let Axle keep you safe. I know it's a lot to ask, but having you here is like having a small piece of Trey back. You can't just be getting an old biker attached and then run off."

Despite the tears in his eyes, he says the last bit with humor, but I don't laugh. I nod silently, unable to trust my voice. I'd promise him anything at this moment, and not only to ease his pain, but because he's reminded me—in the most casual way possible—that I matter. That there are people who care for me. People who would be hurt if something happened to me. And when I thought I had no one, that means *everything*.

I'm on my way to dinner when I see Brianna across the main hall. I'm fully intending to ignore the bitch, but she surprises me by swerving right in my way with a big smile on her face.

"Hey, girl." My face must show my surprise—or more likely disdain—because she rolls her eyes. "I know, don't make it difficult. I promised Axle I'd be nice." Why is she always so connected to Axle?

"And . . .?"

"And I wanted to invite you out with us." I'm about to say absolutely not, and she can obviously tell because she speaks again before I can. "Kace and Jag are already there, and I know the girls would love to see you." I frown at the thought that none of them invited me themselves, but clearly I'm transparent. "They knew I wanted to make amends, so they let me invite you." I guess that makes sense. They're probably bored of me being at odds with someone here.

"Okay, fine." I'm not even a huge fan of drinking, and after how the last time went, I'm not in a rush to repeat it, but a night forgetting everything heavy sounds good to me. Brianna looks relieved and grins, pulling me toward the bar.

"Perfect! Let's get some road-shots in, seeing as we're behind everyone now." She grabs my hand and pulls me toward the bar on the opposite end of the main room, where there's a line of shots waiting. I raise a brow at her confidence, and she shrugs unapologetically. "What? I give a good apology."

"That's generous," I mumble, as she hands me a shot.

"Fair, but I don't think you ever actually wanted to fight." She downs her shot in one.

"No, but someone shitting on my dead father's memory does that to me," I snark before throwing my shot back, and she splutters slightly, having the good grace to look at least a little ashamed.

"Yeah, sorry about that. I don't share well."

Knowing she's talking about Axle sours my stomach, so I drain another shot to distract myself. She thankfully doesn't talk about him anymore, and we both finish the last shot on the bar top. My head swims, and I definitely should've eaten before downing them. Or checked what liquor she was pouring—nothing's ever hit me this quick or hard before. My tongue feels thick and heavy, and Brianna's voice seems to come from the end of a tunnel.

"We're leaving now," she says, although it doesn't sound like she's talking to me. I'd assume it was Kace, but her voice takes on a whole different tone to the usual. Something wrong slithers over my skin and gives me goosebumps. "You ready, girl?"

"Need to grab my wallet," I say, leaning into the way my voice takes on a drunken edge. I do feel drunk, but not in a normal way, and I definitely haven't drank enough to give me this reaction, especially not this fast. The room is starting to tilt and sway.

"We don't really have time," she mutters, but I pretend I haven't heard her and make my way to the stairs. She comes to my side, looking around the empty main room as we reach the door. "I'll wait down here, but be quick, okay?"

"'Course. Two minutes." I drag my heavy legs up each stair and start down the corridor that feels like it's gotten six miles longer. I'm crawling by the time I get to my door, and there's absolutely no way I'm managing to unlock it, so I don't even try. But I can't pass out here. I still don't trust every person in this place, even if I wasn't pretty sure I'd just been drugged.

"Isabelle!" Brianna whisper-shouts from the bottom of the stairs as I give in and lie down. I pull my phone out of my pocket with fumbling fingers and click the only person I can at this moment—most recent on my call log. It rings a couple times before he answers.

"Hey, spitfire! What's up?"

"Something's wrong," I murmur, so slurred I'm surprised he understands me.

"Oh, fuck!" Brianna spits from way closer than before.

"Where are you?" Kace barks in my ear.

"Bedrooms," I mumble, then it all goes black.

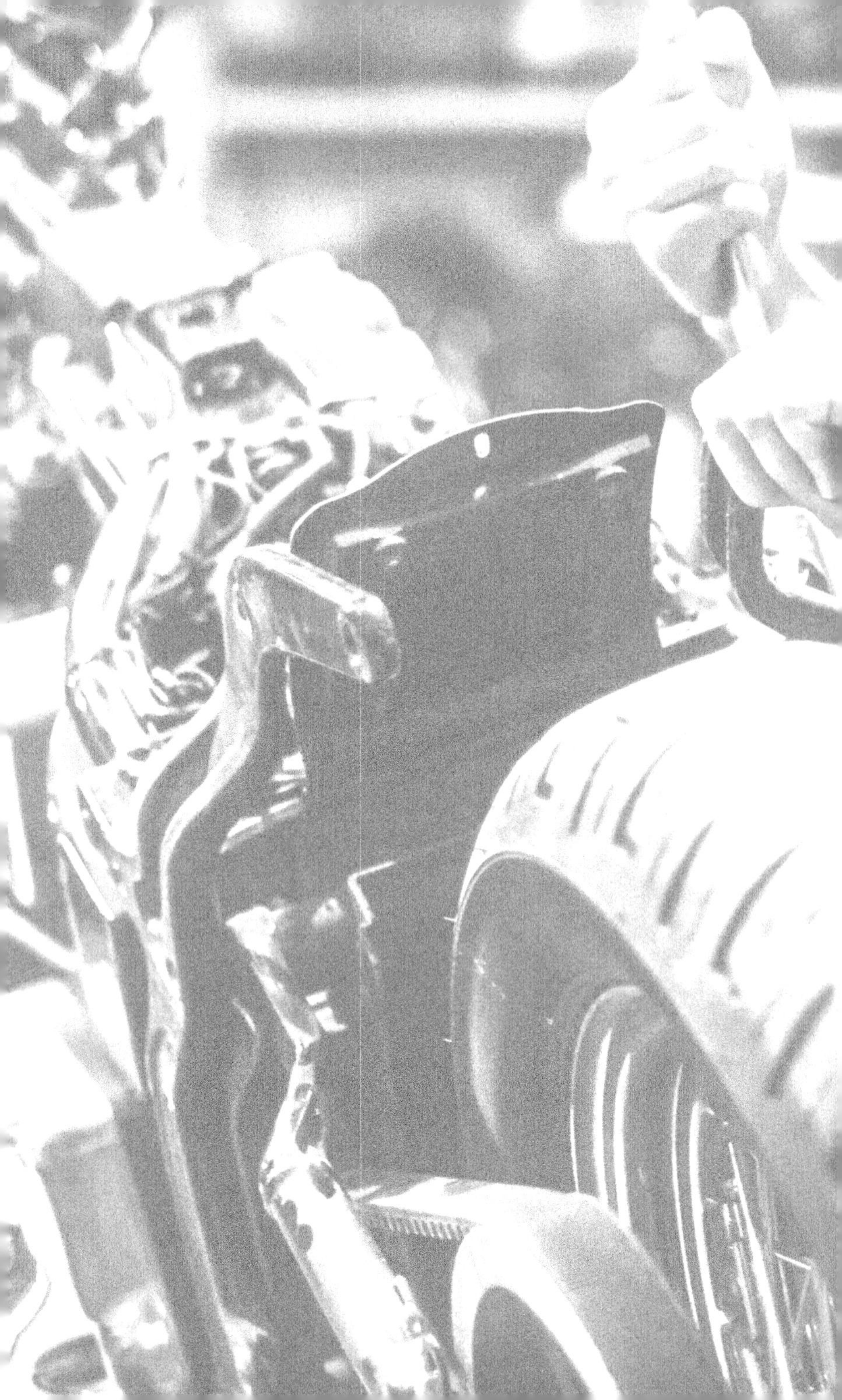

CHAPTER TWENTY THREE

Axle

The second his brows come crashing down, I'm on my feet.

"What? Where are you?" I'm practically vibrating with the need to get to her, and I don't even know what's wrong, just that something is. "She's upstairs."

Unfortunately, we're not at the compound, but we're not far out. Pulling my phone out of my pocket as we head to our bikes, I dial Vaughn. "Prez?"

"Get upstairs and get Isabelle, now," I bark, knowing he'll do exactly that right away without asking time-wasting questions. Dropping my phone back into my pocket, I take off in a blur of smoke and screeching tires.

What the fuck has happened?

We've only been gone an hour and she's calling for help—and calling Kace?

Why the fuck isn't she calling me?

Kace catches up to me as I'm bursting through the main room. "She said something's wrong," he tells me as I fly up the stairs.

We get to the top of the stairs and see Vaughn at the end of the corridor, a shocked Brianna beside him. "What the fuck is going on?"

Vaughn turns when I shout, a limp Isabelle laying in his arms. Without a second thought, my arms are reaching for her, pulling her against my chest. Relief is a palpable feeling inside me, the need to have her close overwhelming all my senses. Her head lolls against my shoulder, but her chest is moving. "I'm asking *you*, Brianna, so start talking right fucking now." I see her flinch out of the corner of my eye but can't bring myself to stop watching Isabelle's chest move up and down, proving she's okay.

"I don't know! She looked funny downstairs, so I came to check on her and found her on the ground a second before Vaughn came up."

"Then what the fuck's wrong with her?" Kace demands to no one in particular. Kace doesn't get angry, usually laid-back and chill, but clearly, he's wound up about this too.

"Kace, come on," Brianna scoffs, as if he's overreacting, but I ignore her.

"Vaughn, ask around. Find out if anyone has seen Isabelle in the last hour and who she was seen with. No one goes anywhere until she's woken up."

If she's a lightweight eighteen-year-old who drank too much, then so be it. But if it's something else, I sure as shit wanna know what. He nods and hands me the keys he's holding, which turn out to be Isabelle's. "I'm taking her home," I tell Vaughn, then turn and carry her down the stairs, Kace opening the doors in my path.

There's no way she can be on a bike right now, so I lay her down in the back of her car and strap two seat belts around her middle and thighs before climbing into the driver's seat. The itch of being in a cage doesn't even feature in my mind—the need to get her home and back in my arms too strong.

Somehow, I make it back to my place in one piece, even with driving ninety percent of the way with my gaze on the mirror, checking on her. We pull up around five minutes after we left the compound, and I carry her out of the car and into the house, up to the main bedroom. Yeah, there's another, but why would I ever put her anywhere that's not my bed? I fret for a second about whether she's comfortable or not, pulling the blanket over her and then folding it back down again. I want to hit something or someone, expel some pent-up energy, but I also want to be still enough to hear the light breaths that exit her mouth.

My phone rings, piercing the silence in the room.

"Yeah?"

"Brianna's gone." I clench my jaw so tightly to avoid fucking roaring that I'm pretty sure I feel a tooth crack.

"How the fuck has she gone? It's been fifteen fucking minutes since I specifically said *'no one leaves.'*"

"She was supposed to be getting the message around and she slipped out somehow. The guys aren't happy about being locked down either." Shit, I need to get back there. I don't want to leave Isabelle while she's still unconscious, but I need to go and be a fucking president, which means protecting her too.

"Okay. Come over and watch Isabelle."

"I'll be five minutes."

I hang up and throw the phone down onto the chair in frustration. Fucking Brianna.

"Now you're definitely angry," Isabelle croaks weakly, and I spin to see her furrowed brow as she blinks up from where she's lying. A huge breath expels out of me in relief, although I can still feel how tense I am, my shoulders rigid. I don't speak or move while she pushes herself to sit, rubbing at her eyes with a groan. "Where are we?"

"My house."

Her brow furrows even more. "I thought you lived at the compound."

"I do, most of the time." I want to go to her, to wrap her in my arms and keep her safe from everything, but instead, I stand there, stock-still as I take her in.

"How did I get here?"

"I drove you."

She tilts her head to assess me, her eyes still half-closed. "I thought you don't drive in cages."

"I do for you."

"Is that why you're angry?"

"No." She raises a brow at my succinct answer, and I begrudgingly continue, getting riled up again just thinking about it. "We found you unconscious in front of your door." She frowns in confusion. "Do you remember anything?"

"I remember... I was going to go out with Brianna. We had some shots for the road." Why the fuck was she agreeing to that? I told her not to go out alone. She doesn't even fucking like Brianna.

"If you had listened to me about not leaving alone, this wouldn't have happened." I'm angry at her, when I know it's not her fault, but I'm fighting the urge to wrap her in cotton wool and never let her out of my sight again. How am I ever gonna relax knowing she defies me?

"I wasn't on my own," she points out, but Brianna isn't one of the people who can keep her safe, and she should know that. It also means Brianna was lying about finding her unwell downstairs, as if disappearing at the first opportunity wasn't suspicious enough. "I was with someone *you* let in. Someone *you* were fucking."

"I never fucked her," I say, not quite sure why that's so important right now, of all times. "She's practically a child," I spit.

"She's my age."

"Exactly," I grunt, disgust at myself leaking through my voice as I run a hand down my face.

"Really?" she asks with an arch of her brow. "You're gonna make me think this is all me? I'm making up how you touch me? How you watch me? How you want me?"

I'm torn between loving how brave she's being with what she knows to be true and flipping out on her for taunting me. I know it's not just her—I'm even worse—but I can't act on it, so what's the fucking point in her rubbing it in?

"What is this?" she continues. "'Cause I'm not going to let you make me feel like an idiot. Clearly you know how I feel about you, and maybe you do think I'm just a child, but I don't think you think of me that way."

I don't—not in the slightest—but it's irrelevant. This isn't the time, even if I could have this conversation with her.

"Is that all you remember?" I ask instead. She doesn't reply straight away as we both stare each other down, and I swear the air cracks between us. How is it like this with her? And how much longer can I help myself?

"Yeah," she says eventually, looking defeated. "What happened?"

"We don't know." Her brow creases again. "How are you feeling?"

"Like shit, now you ask."

That's to be expected. "You'll probably feel that way for a good few hours. If there was something in your drink, the side effects will last longer than the actual effects."

"Oh yay," she mutters sarcastically. "But why would anyone do that?" I don't know. That's what's pissing me off even more. I don't know, so I don't know how to stop it from happening again. I distract her with the thought that won't stop niggling at the back of my brain.

"You called Kace."

"Huh?"

I swallow before I repeat myself. "When you were in trouble, you called Kace."

"Okay?" she asks, furrowing her brow.

"Why didn't you call me?" She flinches at the question and looks away. "Isabelle." I see the shiver that goes through her as she hears her name from my mouth, and my pulse quickens.

"He's my hu—"

"Don't say it!" I haven't got the patience left today.

She looks back at me with a pissed-off look on her face. "Why would I call you?"

"You said—"

But it's her turn to interrupt me now. "Yeah, and *you* said it didn't matter."

It matters.

"You wish it was Kace." She's said it before, but it's no less true now.

"You know what?" she asks, folding her arms with a huff. "Yeah, I do. I wish I felt this weird magnetic attraction to Kace. At least he might reciprocate, and I wouldn't feel guilty all the damn time." A knock on the door makes her jump, and when Kace pushes it open, it's clear he's heard every word she just said. She looks down, chewing her bottom lip, and he looks to me.

"You need to tell her," he says, stating the fucking obvious. It's all going too far, but I can't. Not right now.

"I will. Let me deal with this shit first." He nods, and she looks between us questioningly. "Keep her here until you hear from me. No one else." He nods again, but Isabelle's not happy about that.

"I want to go back to the compound."

"No," I snap, and she flinches. "I can't fucking focus if you're there."

Her face falls, the hurt easily evident before she tries to hide it from me.

"We'll have a sleepover, spitfire," Kace cajoles, and even though he's only trying to cheer her up from where I've upset her, I can't help but practically fucking growl.

"This is all very dramatic for having a bad reaction to some shots," she huffs.

Except I don't think that's true at all, and that's what worries me.

CHAPTER TWENTY FOUR

ISABELLE

I wanted to forget everything heavy, and instead, I've been forced to face it. I've not drowned my sorrows—I've basically told Axle that I wish it was him I was married to instead of his son. Then he left. Without telling me I'm not imagining it all, without admitting to anything himself. Not only did he walk out of the house without saying goodbye, but he disappeared completely. The next day, Kace takes off as soon as he's settled me back into my room, and I quickly realize that Vaughn, Knox, and Axle are all gone too. Vaughn and Knox come back separately, but I don't see anything of Axle for days.

Everything just carries on as normal, as if it's not unusual for the president and VPs to take off for days at a time, and maybe it's not, but I *miss* him. I miss our rides to work, and I miss seeing him over the dinner table. Don't get me wrong, I'm still enjoying the time I spend here. The girls continue to make me feel welcome as I get to know the others, and

Rider and Jag and Satch keep me company, but his absence is always glaring.

I work as normal, then I spend most of my free time in the woods after. Working on the mural just makes me think of him, not that I'm escaping that by drawing in the woods. My pencils seem to take on a life of their own, and instead of forming the canopy above me, they create their own thing. It's more often than not his scowling face that stares back at me from the page.

Why is it I've ended up obsessed with this angry, distant, argumentative guy who wants nothing to do with me? But then, that's not true—I know it's not. I've seen glimpses of Axle when he's caring and gentle, and that's when my heart fizzes in my chest. I know he's just as attracted to me as I am to him. I know he feels this weird connection and feels the pull like I do. So how can he just up and leave, without a word?

I pack up my things as the light falls and make my way back over to the compound. Wanting to put my sketches away before someone sees how many times Axle's face looks up from the pages, I head straight up to my room. Except I'm reaching for the door to the stairway when it's wrenched open, and he stands in the way, nearly barreling straight into me. He freezes just as I do, and we blink at each other, not sure what to say. I've willed him back so much over the last couple of days, and now he's right here in front of me, and I can't function.

His name is called from behind me, and it breaks his gaze as he steps to the side and starts walking straight past me, with *nothing*. Not a word.

"Axle," I blurt as he leaves, desperate to just keep him here for a moment more. And I know he hears me, even if he does ignore me completely, which just pisses me off. "Hey!" I call, but still, Axle ignores me.

In frustration, I throw the object in my hand at him. The pencil sails through the air before it bounces from the back of his head like an insignificant bug. But it works, at least. He stills and turns slowly, gaze locking on the pencil rolling away from him before those eyes come to land on mine. Then he walks ever so slowly back to me, until his chest is barely an inch away from mine, and drops so his mouth hovers over my ear.

"Throw something at me in front of my guys again and I'll bend you over and let them watch as I show you exactly who's in charge."

I swallow heavily as my stomach heats at his words, even if they are meant to be a threat. I couldn't even tell you which of the guys was in the same room as us right now.

"We both know you couldn't bring yourself to do that," I say as he straightens.

"You're so wrong you don't even know."

"Where have you been?" I don't know if it's the question or my sad tone, but his eyes soften, losing their harsh glare.

"Did you need something?"

I scoff at the impersonal question, looking over his shoulder at the guys watching us before straightening my own. "I *need* an annulment."

"It's not happening." He goes to turn, but I catch his bicep and he stills.

"That's not your decision to make."

"What's Kace said?"

I roll my eyes. "He said to speak to you. Repeatedly. Now, why is that?"

"It doesn't matter."

"It matters to *me*. Is that not enough?" Will it ever be? Did I already lose the only man who would ever care about what I want? He doesn't answer, his jaw set. "I don't want to be married to Kace. I want him to be my friend by choice, not by obligation. I want to settle in here as who I am, not as Kace's wife."

I'm getting more worked up as I speak, not caring about the audience as I suddenly feel the rise of anxiety that's plagued me for years as I futilely try to argue for my own identity, something that suddenly seems so imperative to have sorted *now*. "I'm not Kace's, and I don't want to be trapped into it."

My eyes flit between his that are filled with worry, and he rests his hand on my breastbone, but even the warm pressure doesn't help, the feel of his skin against mine only heightening the need to be free. I can't be with Kace when I feel so much for Axle—his dad. He steps even closer, eliminating the space between us, as his mouth lowers above mine.

"No, you're not Kace's. You're not married to Kace," Axle murmurs, and I feel his breath on my lips. I for sure think he's joking—trying to wind me up to alleviate my panic—but he looks deadly serious, and even more worried than before.

"I'm not?"

He shakes his head slightly, and I don't know how to feel. Confused, maybe. I should be relieved, it's exactly what I wanted, but inexplicably, the fact I have no ties to this place now just kind of makes me feel adrift. The anxiety doesn't dissipate. Instead, it ebbs and flows as it fights for space in my mind with bewilderment and doubt. Have I been the butt of their jokes for weeks?

"You assholes!" I step back from him with hurt fury, and his hand drops. "What was the point? Trick the poor idiot with nowhere else to go? Why did you need to lie to me about being married?"

"You *are* married."

"You just said—"

"You're married, Isabelle. To me."

I have nothing to say to that. Absolutely nothing. I am officially speechless. My first reaction is to laugh, but his face is so tight I can't make myself, so I stand there, gaping.

"Breathe."

But I can't remember how to let it go. My chest spasms uselessly without sucking in any air.

"Stop making this into such a big deal," he says flippantly, but there's an undercurrent to his tone, and even his attempt at distracting me, focusing me on an argument, isn't working. My brain is static, and I can't form instructions to tell my body what to do. I quite literally *can't breathe.* Axle is there, cupping my face with one large hand and laying the other over my chest again.

"Breathe in, Isabelle," he says softly, and I do, managing to gasp in a ragged breath. I never can resist the gentle Axle. "And out." I blow it out in a rush as he follows the movement of my chest down with his palm.

He continues patiently coaxing my body into calming down while I stare at him, taking in his eyes that are so full of concern, the pale blue flecks just as mesmerizing as always. Doing what he can to help me, like he has since I moved in here. And now he's not just the president of the club that I have a ridiculous crush on. He's my husband. And he's right here.

I move so suddenly his hand slips from my cheek into my hair as I reach up on my toes and press my lips to his.

His hand tightens where it's tangled in my hair, but other than that, he's as still as a statue. Now it's his turn to stop breathing.

Pulling back so our lips aren't together anymore, I keep my eyes closed, not daring to look at him. The lack of response is embarrassing but would've been understandable when I was married to his son. It's just damn humiliating now I know the truth.

"Axle," I breathe, but I have no idea what to say next.

"If you start something knowing this, know that you're mine," he murmurs, his voice deep and husky. I open my eyes to look up at him, staring intensely down at me.

"You don't want to fuck your wife?" I chide, but it comes out wobblier than I hope. Everything about this situation is overwhelming me.

"Is that what you are?"

"Apparently."

"No, not apparently." His fingers massage the back of my neck where they're still tangled, and my whole body relaxes. It's easier swayed than my mind, although that's not far behind, as stupid as that makes me. "Are you my wife?" He keeps still, not saying anything, and not moving while he waits for my answer. It comes way quicker than it should.

"Yes."

He doesn't kiss me like I'm expecting—like I'm hoping he will. Instead, he takes my hand and leads me out through the main room and over the asphalt to his bike, while claps, cheers and hoots ring out from the club members hanging out in the booths.

He doesn't speak as he puts my helmet on, then takes his seat before helping me climb on behind him. I'm confused and nervous. I was kind of hoping for something a bit more horizontal than a bike ride. Is this where he takes me back and drops me off at my aunt's house? Is he done with my shit? Okay, obviously not, but a girl could use a little reassurance, you know? We're not riding long before he pulls off the main road, winding down little more than a dirt track until he pulls up outside his home in the woods.

It stuns me, just like the first time I saw it—the wooden structure blending into the surrounding trees with huge windows that bring the view into the home. We both climb off, and he pulls my helmet off, cradling my face in both of his hands and tilting my face to his. I take him in as if it's the first time, not actually believing he might be mine.

"The way you look at me is dangerous," he says with awe. "It makes me feel invincible."

I smile indulgently, more than happy that I can give him that. "Why are we here?"

"If I'm going to fuck my wife for the first time, it's not gonna be where someone else has been, or where anyone can hear." Heat floods my stomach as his words hit me.

"Are you loud?" I tease, trying to distract from how my body is already craving him.

"Not me, baby, but I plan to make *you* scream."

The only thing that keeps me upright as my legs weaken are his strong hands, holding me in place as he lowers his mouth to mine. He kisses me as if he's waited his whole life to do it—as if he's worried I'll disappear if he stops. I press my body to his, not able to get enough of the feel of him against me as he snakes an arm around my waist, holding me tight against his chest. His lips are soft but forceful against mine, and I match the fervor he gives.

He hooks his hand under one thigh, pulling me up his body, and I happily wrap my legs around his waist. I feel the steps as he walks through his home without breaking our kiss, holding me to him the whole time. I don't even notice we've stopped, but he bends until my back hits the soft bed and settles between my thighs, his hand sliding up to squeeze my waist. I arch into him, wanting to be closer still, even if it is impossible, and his hands search for my skin, not finding it due to the romper I'm wearing. He murmurs in disapproval before grabbing each side and tearing it straight down the middle. I gasp as he pulls back, looking down at my now exposed body.

"Fuck," he grunts, as he takes in my lacy underwear set. He trails a finger along the frilly edge of the balconette bra. "Do you always wear underwear like this?" I nod, suddenly shy at his obvious approval of what he sees. It's way more modest than some of the stuff you can see at the clubhouse, but he seems to love it. "How am I ever gonna keep my hands off you knowing that?"

I grin, but as he hooks his finger into a cup and pulls it down, freeing my breast and pinching my taut nipple, my eyes close as I tip my head back at the pleasure, and then I feel his warm mouth soothing the sting with soft laps of his tongue. God, that feels good. His hand massages the other while his mouth works magic before he swaps and has me writhing underneath him as I gasp. Trailing his fingers over my stomach, he traces the edge of my panties before drawing a line from where my clit is hidden to where the lace covers my entrance.

"Do you know that since you gave me your show, the only thing I've gotten off to is the thought of what's hidden under here?" The thought of him stroking himself, making himself come while thinking about me has me desperate for him, and I tighten my legs around his waist. "Not knowing what you were doing under your shorts drove me wild. Were you doing this?" he asks, pulling the wet lace to the side and pushing one long finger straight inside me.

My back arches off the comforter as pleasure shoots through me, my pussy clenching around him. He pulls his finger out of me, trailing it over my clit, and I moan at the magical sensation he elicits.

"Or do you like this?"

I'm pretty sure his voice is an aphrodisiac, because having words whispered to me just heightens everything. He stops his slow perusal of my clit and slides two fingers inside me instead. It's a fullness I'm craving, and when he pumps them slowly in and out, I claw at the bedding.

"Axle," I beg, wanting so much more, but he captures my lips with his before adding a third finger. The intrusion is delicious, and when he rotates, hitting my front wall, I swear I see stars, and I whimper into his mouth.

"Fuck, I need to be inside you."

"Yes," I plead. *Yes, please.*

He stands and places his cut on the armchair before shedding the rest of his clothes, and I watch as if it's my favorite show. It just might be. As he unveils all of his taut, tan muscles, I take him in, desperate for him to cover me again. He pulls my panties down my legs and lays a kiss on my stomach before peeling my bra and torn scraps of romper off.

Then he settles himself between my thighs, and the feel of his warm skin against mine is heaven. He kisses me until I feel like I'm spinning as he hikes my knee up by his hip, opening me up for him. I feel the pressure of him at my entrance, and when I might tense, he pinches my nipple, kissing the gasp from my lips. Then he pushes in, and I think I pass out. I've never felt so full, so good, so right.

He pulls back out until just the tip is in, and then he pushes all the way to the hilt again, and I love it. I'm so wound up that every time he pushes in, my toes tingle, my orgasm just on the edge, but he drives me insane by drawing it out.

Axle pushes up on his hand and looks down to where we're connected, where he's pushing in and pulling out of me right now. His jaw tightens, and I know he's trying hard to control himself.

"That is such a pretty sight." He sounds so full of awe that I feel like I'm missing out.

"I wanna see."

"Yeah?" he checks, and I nod. He kisses me before pulling out, then lifts me up and takes me into the bathroom. He stands us in front of the large vanity mirror and bends me over the counter, pushing into me as he sucks in a breath through his teeth.

When he's deep inside me, he pulls me up to standing, hooks his hands under my thighs again, and picks me up as if I'm sitting. I wind my arms around his neck behind me and put my feet up on the counter. Then he parts my thighs, and I can see the exact place we meet. He slowly pulls out until it's just the tip hidden from view and then pushes all the way back in, and we both watch as I take him fully, matching groans filling the space as he resumes teasing me with shallow thrusts.

"You like that, baby? You're squeezing my cock so fucking hard."

"Yes," I breathe, desperate for him to do it again. It must feel as good for him as it does for me, 'cause he groans like he's in pain.

"Okay, show's over." He places my feet back on the ground and pushes me to lean over the counter again. This time, he pulls all the way out but then he plunges into me so deep, hard, and fast that my orgasm crashes over me like a wave and my vision goes hazy. All I can focus on is the way he pounds relentlessly into me, keeping the pleasure pulsing through my body from fading away and sending me into a second explosion before I've even come back to reality.

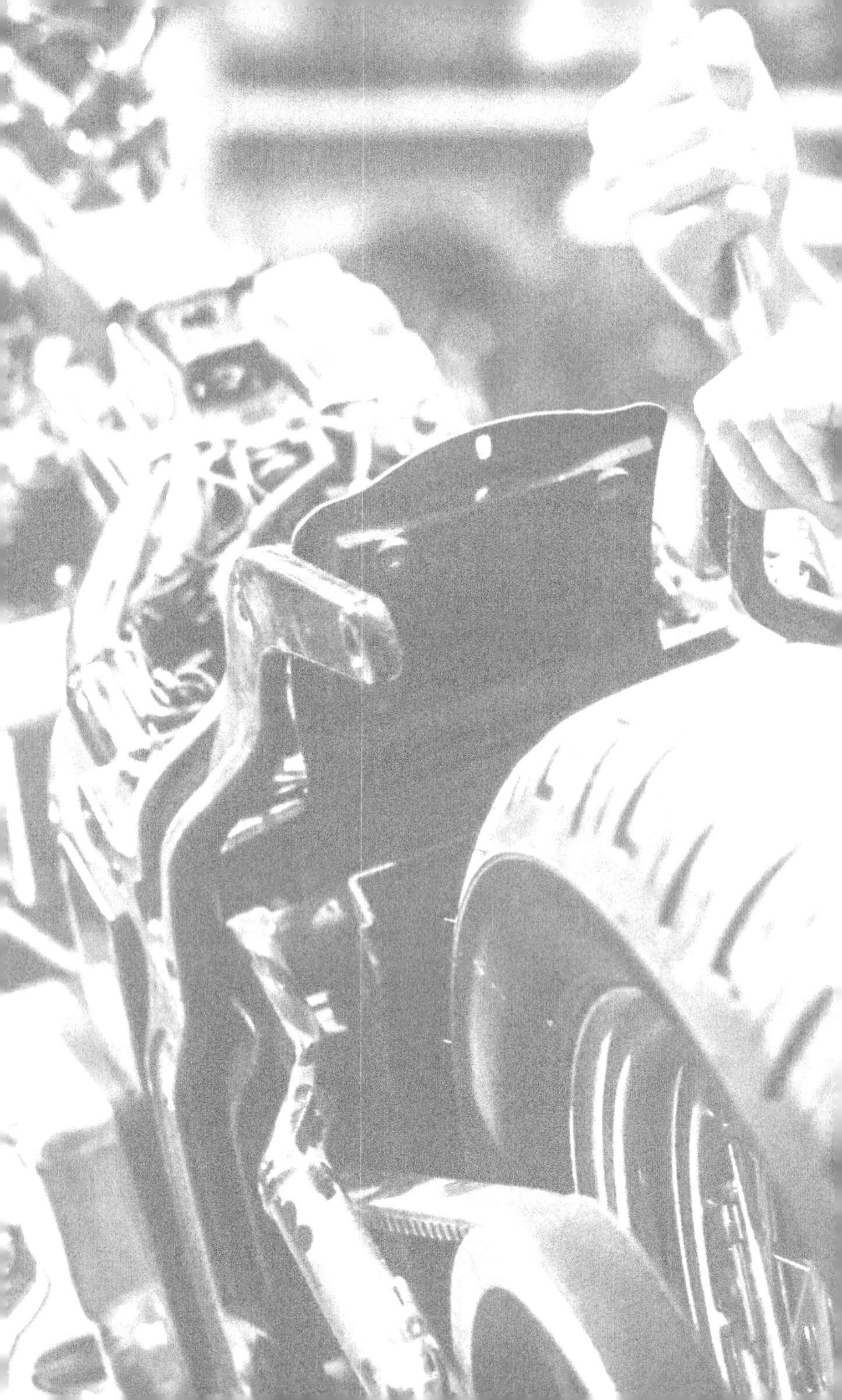

CHAPTER TWENTY FIVE

Axle

I watch her start to stir long before she fully wakes. I can't stop watching her. Like maybe if I take my eyes off her, she won't actually be here, and this would've all been a dream.

When I got back to the clubhouse yesterday, I wasn't even expecting to see her. I was happy to avoid her and slink off again. Well, not happy, but that's what I'd decided. I missed her so fucking much, but focusing on finding Brianna and figuring out why she was targeting Isabelle kept me busy and from saying "fuck it all" and taking everything Isabelle seemed to insinuate she was willing to give.

I may have thought about her—about what she said—every second of the day, but the physical distance meant I couldn't act on it, especially when I got too weak to remember the reasons why I was.

But seeing her yesterday and thinking I was causing her any kind of unhappiness instantly broke through those walls I was putting up. I simply can't stop myself from fixing everything I can for her. I had no idea what she'd say or do when I told her the truth—well overdue as it was—but Isabelle kissing me would not have been within my wildest dreams. Her lips tentatively pressing against mine fucked all my reasoning, smashing through my barriers in an instant. It was just me and her—all I could ever want. And now she's in my bed, naked in my arms, as my wife.

It's still early when she slowly blinks her eyes open before focusing on me.

"You're here," she says huskily. From the sleep or the screaming, I'm not sure. I frown down at her.

"Where else would I be?"

"I don't know. I kind of half expected you to pretend it didn't happen." She looks at my mouth rather than my eyes, and I know she's avoiding me as best she can, which she should know by now I hate, but I don't blame her. I've been the worst kind of hot-and-cold asshole. Everything Vaughn said was right, but I wasn't strong enough to deny myself Isabelle, not fully. I pinch her chin lightly and tip her head back so she has to look at me when I speak.

"I'm sorry."

"Why? Why did you tell me I was married to Kace in the first place?" Her eyes are shining, but she doesn't look accusatory, just curious, and answers are the least I owe her.

"Technically, I didn't. You assumed it was him, as I planned, because I'm thirty-seven and you're eighteen. Because my best friend was your dad. Because I've pretty much watched you grow up and should be ashamed of myself for forcibly tying you to me." She frowns as if I'm out of my mind.

"But I don't care about any of that." A small smile breaks free at her earnestness.

"I know. And if you don't care, then I'll work on caring a little less."

"Can your wife help?" My smile turns into a full-fledged grin at hearing that name from her lips, as well as the satisfied smirk that she's wearing as she says it.

"You like that, huh?" I say. She blushes and presses her face into my shoulder, but I wind my hand in the hair at the nape of her neck and pull her lightly back. "Nuh-uh, you're not allowed to hide from me anymore."

"I like it a lot more than ol' lady," she admits as she looks up at me with wide eyes, and my breath catches.

"You're so fucking gorgeous." Her blush deepens, and I press my lips to her warming cheek.

"I always preferred the nice Axle," she murmurs, as I move to kiss the corner of her mouth, her lips always so inviting.

"I guess I didn't realize how tense being so close yet so far from you made me. I hated not knowing what was going on in your head or knowing how you were feeling."

"Or how I felt," she teases, and I grin against her skin.

"Yeah, that too."

We don't talk any more about why I stayed away or what her dad would think, although it's still in the back of my mind. I want to not give a fuck, to have her anyway, but what if I'm taking more than I'm able to give? Instead, I move my lips to her neck, leaving open-mouthed kisses on the soft skin over her pulse point. When she grips my biceps, I suck lightly and hear the breath she pulls in, my dick already hard at how she reacts to me. Pulling back, I admire my handiwork, loving the red stain left behind that marks her as mine.

"Pee on me, it might be easier," she jokes, and I laugh, not embarrassed at all that she's caught onto my thoughts of marking my territory so quickly. Moving my lips to the hollow at the base of her throat, I murmur against her skin.

"Maybe I'll leave seven of them."

"That's not going to move you up," she quips, and I meet her eyes, narrowing my own.

"No? What's a guy gotta do to get to number one, then?"

For some reason, that's hilarious to her, and she throws her head back and laughs freely. I'm confused. "What?" I ask, chuckling at her mirth despite my annoyance as she caves in on herself, wrapping an arm around her stomach as she continues to laugh. "Share the joke, Isabelle," I urge, and I brush her sides with my fingertips, but when she squirms, I grip harder, tickling her ribs until she's fighting me off and trying to catch her breath.

"Okay, I give up," she pants, her back now to my chest, and I ease my attack, letting her recover. "You weren't ranked like that. It was just who I saw the most." I'm quiet while I process that. So I was seven because I tried to keep away from her as much as I could. She rolls to look at me face-on, and I steal a quick kiss from her lips, keeping my arm wrapped around her waist.

"So not your favorites?"

"Oh, no, you'd definitely be number one then," she says very seriously as I pepper her with soft kisses, but her cheeks are wide with her smile. It's a minute before she speaks again, softer this time, cautious. "Who would your numbers be?"

"What do you mean?" I ask, looking back at her.

"I don't know," she says, taking my lips with hers. I let her for a minute because I'll never not take a kiss from Isabelle, but then I draw back slightly.

"No, what did you mean?" I wait until her eyes come to mine of her own accord. "Be brave, baby."

"Like, if you had to pick from the club, who would it be? You said you wanted me somewhere no one else had been, so I assume . . ." She trails off, but I don't make her finish. I know what she's asking, and if I can reassure her for even a second, I will. I'm not about any games with her any more.

"Your bed was actually new for you. I just wanted you to myself. And no one has been in my bed either—not since it's been mine, anyway—because I haven't slept with any of the club girls."

"Yeah, sure," she says quickly, with a roll of her eyes.

"It's true. I've slept with a lot of women *outside* the club, but I didn't want to get into that drama as the president."

"So not even—"

"Don't say her name," I warn, feeling the anger resurfacing at the fact we were still failing Isabelle by not finding Brianna. "But no, not even her." She tries to fight her smile, but I'm glad she's possessive, it's hot as fuck.

"What about before you were president?"

"Before that, I had Kace's mom, and if anything was going to teach me not to shit where I eat, it's that shitshow." She nods in acceptance, not pressing for any more information, content with my explanation.

"That's why I was in your room, you know," she says, and I frown, but she carries on without any prompting. "I was looking to see if Br—her stuff was in there. Anyone's."

"There's no one but you, baby," I tell her truthfully, pulling her to me with my arm around her. Wrapping her leg around my waist, she winces as she does so. "Are you sore?"

"Kind of," she whispers, but tightens her leg anyway. "But in the best way."

"Yeah?" I stroke over her gently and she practically purrs. "Shall I run you a bath?" She shakes her head, her eyes sparkling as I roll her underneath me. "What will make you feel better?" My fingers continue to explore her with gentle strokes, but when her hips start rocking, I almost groan at her eagerness.

"You," she declares, and *fuck*, I can do that. I drop kisses down over her chest, the swell of her breasts, her stomach, until I'm settled with my face between her thighs. Holding them apart, I blow on her swollen lips before soothing them with my tongue. I feel her thighs flex under my hands, but I keep them against the mattress, taking my time to savor her taste as it explodes on my tongue. She's so sweet. Everywhere.

Using my tongue to gently fuck her, I ignore her clit, even though I know she's already wanting to come, but I want to build her up. Patience is key. Even as my dick throbs and her fingers scratch along my hair, I continue driving her, and myself, crazy by slipping my tongue in and out of her.

"Axle," she begs, and I nearly snap, loving the way my name sounds so desperate coming from her right now. Instead, I stretch back over her, lining myself up with her soaking entrance.

I go slowly this time, not wanting to make her any more sore than she already is, but as I slide inside of her, her fingernails dig into my back and my ass, urging me to go faster. Knowing she wants everything I give her and is desperate for more makes me want to bury myself inside her harder and faster.

Taking her hands off me before I snap, I hold them in my own above her head, continuing with my leisurely pace. She writhes beneath me, her pussy clenching around me as I sink inside. Her back arches, and she gasps at the friction as her nipples drag against my chest. Moving her hands to one of mine, I use the other to pinch at one of her nipples, and she mumbles something incoherent.

She's unraveling slowly beneath me, and it's the hottest thing I've ever seen. I roll the same nipple between my fingers, and she moans my name in a plea, breaking the last of my control. I lower onto my forearm, pressing my pelvis to hers as I grind myself against her clit.

"Come for me, baby." She takes the permission and rolls her hips, welcoming the orgasm as it hits her, squeezing me so fucking tight that she drags me under with her, milking every last drop of cum from me with her spasming pussy.

CHAPTER TWENTY SIX

ISABELLE

I wake slowly a bit later, cocooned in comfort and warmth and horny as hell. As I come to my senses, Axle's arm loosely over my waist, I realize why. Not only is he pressed up behind me, but I'm still full of him, and he's clearly as ready as I am. I tense as I wake fully, and he moans sleepily against my hair. Wiggling my ass, I press back into him, and his arm tightens around me.

"Isabelle," he warns huskily, but I'm not sore—or if I am, it's been pushed out of my brain by need, and what I *need* is him.

"Axle," I reply, letting my voice show exactly how much, with no shame at all.

"You need me, baby?" he growls, and I moan, clenching around him again.

"Yes. Please." He rolls onto his back, pulling me upright as he bends my legs all while keeping himself inside me. I end up straddling his lap but facing away from him.

"Take what you need, Isabelle." I roll my hips, lifting up slightly and sinking back down as he slips the last couple of inches until I've taken him fully again. As I rock my hips, finding which angle feels the best, he palms my ass with his large hands, parting my cheeks so he can see where he enters me. He uses his grip to lift me up and slam me back down as he thrusts, and it hurts deliciously. I want more. I want harder as he jolts my insides. I want to explore every single way I like it with Axle.

He continues moving me as he likes, and the fact he's taken control makes me even hotter. As his hands squeeze my ass, his thumb slips between my cheeks, and a shudder runs down my spine as I tighten around him.

"I'm gonna fuck this ass, Isabelle," he promises from behind me as he presses against my tight hole. "Your ass, your cunt, your mouth. They'll all give me pleasure."

His words are my undoing, and my orgasm crashes through me as he pushes his thumb inside, the foreign, full feeling only heightening my bliss. He continues fucking me from below as I ride out my orgasm, only holding himself still and spilling himself inside of me once I've come down the other side.

I probably should be worried about that a bit more, but I just love the feel of him inside of me with no barriers, and feeling him pulse as he empties into me is all the satisfaction I need.

He spins us both so we're lying on our sides before pulling out and arranging me like his own doll until I'm splayed over his chest. I lie there catching my breath and feeling his own heartbeat slow under my cheek.

"Do I still have a job?" I mumble into his chest a few minutes later. I kind of want to stay here forever, but I know that's not possible, and I try to think about how long I've actually been in this little bubble. I'm pretty sure it's only been a night. His chest rumbles as he chuckles.

"Yeah, baby, I'm pretty sure you do." My skin heats as it does every time he calls me that, and I wonder if I can physically take another orgasm so soon, but the ringing of his phone interrupts that thought. I didn't realize it was on, and it surprises me we got so long without it going off before. "I need to get that," he murmurs, but makes no move to do so.

"Reality beckons, huh?"

He must hear the downturn in my voice because he rolls me onto my back, looking into my eyes. "Yeah, but it changes nothing. You're mine now, and I'm yours, okay?"

My heart soars and tries its hardest to burst out of my chest.

"Okay," I agree simply. Then he lowers himself and kisses me until I'd agree to anything he asked. He only pulls away with a longsuffering groan when his phone starts ringing again. He doesn't roll off me, instead reaching for it with our bodies still pressed together so I can feel the vibrations when he speaks, barely taking his eyes off me for a second.

"Yeah?" I don't pay attention to whatever is being said on the other end of the line, preferring to explore the lines of his face, but his brow creases. Reaching up, I lightly stroke where he's furrowed, and his face relaxes again, a soppy smile taking over. "Give me an hour," he grunts, then drops his phone back on the nightstand.

"I don't need that long to get ready if you're in a rush to get back," I explain, never wanting to get between him and his responsibilities with the club. His house is only five minutes away.

"*I* need that long to shower with my wife," he says with a grin, kissing my lips lightly before pulling me up with him and carrying me over his shoulder to the bathroom.

I'm oddly nervous to walk back into the main room, especially so with Axle's arm slung around my shoulders, but no one bats an eyelid. I guess we weren't all that inconspicuous, eh? Did they all know about Kace?

"There you are," Jag says as he spots me. "Was starting to miss my favorite girl." I feel Axle's hand tighten around me, and Jag does a double take with a frown at the way it's wrapped around me. "What's going on?" he asks. I guess not.

"Isabelle is mine," Axle tells him before I can, and I try not to preen. "She was always mine. In every way."

"And Kace knew?" His eyebrows flatten as he looks angrier than I've ever seen him. Axle nods, and Jag storms off.

"What's going on there?" Is he mad at me or Kace?

"God knows when it's between them." He steps in front of me, his hand finding its way to the back of my neck. "I've got some shit to do. What are you gonna do?"

I shrug. "I'm sure I can keep myself entertained."

"Doing what?" he barks, and I frown at his change in mood.

"I'm not into this bulldog shit. I thought you'd have realized that by now."

He sighs, rubbing a hand down his face. "Sorry." He leans in and leaves a kiss on the corner of my mouth. "I can focus more when I know exactly where you're gonna be, and who you're with."

"I think I'm gonna work on the mural," I concede, because that's kind of sweet, and I wasn't expecting him to explain himself to me.

"Are you going to get it finished? I can't wait to wake up to it."

I hadn't thought far enough ahead to wonder where we'd stay or if it'd be together. I guess I kind of assumed his house would be the secret fairy tale, and it might change now that we're back at the clubhouse.

"Are you staying with me?"

He frowns in confusion. "Of course I am." Just then, Vaughn struts over, nudging Axle with his shoulder.

"Nice of you to deign us with your presence, Prez," he jokes. There's a smile on his face as he says it, but it makes me worry again about keeping him from the club. That's never my intention, and I'd never ask that of him. I've already inadvertently taken it from one man, and I hate how that left me feeling out in the cold once I realized his life was split in two.

"I'm gonna get working on it," I say with a bright smile, taking a step back. "Hi, Vaughn. Bye, Vaughn."

I head through the double doors and am jogging up the stairs when Axle calls out behind me. "Isabelle."

I stop and turn, and he takes a few steps up so he's in front of me, putting us almost level. I remember the last time we were in this position and how much I wanted to kiss him, and marvel at the fact that if I wanted to now, I could . . .

So I do.

I clearly take him by surprise, but he catches up quickly, grasping the back of my head as I go to pull away and deepening the kiss, turning it from a loving peck into something way less appropriate for a public stairway. We're both breathing heavily by the time he pulls away, our panted breaths felt against each other's lips as he looks at me. "You're not mad?"

I know I've just had my brain scrambled, but I don't follow his thought process. "Why would I be mad?"

"You ran off out there."

"Vaughn needed you."

"I don't care," he says with a frown, and I roll my eyes. "I mean it. Nothing is more important to me than you."

"I don't want that."

His fingers twitch at the back of my head as his jaw sets. "What does that mean?"

"It means I don't want you to give anything up for me."

Awareness softens his face. "I'm not giving up anything. You're giving me *everything*. I can be a great president *and* a kickass husband. Just watch."

"How are we married?" I ask suddenly. Last I remember, I was unconscious when it should've happened. "Like, is it all legal?" For some reason, I think I'll be disappointed if it's not.

"Of course it is." He frowns like I've asked him if the sky is really blue.

"But how?"

"I'm the president of an MC. I can get most things done I want. And I wanted you to be mine from the first time I saw you grown. It needed to be done, and no one else was getting a look in." I kiss him again because I can and because I want to.

"Ask me your question before I go," he urges, so I ask the first one I think of.

"How come you're all so young? The main guard?"

"Young is subjective," he says with a scoff, and I roll my eyes, knowing he's thinking of our age gap. "But Presidents get voted in, then they pick their own crew. Any prez needs to be surrounded by their closest friends and allies." I nod because that does make sense. For some reason, I'd just assumed the ones in charge would be the older of the club. "Tell me what you want to do for graduation," he says.

My eyebrows shoot up. I was not expecting that question. It's going to be here soon, and truthfully, the answer is I don't know. I know I could go and some of the guys might come and cheer, but that was my dad's job. I'm looking to exist without him, but I'm not replacing him.

"Can I get a raincheck on that answer?"

"Of course. Now, I'm going to go sort this shit out and then crawl into your bed and watch you come undone around my dick." I shiver against him at his words, and with one final kiss, he leaves.

I jog up to my room full of pure, unbridled happiness. Opening the door, I'm greeted with gorgeous light as the sun is just starting its descent, and I decide it's much too nice to be cooped up in here, even if I only get an hour out in the woods.

I grab my current pad and a handful of pencils and make my way out of the clubhouse and across the asphalt. I smile at the prospect on the gate before blending into the trees and finding my favorite spot.

CHAPTER TWENTY SEVEN

Isabelle

I assume the creaks and cracks are Axle joining me, and my heart rate picks up. I have no idea how he was so quick with whatever he needed to get done, but I'm certainly not complaining. When the light is blocked, it's not his face I see, though—it's Brianna's. I haven't seen her since the night we had shots, and no one's said much to me about her, but even I know it's suspicious as fuck for her to just up and disappear from the compound completely.

Bolting upright, I spin to face her, not loving the fact that she's towering over me when I'm sitting on the ground, but she just watches as I get to my feet. I glance toward the compound but can't see anything through the trees, just like anyone looking over wouldn't be able to see me either. It's why the place is perfect for alone time . . . but now, maybe that isn't such a great thing.

Brianna still doesn't speak, and I take the opportunity to appraise her. She looks like shit. Her eyes are red and puffy, and even in the dim light, I can see the dark bruising over her face.

"What happened to you?" She shrugs as if it doesn't matter, but winces as she does. "Brianna." She instinctively looks toward the compound, just like I just did, as if someone will hear me saying her name and come for her. "Why are you here?"

"I've come for you," she finally says, her voice devoid of any emotion, though I can see waves of it swirling in her eyes.

"Well, you can leave," I say, folding my arms defensively. As if I'd go anywhere with her.

"I can't." Her voice cracks on the last word, as if she's fighting to keep it steady.

"That's your only choice. Leave before I call the guys." I pull my phone out of my pocket to prove my point, scrolling through to find one of the guys' numbers, but her words stop me in my tracks.

"He sent me pictures of my sister," Brianna says with a stifled sob. "She's only twelve." I stare at her dumbfounded, and even as I ask, I know. She's not here because she thinks she can win—she's here because it's her only choice.

"Who?" I ask, not really needing an answer. There's only one man I know sick enough to entertain that thought, and if Brianna is here, that means he wants me. I don't bother waiting for her to say his name. "What does he want?"

"I'm so sorry," she whispers, her eyes dropping to the floor. She looks broken and defeated, and I can hear the genuine sorrow in her voice. Whatever she's here for, it's clear she doesn't want to do this but thinks she has no choice.

"What does he want?" I ask again, desperate to get the facts so I can see what we're working with. I feel like if I call Axle, she'll bolt, and I want to know what the sick fucker is thinking.

"You." A shiver runs over my exposed skin, even though it's balmy out.

"And then he lets your sister go?"

She nods meekly, but it's as if she doesn't actually believe that, she's just doing what she can right now in the hope it happens. "He doesn't have her—she doesn't know. He sends me her location and photos every so often. I can't let her know."

"You should've gone to them," I say. She should go to them now. I know she's already fucked up, but they're not monsters—they'd still help her. I should call Axle.

"I know." She wipes her nose on her wrist, glancing once again toward the compound before looking back at me with watery eyes. Her cheeks are tear-stained, and she looks so young. Gone is the cocky, impossibly cool chick from the club, and it wanes my hatred. You can't hate someone so in need. "I panicked—and then it was too late. The thing is, I know they would've helped me. I don't know why I didn't ask." You can see in her eyes the pain her wrong decision is causing her.

"Let's tell them together now," I offer, but she startles like a deer in headlights. Wrong move. She shakes her head, tears flying onto the mossy floor.

"It's too late now."

"It's not," I promise, but she's not listening, still shaking her head.

"I'm so fucked." She turns and runs before I can say another word, and without thinking, I take off after her. I should stop, go back to the compound and let someone know—anyone. I should call Axle and explain. But Brianna's faster than she looks, and I can't hesitate in case I lose her. If I lose her and she goes back without me, what does that mean for her? I've seen the bruises on her face.

What does that mean for her sister?

I will never let another woman suffer for me, not even Brianna.

She runs all the way to the other side of the forest, climbs into a beat-up car, and starts it with the keys already in the ignition. I wrench open the door and throw myself into the passenger seat.

"What are you doing?" she asks, aghast.

"I'm coming with you."

"Why?"

"I'm not about to let that sick fucker take out his frustration with me on someone else." She blinks at me. "I know exactly the kind of thing he would've threatened your sister with. You think I could live with myself if I didn't try to stop it, knowing it's really me he wants?"

She stares a little longer before she pulls away from the trees and exits onto the road. We're quiet for the drive, and my fingers itch to grab my phone and call Axle, or even text him. He's gonna flip when he finds out. Will I live to see that?

As the sky darkens and we continue to drive, my adrenaline slows and my confidence disappears. What the fuck am I riding toward? Why did I think I could do this? We're just two scared girls driving toward evil.

Brianna pulls up outside an innocuous house in some part of town I don't frequent very often, but she makes no move to get out. I stare up at the plain double-fronted home, only able to see from the in-ground lights along the front, as the sun has set on our drive.

"I love them, you know," she says softly, pulling my attention to her. "Some of them too much. It's why I was such a bitch to you."

"Why?" I ask with a frown. "I know you weren't with Axle."

"No, but you had who I wanted, so I made you think I had who you wanted." Kace.

"I get that," I acquiesce, because it seems kind of pointless to hold a grudge now. "He's pretty lovable."

"Who would've thought? An MC with better men than most I've ever met." Her eyes lose focus but she continues, and I'm happy to let her as she obviously wants to get it out. "They accepted me easily, and I know they'd have dealt with anything thrown at me. They're like that for anyone who joins. They accept all the strays, no judgment. They'd do most anything for one of their own."

"You didn't want that?"

She shakes her head lightly. "I wanted to show I belonged there. That I wasn't a stray—I could deal with my own shit. I could stand *with* them."

"You didn't want to need saving."

"But I'm an idiot. All I've done is make it worse. They'll never look at me again."

"We can just—" I'm trying to offer to stand with her against them, to explain it together, but my words are cut off as the door to my back abruptly opens. I would've fallen had it not been for the body behind me, the arm that bands around me.

"Wait!" Brianna screams as I'm unceremoniously dragged out of the car, but her plea is ignored.

She scrambles at her door, jumping out as I'm pulled toward the house, my limbs flailing pointlessly. For as much as I struggle and fight, the arms just pull tighter around my throat and stomach until my view goes hazy.

I'm trying to scream at Brianna to run, but I can't push my words past the restricting forearm as she follows us inside. I'm thrown to the ground in the foyer, and I greedily inhale as I crawl away from Gary, pressing my back against the far wall as I gasp. He slams the door shut, and Brianna crouches in front of me, sobbing again. "Are you okay?"

I nod weakly, but her tears don't stop until she's yanked away from me, flying until she falls and smacks her head on the bottom step on her way to the floor. It sounds with a sickening thud, and I cringe, getting to my feet to check on her.

"Leave her," he demands, and my body freezes. My eyes strain on her chest, hoping like hell to see movement, but I can't tell. My whole head pulses with the ferocity of my heartbeat, and my eyes won't focus. I'm officially freaking the fuck out. Dragging my eyes away from Brianna, I finally lock my gaze on to the man that's caused all of this.

"Welcome home," he smirks manically, but I don't know what he's talking about. I've never been here, but the thought that he's referencing *himself* makes my stomach roil.

"What do you want?"

"What, no small talk? Like, *Hi, Uncle, how you been? Sorry for throwing you down the stairs and getting that ape to threaten you!?*"

"What do you want?" I repeat through clenched teeth.

"Fine." The tight smile on his face stretches into one of glee. "I want to finish what we started; to get what I deserve. What I'd patiently waited *years* for, until you decided to be a whore and give it out willingly to someone else." My heart races so fast in my chest I think it might come out of my throat.

"I don't know what you're talking about," I say—anything to keep him talking. I feel the panic rising, and the longer he rants, the longer I have to figure something out, not that I'm coming up with anything right now.

"Then let me make it simple for you," he says leisurely as he makes his way over to a bureau, his back to me. Do I run? Will I make it? But one look at Brianna in a crumpled, bleeding mess crosses that option off my list. Good thing, really, because when he turns with a gun in his hand, I wonder if he would've shot me. The breath evaporates inside me at the sight of the gray metal in his hand, my chest tightening and my head going light. "Undress."

I don't even register his command for a moment, processing everything as if I'm thinking through thick mud, and when the front door opens, I jump.

"What the fuck is going on?" my aunt asks, pushing the door closed behind her and regarding me through narrow eyes as if this is somehow my fault. As if her partner doesn't have me literally at gunpoint.

"Surprise!" he says with an unhinged cackle, but she rolls her eyes.

"What do you even see in her?"

He shrugs as if they're discussing the weather before turning back to me. "Fucking undress!" he suddenly bellows, making me jump even higher as he waves the gun at me. But I can't. My body is frozen, my skin clammy. Is this how I'm going to die?

"Go and do it for her," she says lazily, holding her hand out, and he smirks as he hands the weapon over. These two are surely what pure evil looks like. I can't believe that someone would speak so callously about anyone, let along their own flesh and blood. But Gary's barely taken a step, though, before she ejects the cartridge and bullet like a damn pro.

"Are you fucking insane?" he asks, whipping round to her.

"Me? You don't think shit through!" she hisses in his face.

"I'm owed—"

"You're owed fucking nothing. If you can't get it right the first time, then that's on you. On the fucking *stairs*? You missed your chance, and I'm not going to deal with those fuckers so you can get another one."

"Celia!" he bellows, but she stops him with a scream of her own.

"No! Get the fuck out of here and let me clean up your shit, as per usual."

He's fuming, his face screwed up, and I'm worried he's actually going to lunge at her, but he storms past, slamming the door behind him. She exhales as he goes, not even bothering to look at me as she picks the bullets up, moving into the attached kitchen where she deposits them on the counter, along with the gun.

"Get your friend and get out," she drawls. "And make sure he knows nothing fucking happened here."

She must be talking about Axle, but I don't want to stick around to double-check. I lean down to check on Brianna, who is just starting to stir. Relief floods through me as I sweep her hair from her eyes.

"Hey, can you hear me?" She mumbles something, but it's not coherent. "I know you're in pain, but we need to get out of here," I say in a low voice. "I'm gonna pull you up."

I sit her up against the wall and give her a moment as she breathes deeply with her eyes shut, her head leaning back. Celia comes back to use the stairs and, finding us blocking them, rolls her eyes as if we're inconveniencing her.

"Hurry up before I call Gary back to finish what he started." Her spiteful words stun me, although I really shouldn't be surprised at how vile she is by now. There's just one thing that's bothering me.

"Why did you even keep me for so long?" I ask her, keeping my eyes on Brianna. It's something I often wondered.

She could've kicked me out at eighteen and been justified. She clearly couldn't stand the sight of me.

"For the money," she says, as if it's obvious.

"What money?"

"They haven't told you? That's interesting . . . Your guardian gets a certain amount every month until you reach twenty-one, which explains why they were so keen to take that over. Although they went one step further than I could've by locking you down."

"What?" I'm trying to pay attention, but she's speaking in riddles, and I'm also focused on getting Brianna out of here alive.

"God," she sighs. "Do I have to spell it out for you? I've seen you at the shop, so don't act dumb." I frown. The bike shop?

"I intern there."

She laughs cruelly at that. "You don't intern. How can you when you *own* it?"

"What?"

"Your dad left you multiple businesses. Not the ones they launder money through, but the legitimate ones. They're probably the most profitable, seeing as they're meant to *make* money, not clean it. I guess the MC realized just how profitable you are. Why else would they marry you into the club?" My face flames.

"You hated me all this time and left me with nothing, *for money?!*"

"Use your fucking brain!" she seethes. "You think any of them actually want you around? I bet they barely tolerate you, just as I did. *For money.*" I shake my head, not able to vocalize the denial because the doubt is making my stomach ache, but she latches on to it, of course. "No? Then why did they wait for you to be unconscious to make their move? Because they knew you'd never agree to marriage."

"What's that got to do with anything?"

"Your guardian gets the allowance, but your husband has the right to half of all your assets once you turn twenty-one. All of it if you were to tragically die an accidental death, and at a young age. How sad."

"I don't have anything," I mumble stupidly, because it sure sounds like I do actually have quite a lot. She rolls her eyes at me.

"You have a lot more than nothing, even without the stores. I'd have killed you for it, but your fucking useless father made sure that it still wouldn't have come to me. Still, I was happy taking the babysitting cash, until he fucked it all up."

It's not even the casual way she discusses my murder that enrages me but the insult toward my dad. "He's not useless!" She tuts as if I'm being insolent.

"He didn't give a fuck about his family. He'd have always chosen the club. You should be grateful he didn't stay alive long enough to disappoint you."

"You're a fucking liar." About him—about all of it. Why, I'm not sure, but she's got to be saying this to fuck with me, or she's completely crazy.

"Why would I lie? I kept it quiet when I wanted the money, but what's the point now? Clearly the bikers had the same thought, because I guess you're still not seeing a penny of the cash."

This is of course true, and she must see the realization on my face that maybe what she's saying isn't so crazy. Axle hasn't told me a thing about any of this. Is he playing me until I'm old enough that he can take his part? "Oh, honey, you didn't think he actually cared, did you? You're more pathetic than I thought."

"She's not pathetic," Brianna fumes, and I'm surprised to see she looks like she's actually following the conversation. But I don't need her to stick up for me. I need to get us out of here before Gary decides he's not taking instruction from Celia anymore.

I haul Brianna to her feet, and Celia huffs impatiently. With a crash, the door behind her breaks through in a crack, and splinters of wood come flying in. She squeals as she drops her glass, and I nearly drop Brianna back to the ground. Celia backs up as Axle appears, his eyes landing straight on me.

He scans the room as he makes his way over to me. He doesn't even speak before he's looking me over, checking for injuries. When he reaches us, I know he's going to tilt my chin, but I'm too raw and vulnerable from what I've just found out. I grab his fingers before he can touch my face, pushing them back down with a slight shake of my head, and his jaw tenses before he finally speaks.

"What the fuck is going on here?"

"We're just talking," I say. I don't know why I lie.

"You were supposed to stay the fuck away from her," he fumes, turning to Celia, and I take the chance to leave, supporting Brianna with her arm over my shoulder as we make our way to the door.

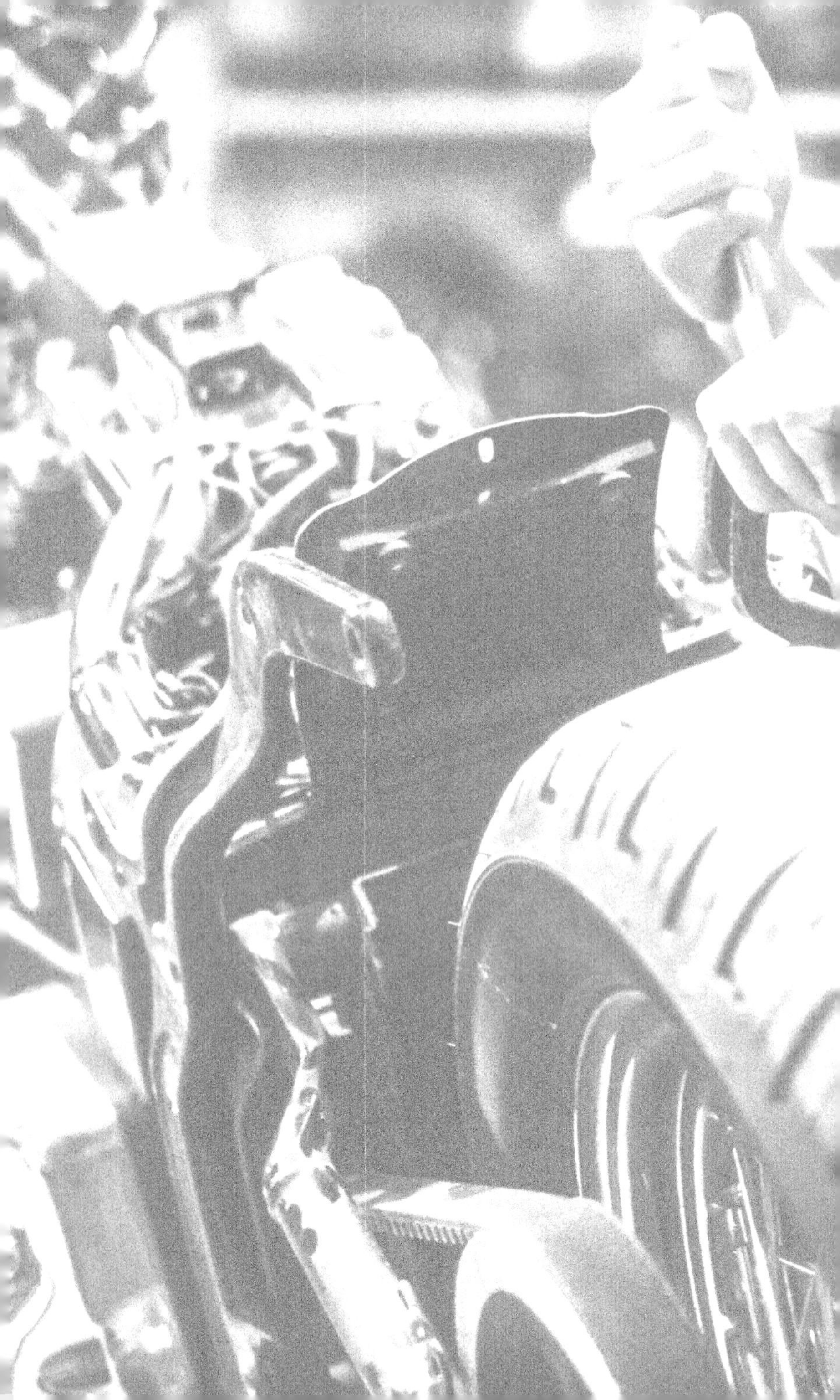

CHAPTER TWENTY EIGHT

Axle

My heart only starts beating again when I have her in my eyeline. I've never felt fear like I did when I saw she wasn't where she should be. I don't know what the fuck she's thinking being here, but she *is* here, and I've got her now. Even if she won't look at me.

My body remains tense and coiled, and I long to reach out and wrap my hands around her. Or her aunt's throat. If Isabelle won't let me touch her, then I need something to keep them busy, and they're itching to squeeze the very life out of someone.

"What, you're acting like you care about her now?" Celia asks, bringing my attention away from Isabelle. As if I didn't already hate this bitch.

"There's no fucking act," I growl. "Of course I care for her. I'm in love with her." Maybe that's something I should've told Isabelle first, but I'm ready to shout it from the fucking rooftops. Her face turns up in disgust, but I couldn't care less.

"You're fucking sick. You should be ashamed of yourself."

And I realize I'm not—not one little bit. I laugh at the fucking audacity she has, to judge *me* on how *I* love.

"Well, I'm not, and I've got you to thank for that. Your love—the love of *family*—is supposed to be *right*, and look what a shit show you're making of it. My love might be wrong, but no one will ever love her harder. My guys—her true family—will give it a good go, but they won't succeed. Until my last breath, I'll worship her, even if that comes decades before hers. I'll give her kids, a house—whatever she wants, because she's what I *need*. She's my everything."

Celia is putrid red with fury, probably at the idea Isabelle gets anything that Celia thinks she deserves. "Trey—"

"Trey would approve because he knows me." The moment I say the words, it hits me that they're completely true. Trey would approve, because he knows I'm what she wants. I'm what will make her happy, and that's all he ever wanted. I look to where Isabelle was, but she's gone, taking Brianna with her. "Stay the fuck away from her," I call over my shoulder as I go to find her.

She's standing outside with Kace, who already has her wrapped in his arms just like I want. I can see the others itching to hug her, to feel she's still here and safe themselves, but I'm a selfish motherfucker.

I stride straight over to where they're embracing and pull her from his hold, wrapping her in mine instead. I inhale her scent, my nose buried in her hair. She doesn't hug me back and remains stiff, her hands loosely at her sides, and when I pull back, she's guarded.

"What did she do?"

"How did you know where I was?" she asks, instead of answering my question.

"You're crazy if you think you've ever been out of my sight."

"Afraid to lose your investment?" One eyebrow rises, but there's a hurt in her eyes I don't understand.

"What are you talking about?"

"She told me about the money. About how you have access to it now. Is that why you're with me? For your half?"

The accusation stings, though I don't think she truly believes it—at least, I fucking hope she doesn't—but I do think she's feeling vulnerable and unassured. She's got it all twisted, but that doesn't make my decision the right one. I should've been the one to tell her about it. I kept it quiet to benefit me even if it's not the way she thinks.

"I was trying to give you somewhere to lean—people to lean *on*."

"I don't need that. Or them. Or you."

I hold her chin between my thumb and forefinger so she has to look at me when I say the words so she sees the honesty that comes with them.

"I know you don't. You could live this life looking out for yourself, and kick ass, but you don't *have* to. I want to be there, fighting your battles with you. It's not about not being able to, it's about me wanting to do it for you." I flick my eyes briefly over my guys, all watching us closely. "Them too." She follows my gaze and blushes, trying to step away, but I don't relinquish my hold on her, so she continues despite the audience.

"She hid it, and you're just as bad."

"I'm nothing like her."

"No? You didn't keep me for what I have?"

"The complete opposite. I kept it from you so you had to stay. I know that's no better, but I was desperate to keep you close. I just didn't know why."

"You didn't want me to have a way to escape, but the thing is, I *want* to be here. I wish you'd have respected me enough to let me make that decision." She's right, we both know it, so I don't even fight it when she pulls away to look at Kace. "Can you please go with Brianna to her house?"

He nods stiffly, even though he doesn't look happy about it, and I'm not surprised. But I trust Isabelle, and so does he. Of course, Jag peels off with him once Brianna is safely on the back of Kace's bike. Vaughn's restraint clearly breaks, and he ruffles her hair, relief all over his face.

"Glad you're okay, Little T," he says softly, and she smiles up at him. I lead her over to my bike, and the others acknowledge her with nods and waves as I help her climb on behind me. She holds on tight, but I'm sure that's for the safety rather than anything else, and my chest aches.

When we get back to the compound, I take her hand and lead her to my office, not the bedroom like I really want. She stands quietly while I rifle through the filing cabinet, pull a fat document wallet out, and hand it to her.

"This is everything. I gave you what I could. I will always give you what I can," I promise.

"Okay," is all she whispers before turning with the paperwork in her arms and leaving me there. I hate it. I want to follow her and force her to forgive me, but I know that will just make her defensive. I have to let her process. I made a decision to benefit only myself, and if giving her space is my punishment, then I'll take it.

I'm still there three hours later when Knox finds me staring into space. There's absolutely no fucking way I'm going to bed alone, so I was content to wait for Isabelle to come and find me—stupidly hopeful, perhaps—but she hasn't.

"You need to see this," he says cryptically before leaving again, giving me no choice but to follow him through the main hall and across the lot to the bikes where he mounts his and peels off without saying anything else.

Following his lead, we head back to the house we just came from. The one I found Isabelle in. Except this time it's not quiet, with only one beat-up car in the driveway. Now, it's a hive of police activity, tape at the bottom of the drive and officers milling around everywhere, lights flashing. We pull up between the cars, right up to the tape, and the chief is there before the engines are off.

"Axle, I didn't think you'd be back." How did he know I was here in the first place?

"What the fuck happened?"

"I thought you might be able to tell me that." Nodding toward a large police SUV, he stops at the open door and I follow him over. There's a small screen leaning on the chair, a black and white grainy image filling it. The chief presses play, and it's not until Isabelle is dragged through the front door that I register it's footage of the house in front of me. I didn't recognize it, especially not from this angle, having not exactly paid much notice to the decor when I was there mere hours ago.

I nearly lose my temper as Brianna is thrown across the floor like a fucking ragdoll. My eyes are trained on Isabelle, as always, so when the chief hands me headphones and I hear Gary's voice, my temper flares again. I watch and listen with my teeth grinding together and my hands balled up into fists as Gary demands that my girl get undressed *at gunpoint*, to all the sick things Celia filled her head with after he'd left. Then I watch Isabelle leave with Brianna before the video freezes on the image of me and Celia facing each other.

"Is that it?" I ask, vibrating with the need to hunt Gary down like an animal.

"No, that's not it. I need you to tell me what happens after this point right here." My brow furrows at the question.

"What do you mean? That's the end. I came out after Isabelle. Surely you can see that?"

"Actually, I can't. The footage from that moment on is deleted, and the camera never comes back on."

"Is there a point to this? I've got shit to do." Like go and convince Isabelle that not one word her vile fucking aunt said is true. And get a reason for why the fuck she told me they were *just talking*.

"The point is that you were the last known person inside that house with Celia, and now she's dead."

CHAPTER TWENTY NINE

Isabelle

All I want to do is cry. This is what acknowledging your emotions does to you—leaves you vulnerable to feeling like your heart has been driven over by a two-ton Harley.

I open my arms and let all the paperwork fall to my bed, covering my comforter with the sheets of paper. I should look through it—clearly there's information in here that everyone is so desperate to keep from me—but it all seems so overwhelming, and none of it really matters anyway.

I never wanted anything from my dad; there's nothing he could leave me that would make up for him not being here. But clearly, he thought it was important. And my aunt thought it was important enough to hide it from me. At least I know now why she bothered to keep me around. Unfortunately, it looks as if Axle did for the same reason.

But that can't be true, right?

He can't have done all of this—gone as far as to *marry me*—just for a bit of money.

I move the pages around with my fingertips, kind of wanting to burn the lot. I never wanted any of it, but it seems like everyone else did. They can have it. I don't care. I'm about to scrunch the whole pile up and throw it away when a handwritten letter catches my eye.

Dad's handwriting.

I pick it up with trembling hands before swiping the lot off the comforter and sitting down. I curl into a ball as I stare at my name written in his scrawl until my eyes blur. I wish Axle was here, that he'd told me the truth from the beginning . . . that I didn't have any reason to doubt the way he feels about me.

I must drift off, as the room is lightening when my eyes peel open. The letter remains in my hand, crumpled against my chest. With a deep breath, I flip it over, hesitating for a moment before peeling the envelope open and pulling the paper out.

To my darling Belle,

If you're reading this, then I'm no longer with you. Know that I will miss you from the second I'm gone, and I'd never choose to leave you. Sometimes life is just shorter than we think.

I hope you still are and remain to be the courageous, sympathetic, caring, confident, loving girl I know. You love hard and out loud, and I want that for you forever.

I guess by now you know my secret. I know you're not used to them, and that's my fault, but you've always known they were there for you. They protect us. I promise you that no one is perfect. You can be a good person and do bad things, make mistakes. Just remember your intentions, and make sure they're always for the best of someone.

You can't fix everyone, but you can try your hardest. That's what I've learnt from being a president, and more importantly, your dad. I stepped down for you, and I'm still not convinced that was the best idea—depriving you of this family—but it's what I thought would keep me with you. People make mistakes when they're scared of losing something precious. Give them the benefit of the doubt, sweet girl.

Trust your gut, and don't be afraid to be wrong. I'd rather see you brave and disappointed than never hopeful. Above all, my precious Belle, be happy, however that looks for you. Know that I'm forever proud of you, and I love you more than life itself.

Dad x

Tears stream down my face when I read the end, droplets falling onto the paper. I don't try to compose myself, feeling all of my dad's words as I grieve for the fact he can't say them to me. It will never get better that he's not here, but maybe I need to acknowledge and accept it, live alongside my grief. Pushing it away and hiding from the memories isn't helping.

He wasn't perfect. No one is.

He didn't make the best choice every time, just the one he thought would be best for me. That's what Axle has done. He made the decision to keep me with them all, to bring me home in the first place, where I belong.

I swipe the tears off my cheeks and jump up, desperate to find him. Pulling open the door, I find him already here, his hand poised to knock. He looks surprised, but I only give him half a second before I'm leaping at him, wrapping my legs around his waist and my arms around his neck. His hands are around my thighs a moment later as I murmur against his skin.

"I'm sorry."

He kicks the door shut and steps over the discarded paperwork on the floor before kneeling on the bed, bending over so my back is against the comforter. Then he moves his hands to my face, running his thumb along my bottom lip as he gazes at me with those pale blue eyes.

"Don't you dare be sorry. *I'm* sorry. I should've let you make your own choices and figured out how to follow you from there. I don't want to stifle you. I didn't know what this was, why my chest fucking ached when I looked at this girl that was too young and too off-limits. I didn't know why I craved having you around and needed you safe to function. I went too far. I said I will give you what I can, and I mean it—I just couldn't risk you running so soon after getting you. But it's yours, all of it. I never wanted or needed a cent."

The adoration shining from him makes me melt into his touch, my legs tightening around his waist.

"I don't want it either. I don't need it. I just want to be happy with you." I stretch to capture his lips with mine, and he whispers against them.

"Isabelle."

"I want *you*. Us, Axle."

"Say it, baby. Say it first so I'm not trapping you."

It's on the tip of my tongue, and I know he knows it because when the knock comes from the door behind him, he growls in frustration.

"Prez, they won't wait," Vaughn calls through the door, and Axle lowers his forehead to mine.

"The police are here," Axle says to me. "I wanted to be with you when they told you."

My forehead crumples against his. "Told me what?"

"Your aunt. Come on."

He doesn't explain, just pulls me up by my hand and walks me down to the main room, tucked in beside him. It feels like most of the MC is here, despite the early hour, but when Axle nods at the room, most of them clear out, leaving Knox and Vaughn standing next to a booth where the chief sits.

Panic swirls in my chest as Axle leads me to the booth, letting me slide in before sitting beside me with his hand reassuringly heavy on my thigh.

"Hi, Isabelle," the chief starts, and I murmur a hi back. Why am I so nervous? It's like my body knows this is bad news. Worse than questioning me on my attack. The way Vaughn and Knox are so solemn at my side ramps up the tension. "There's no easy way to say this, but unfortunately, yesterday evening, your aunt took her own life."

My eyes shoot up from the stain on the table I was focused on, meeting his sorrowful ones. That is not what I was expecting him to say.

"What?"

"It seems like once you left there, she used the gun that was present and ended her own life. I'm so sorry for your loss." There's no way. No way in hell was that the course of events. But my train of thought gets stuck on the fact that he knows I was there yesterday. How?

"How do you know I was there?"

"There was a camera set up at the property." My stomach roils at the realization of why that was, and Axle squeezes my thigh as he feels my tension. Not that he's exactly calm—anger still radiates off him. But this is different to a security camera. He'd set one up? "We will also want to talk to you about the events leading up to that, but for now, I just came to deliver the news and offer my condolences." I nod in acknowledgment, not exactly excited to make another visit to the police station but wanting to answer the questions right now even less. "I'll be seeing you," he says with a nod, and stands from the booth.

"I'll be right back, baby," Axle says to me before standing with him, but by the time I register it, he's already gone.

"You okay, Little T?" I'm expecting it to be Vaughn who asks, but when I register that it's Knox's voice, I unexpectedly want to cry and frantically try to blink the tears back. He holds his arms out, offering me warmth and comfort, and I take it, standing and pressing my face to his chest as he rubs gentle circles on my back. Vaughn's hand soothes my hair as I try to keep myself together, wrapped in Knox's arms, feeling overwhelmed with their affection. These guys care for me. I know they do. They want to know that I'm okay. And I think I am, or, at the very least, I will be.

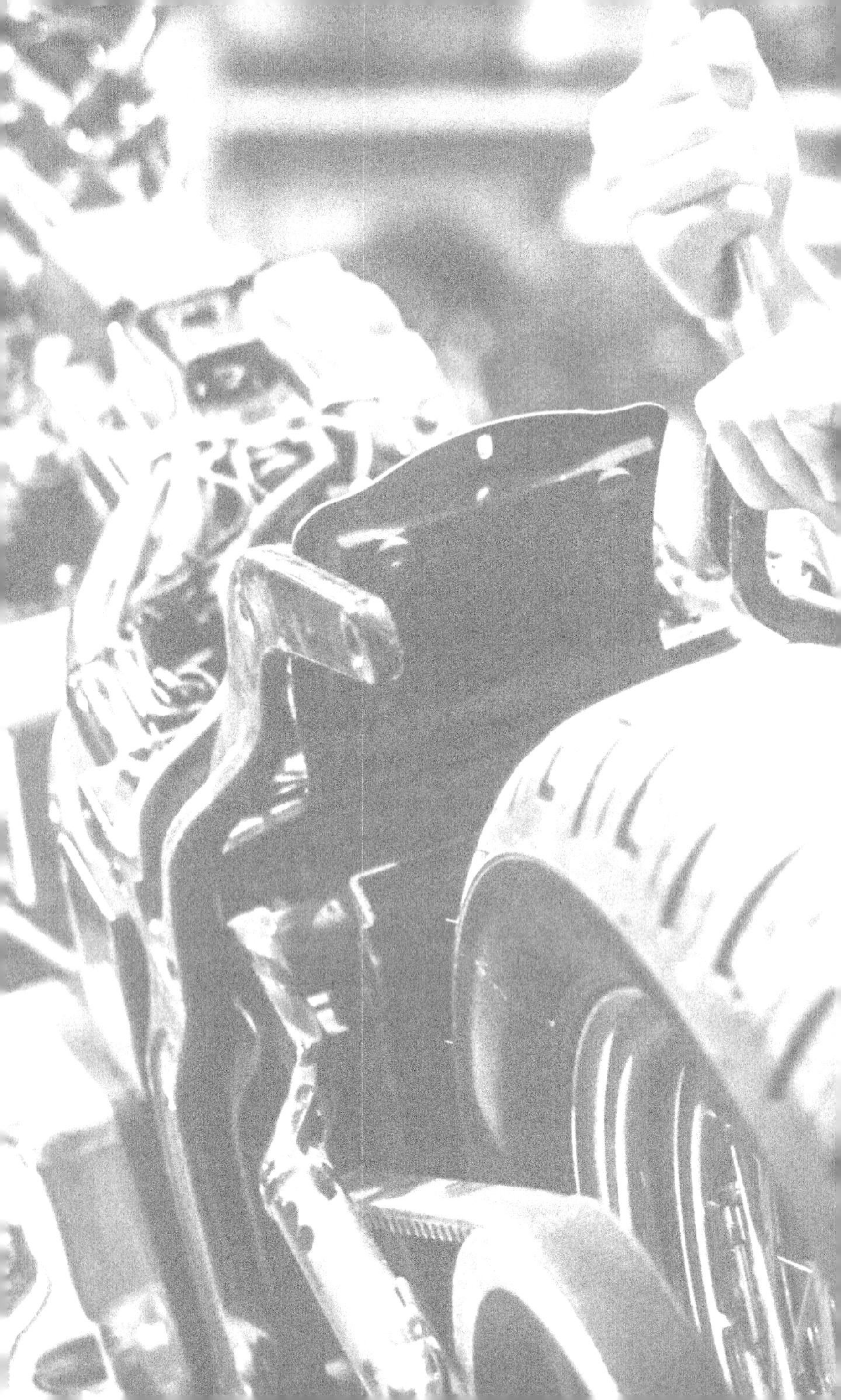

CHAPTER THIRTY

Axle

Isabelle is completely still while the chief is escorted out and I reluctantly follow him.

"Did you even check with Gary?" I ask, bitter at the lie Isabelle was just told.

"Yeah, he has an alibi, not that he needed one *because it's not suspicious*," he says pointedly. We both know that's bullshit, but I don't want Isabelle being dragged into an investigation. As one of the last people to see her aunt alive, she'd be questioned, and after seeing what was caught on camera, there's no way I want her to have to relive it. The agreement to accept the death as a suicide is one that sits heavy in my gut, but I know it's needed for now. Let Gary think he's walking around scot-free.

"Where is he?"

The chief shakes his head. "Not a chance, Axle."

Instead of responding, I shrug. That's okay. We'll find him eventually. I go back to Isabelle, and the others make themselves scarce.

"You okay?" I ask her gently.

"I think so."

"Come on, let me make you breakfast." I hold my hand out to her, but she doesn't acknowledge it, her eyes glazed.

"I'm not hungry."

"You need to eat something." I take her hand and gently pull her out of the booth. She follows behind me into the kitchen, and I sit her on a stool by the stove and pull a plate and some bread out. "What's your favorite sandwich?"

"A toasted Cuban," she says distractedly.

"I can do that." She looks at me then with a raised brow. "What? I can whip up a glorified grilled cheese."

"Blasphemy," she mutters, with a small twitch of her lips.

"There it is. My favorite smile." She rolls her eyes, but her smile grows, so I'll call that a win. "What do you wanna do today?"

"I think I want to go to work."

Trying not to flinch at the thought of her being away from me, I busy myself with collecting the fillings. "Yeah?"

"Yeah. A little bit of normal sounds good."

"Okay. You get an escort though."

She doesn't argue or reply at all, and when I look up at her, she's looking down at her hands guiltily. I stop what I'm doing and wait for her to look at me, which she eventually does. "Why didn't you call me?" I ask.

"I wanted to," she says quickly, "I swear." I know she means it, but the fact is she didn't. "Brianna ran, and I thought I'd lose her."

"So?" I ask incredulously, still not certain of the events that led up to last night.

"So, I won't let someone else suffer for me," she says determinedly, and I try not to scoff.

"Yes, you will. Especially when you're mine."

"Axle—"

"No," I interrupt her, and I know I'm being an asshole, but I don't care. "There's nothing to discuss. You fuck over whoever you need to, and you come to me."

"You're being awfully bossy," she gripes, folding her arms.

"Considering I know exactly what actually happened in that house, including the fact that Gary was there threatening you with a gun, I think I'm being really fucking reasonable." Her defensiveness drops as I try to keep my volume even.

"You saw the footage?"

"That's not the point, Isabelle. Why didn't you tell me?"

"Because I thought you'd be angry," she mutters, and I scoff in disbelief.

"Yeah, of fucking course I'm going to be angry!" How I've managed to act like a normal person since I saw that tape, and talking about it with her now, I have no idea.

"Exactly, and then what? You'll go find him?"

"He's going to pay," I promise her. "He already had one chance, which is way more than he should've."

"What if you don't win? He seems to come out on top every time. Look at my Aunt Celia. I know it wasn't suicide—she was way too self-obsessed for that."

The anger leaks out of me at the worry on her face, and I itch to touch her. Coming around the island that separates us, I hold my knuckles under her chin, making sure she keeps her eyes on me. "You don't get it, it's not me against him. It's *us* against him. The whole club. I will never put any of them in reckless danger, and I will always come back to you."

"You can't promise that," she whispers softly.

"Then watch me prove it." I kiss her gently to seal the promise she won't believe before going back to her sandwich, giving her some space to think, even though it's the last thing I want to do.

She watches me silently, but I catch her opening her mouth a couple times before she thinks better and closes it instead, biting her lip to trap the words. When I'm done, I put the plate in front of her and tug her lip free, kissing it gently.

"What's going on in that head of yours?"

She shrugs lightly, turning her attention to her food but not making any move to eat it.

"You can tell me anything, Isabelle."

"I don't feel sad," she says finally.

"About your aunt?"

"Yeah. I mean, anyone losing their life is awful," she quickly clarifies, "but I'm not grieving."

"You don't have to be grieving right now. You can take a few days, weeks, months to process and then grieve, or you can not grieve at all. There's no right way to do it."

"But what if I never do? Does that make me a terrible person?"

"No. *She* was a terrible person." Even the thought of Isabelle holding any guilt about that woman makes me angry. "However you feel is valid."

"How do I feel?" she asks, looking to me with lost eyes for an answer.

"You don't have to feel anything. You don't have to do anything. We can throw her in the sea for all I care."

She mulls my words over as she finally takes a nibble of the sandwich in front of her, albeit a tiny one. "I want her to have a funeral. She's still a human." *Barely*. "Can it be organized without me?"

"Of course. Whatever you need."

I set Bishop on the case to organize a modest funeral. The coroners officially rule it a suicide, so it's only a few days before it comes around. Those days are filled with Isabelle. She goes to work, and I count down the minutes until she's back. I don't get to take her or pick her up seeing as I'm not babysitting her. I tried, but she's way too distracting when she furrows her brow or bites her lip in concentration, and Satch kicked me out when I nearly busted a boner in front of him. Fair enough.

We haven't spoken about the fact that the shop actually belongs to her, or any of the other things she must've learnt from that paperwork I gave her. I guess she'll come to me when she knows what she wants to do, but until then, it'll carry on going like it has for the last five years.

Isabelle spends a lot of time finishing the mural. I've offered to go to the woods with her every day, but she's declined, opting to finish the beautiful canopy in our room. I'm okay with that, knowing she's inside where she can't be hurt, but I secretly hope she gets her confidence back and continues doing what she loves soon. The idea that Gary could've taken anything from her makes me furious.

She joins in with conversations at dinner if someone brings her into one, but she's unusually quiet—withdrawn and inside her own head. It makes sense that she's distracted with everything that's happened and is coming up, but I also wonder if it's because Kace and Jag aren't here right now.

They're still with Brianna, at Isabelle's request, but having her two friends she was most comfortable with gone must be having an impact.

We've just got the service to get through, and then we can start getting used to our new normal.

CHAPTER THIRTY ONE

Isabelle

I smooth a hand down the front of my black wrap dress and blow out a breath. I haven't been to a funeral since my dad's, and I don't really remember that one—the whole day was a grief-filled black hole.

Funerals are hard to dress for. You don't want to seem like you put too much effort into looking good, but you also want to be smart enough. I've put my hair in a neat bun with minimal makeup, but for some reason, I'm still fussing.

Maybe if my look is perfect, no one will notice I'm not sad.

A soft knock comes at the door before it pushes open and Axle is there, looking far too hot for someone about to attend a graveside. He's swapped out his normal blue jeans for a black pair, and paired with the black shirt under his cut, it's a great look on him—one I eagerly drink in. I bite my lip on a flush and turn back to the mirror. He comes up behind me and wraps an arm around my waist, pulling me back against his hard chest. "You look perfect."

I smile gratefully up at him in our reflection, and he drops a kiss to my shoulder. Everything is so natural with us now, even though it's been such a short amount of time. The way he touches me, and the way I lean into it—it's like it was always meant to be this way.

"You ready?"

"Yeah," I reply, and he steps back, takes my hand, and leads me downstairs. It's a weekday, so I expect the main room to be pretty empty, but I'm stunned when Axle pushes through the doors and we're met with what looks like every member of the club. Knox, Vaughn, Ashton, even Satch. It's just missing Kace and Jag. I tug lightly on his hand, and he turns to look at me.

"What's going on?"

"The guys wanted to see you off."

And that's what they do. Every member of the club present either nods, salutes, or smiles as I self-consciously walk past with Axle, until we get to the end and Satch drags me in for a hug that feels like a bear wrapping his arms around me. I'm pretty sure I hear Axle growl, and a giggle bubbles up inside me as Satch lets me go.

"We'll be here when you get back," he says, and all I can do is mouth "thank you."

Axle parks his bike by the graveyard gates where Knox and Vaughn will wait for us. They're not attending, but it's nice to have backup. As we wander through the gates toward the location we've been given, I see Gary before Axle does. I know because the exact moment Axle notices him talking with someone I don't know, energy zips through his body, and his hold on my hand tightens as his posture tenses.

"Can we please just get through this and go home?" I ask quietly, wanting to be here even less now that Gary is. I expected him to show up, but that doesn't mean I'm comfortable with it. Axle doesn't offer his agreement, but I hope he hears what I need today.

The funeral is a small, short affair. The priest says some lovely if impersonal things, and we're invited to throw a handful of soil onto the coffin at the end, but it's quite generic—it could have been a funeral for anyone.

I try to muster up some sympathy that there's no one here who loves her, but I can't. There's probably no one in the world that she didn't push away. The fact that she lost her life, and in the way I suspect, is horrible, but that's all the sadness I can find for the situation. I can't even muster any gratitude toward her for saving me from Gary, knowing it was only to save her own skin in the long run. Not out of any loyalty to me, or common decency.

It's over before it really begins, and the few attendees mutter their condolences to me as if they mean anything before quickly leaving. I turn to Axle with a sigh, but it gets caught in my throat at the sight of Gary coming up behind him.

Grabbing his arm, I tug Axle so he's standing next to me instead of with his back to Gary as he comes to stand at my side. Axle turns us again so we're facing him together, which puts Gary between us and the grave, but he doesn't even give it a second look, his smile smug. The monster only has eyes for me.

"You're awfully fucking brave to be this close to her," Axle grits out with barely restrained fury, but Gary barely glances his way.

"Isabelle, so lovely to see you."

His tone is conversational, but there's something lingering in the depths. Axle tenses at my side, as on edge as I am, but I squeeze his hand, knowing I need to hear what Gary clearly has to say. If I don't, I'll only have a lifetime of wondering what and why.

"What do you want?" My voice doesn't waver, even as a tightness spreads over my chest and I try to focus on the warmth of Axle's hand in mine.

"I wanted to let you know that I'm always going to be there, even when you least expect it." His words take a second to infiltrate my brain as he uses such a casual tone, completely at odds with the threat it actually is. "Your *hus-*

band can't be everywhere to protect you. One of these days, he'll turn up too late."

My whole body is shaking as the ice-cold words flow through my veins. I'm frozen to the spot with fear when Axle steps between us, right up to Gary's face, halting his speech. Axle mumbles something so low I can't hear over my heart pounding in my ears, but my eyes stay locked on Gary's, and the same fear he just injected into me flashes in his eyes. It's euphoric.

Gary's lips part on a silent gasp, and as Axle steps back, he falls . . .

He doesn't trip, he simply falls backward, his body crumpling on itself until it crashes into the top of the coffin then slumps off the side. A bloody trail is left over the wood, so dark it looks almost black. It happens so fast, I'm not convinced I don't imagine it, but there he is, lying wheezing in the dirt in my aunt's grave. I'm still gaping at the mess when I feel a presence behind me, which snaps me out of the daze.

Someone's here. Someone's seen it.

I whip my head around and search, but all I see is Knox and Vaughn, standing behind us like sentries. The rest of the graveyard is quiet and still. Axle cups my cheek to stop the incessant swiveling of my head and speaks against my lips.

"It's okay, baby," he murmurs reassuringly. "He's gone."

Knox and Vaughn move around us and start shoveling the huge pile of dirt into the hole, covering the coffin and the man who's probably still alive with soil and stones.

"Is he—"

"He will be soon." I look up into Axle's eyes and I see worry. "No one will ever make you feel fear like that again. I'm here, always." I nod numbly before capturing his lips with mine, wanting to feel something other than terror. His kiss grounds me, as it always does, showing me what's important and what to focus on. "You okay?" he asks, with his forehead resting against mine.

"Yeah." I am. I think. Maybe I'm in shock.

"Let's go home," he says, winding his arm around my waist and turning me toward the exit.

He doesn't take me back to the clubhouse, heading straight to his place instead, and although I feel a tiny bit guilty at them all waiting, I can't deny that I'm not glad of it.

We're both quiet as he sits me at the kitchen counter, then pulls some drinks out of the fridge and places one in front of me.

"I'm going to shower, okay?" he says, and I nod, feeling his lips against my forehead before he heads up to the bathroom.

He still looks worried as he goes, and I guess killing someone does leave its toll. It doesn't even seem real—I can't believe that just happened in front of me. But I'm not the one who took his life. I have no idea about what the MC does aside from the businesses, and honestly, I don't want to know. I'm happy just knowing who they are as men. I don't know if Axle has killed before or how he deals with it, but I want to be the one who comforts him after anything, through anything. I'm not some scared little girl he needs to shelter. I can be there for him, stand beside him through anything the MC brings to his door. He can have them *and* me.

I take a long sip of my drink before climbing the stairs, following the sound of running water to his master bathroom. Toeing open the door, I can see the blurry shadow of him behind the fogged-up glass, leaning his head against one arm that's propped against the tile.

I shimmy out of my dress and underwear and release my hair from its tie before softly opening the glass shower door. He doesn't even seem surprised when I step in front of him, wrapping me in his arms and burying his nose in my hair.

"Are you okay?" I murmur against his chest, and he pulls back, the water spraying against his back, his body sheltering me from it. I take his shower gel off the shelf and squirt some into my hands, lathering it up in my palms.

"I'm fine, baby. How are you?" he asks, and I start to clean his chest, working the suds from his pecs over his abs and around his sides. He ignores the way he grows harder between us, so I do too, although what I really want to do is drop to my knees and taste him.

"You seem tense. Have you never done that before?" I ask.

He frowns. "More times than I'll ever admit to you."

I grab some more shower gel, then wash over his shoulders and down one arm. "Are you scared you'll get caught?"

"No." I finish the other arm and signal that I want him to turn, which he does, but he doesn't continue. That's fine. He needs quiet.

Adding more shower gel to my hands, I swipe them over his back, taking my chance to drink in his tattoo properly this time. The talent is astounding—it even puts the motif on the back of their jackets to shame—and I'm filled with pride that my dad created this. Knowing he spent hours, possibly days, inking this into Axle's skin helps me feel still connected to my dad in some way. I'm so engrossed in the details that Axle's voice causes me to jump. "I shouldn't have done it in front of you."

So he's worrying about me? "I'm fine, Axle."

He pulls me around to his front so the warm water is against my back, smoothing my hair back as it wets. "You're always fine."

I get what he means. "Okay, when he was saying those things, I was terrified, and I probably never would've told you that. But I didn't need to. You knew, and you fixed it for me."

"Fixed it?"

"Yeah." That's a pretty reductive view of what happened, but the point remains the same. "I love that you protect me so fiercely."

Relief softens his face as his arms tighten around me, making it impossible to miss how hard he is now. "Always."

I snake a hand between us as heat pools in my stomach, wrapping my slick, wet hand around his length as his jaw ticks. His eyes are full of so much comfort and warmth and devotion that I hope he sees it mirrored in mine too. When he parts his lips, I know what he's about to say.

"I love you," I say quickly, wanting to beat him to it, just like he asked.

He freezes, searching my face for any hesitation or lie, but of course he doesn't find it. What he does find spreads a huge grin across his, and he kisses me hungrily, his lips forceful against mine.

His fingers move between my legs, stroking and coaxing, but he doesn't give me what I want, silencing my attempted protest with his tongue as my lips part. Lifting me by my thighs, he lines up and thrusts into me in an instant, stilling when I gasp and arch my back at the delicious intrusion. Then he presses me against the tile and pushes all the way in as I clench from the cold sensation. He groans against the tight fit, and I climb higher at the way he pushes against my walls, creating incredible friction.

How we went from a funeral to almost coming after one stroke I have no idea, but I hope he always has this effect on me. He doesn't slow down, pulling out and pounding back in as if he's lost all control, and I love it.

This is somewhere I might prefer feral Axle, because as he roughly takes what he needs from me, I only climb higher and higher. I don't even manage to choke out a warning before his fingers come between us, rubbing circles against my clit, and I come undone spectacularly.

He swallows any sound I may make with a hungry kiss, his moans mixing with mine as he thrusts once, twice more into me as I spasm around him before he stills and empties himself inside me. I'm still fluttering and he's still pulsing when he pulls his mouth away from mine, staring at me with adoration.

"I love you too."

CHAPTER THIRTY TWO

Isabelle

I wake up warm and comfortable but alone. I know that even before I roll over and find the huge bed empty. In the handful of times we've slept together, it's never been without Axle wrapped around me.

Despite this, I feel lighter than I've felt in years, knowing there's nothing left to weigh me down. No days I hate, no lingering obsessive psychopath, no family that hates me more than they tolerate me. Not even the all-consuming grief that threatens to drown me. It's still there, of course, but somehow and somewhere in the last month, I've learnt to co-exist with it and keep living without it weighing me down. How much can change in a month. And it's all down to him.

Speaking of, I climb out of bed and throw on a T-shirt I find in the first drawer I open. It's only plain white, but it hangs below my ass, so I'll take it. Climbing down the stairs and leaning against the door frame that leads into the kitchen, I have to stop and stare.

Axle has his back to me, working over the stove in a pair of low-slung pajama pants and nothing else. I'm pretty sure I'm blushing. Even after all the things he's done to me in the last week, I'm not used to seeing him in all his nearly naked masculine glory.

"This looks a lot like my fantasy," I admit, and he's grinning when he turns to see me perving over him. He pulls the stool closest to him away from the island and pats it, and I happily make my way over.

When I'm seated in front of an empty plate, he turns back to his project, brow furrowed in concentration, and I didn't think I'd ever think this about an MC president, but he looks *adorable*. I'm about to tell him as much when I notice what he's so focused on. He's making pancakes. As he turns with the pan in one hand and a spatula in the other, he stills at my expression.

"Is this okay?" he asks, and I nod. Does he know? "Pancakes on the last day of May Mayhem, right?" he checks, putting the first perfect pancake onto my plate. The Mayhem makes a lot more sense now—Dad must have named it after the Knights.

"How did you know?"

"Are you kidding? Trey used to disappear for the whole month. Happy birthday, baby." Holding the pan and the spatula in one hand away from me, he cups the back of my head in the other and kisses me lightly, and the mention of my dad's name doesn't even cause any pain, just a bit of sadness. It's not that I'd forgotten what day it was exactly; it just didn't seem as important. I haven't celebrated properly in years, and I wasn't expecting anyone to know.

He pulls away way too soon for my liking, turning back to the stove and pouring more batter into the pan. "Eat up. We've got plans."

"We do? What?" He taps his nose, and I grin like an idiot and tuck in to what becomes a steady stream of pancakes.

"This might not be the best idea," I complain, as he places the helmet on my head and chuckles.

"You've ridden it loads of times now."

"Yeah, but not after you've fed me six pancakes." Six. I'd really eaten six, but they were so good. I turn to the side and stick my stomach out to accentuate how full I am, but when I look back up at him, he's not laughing, his eyes locked on my midriff. "I'm joking, I won't vomit on your pride and joy . . . probably."

He snaps out of it and moves my bangs out of my eyes. "You are my pride and joy." Then he gets on the bike and holds a hand out to help me on behind him like that wasn't the cutest thing anyone's ever said to me.

I assume we're going to the clubhouse, but he bypasses that road completely and continues on to the other side of town. When we're a couple minutes out, I guess where he's taking me, and my chest warms as I squeeze him tighter. We pull up outside the cemetery, and he helps me off, taking the helmet and leaning against the side of his bike.

"You're not coming in?" I ask when he makes no attempt at moving.

"No. This one's for you, remember?"

As I make my way toward Dad's grave, I marvel at how different I feel in just a month. Where I used to think this was the only place I could be close to him, I now know that's not true. He'll always be with me, in the way I think and see the world, the men I'm surrounded by, and the way I treat people. He made me into who I am, faults and all, and I couldn't be more thankful.

I sink to the grass with my back against the stone, as always, lean my head back, and close my eyes. I miss him. I really, really do. Especially on days like today, when he should be celebrating with me. But I can know this and not let it drown me. Not anymore.

"I did it, Dad," I murmur. "I kept on living. Sorry it took me so long. I bet you were losing your shit, eh?" I chuckle at the thought of him knowing I indulged my sadness for so long.

"But I can breathe again now, Dad. I learned how to do it without you." A tear slips down my cheek from behind my closed lids. Just because I can now, doesn't mean I'd ever choose to.

"I can see why you and Axle were friends." Is that an odd thing to think? Doesn't seem like it. "He makes me feel like I'm exactly who I'm supposed to be." He makes me feel perfect. Loved. Accepted. "He makes me happier than I remembered was possible." I know Dad would approve. That's all he ever wanted for me.

"I want you to know that I don't think it was a mistake—keeping me away. I think it all happened this way for a reason." Not that there's ever a silver lining to my father's death, but staying away from the club until I was an adult? I can see the upsides to that. "Because now I get to choose. I get to choose to stay and choose Axle, and he can choose me."

My voice breaks, but I know I want to get the words out. I stifle a sob as I say, "Thank you for everything, Dad. For always encouraging me to grab on to things with both hands and reminding me that good intentions mean the world. For making me courageous and caring and showing me how to love so fucking hard." I swipe my sleeve across my cheeks to dry the tears that have escaped. But they're melancholy, therapeutic tears. Instead of drowning me, they leave me feeling lighter.

Getting to my feet, I take another look at the headstone—the one that's only for me. "I'll miss you every second of forever," I promise. And then I turn and start making my way back to my other forever.

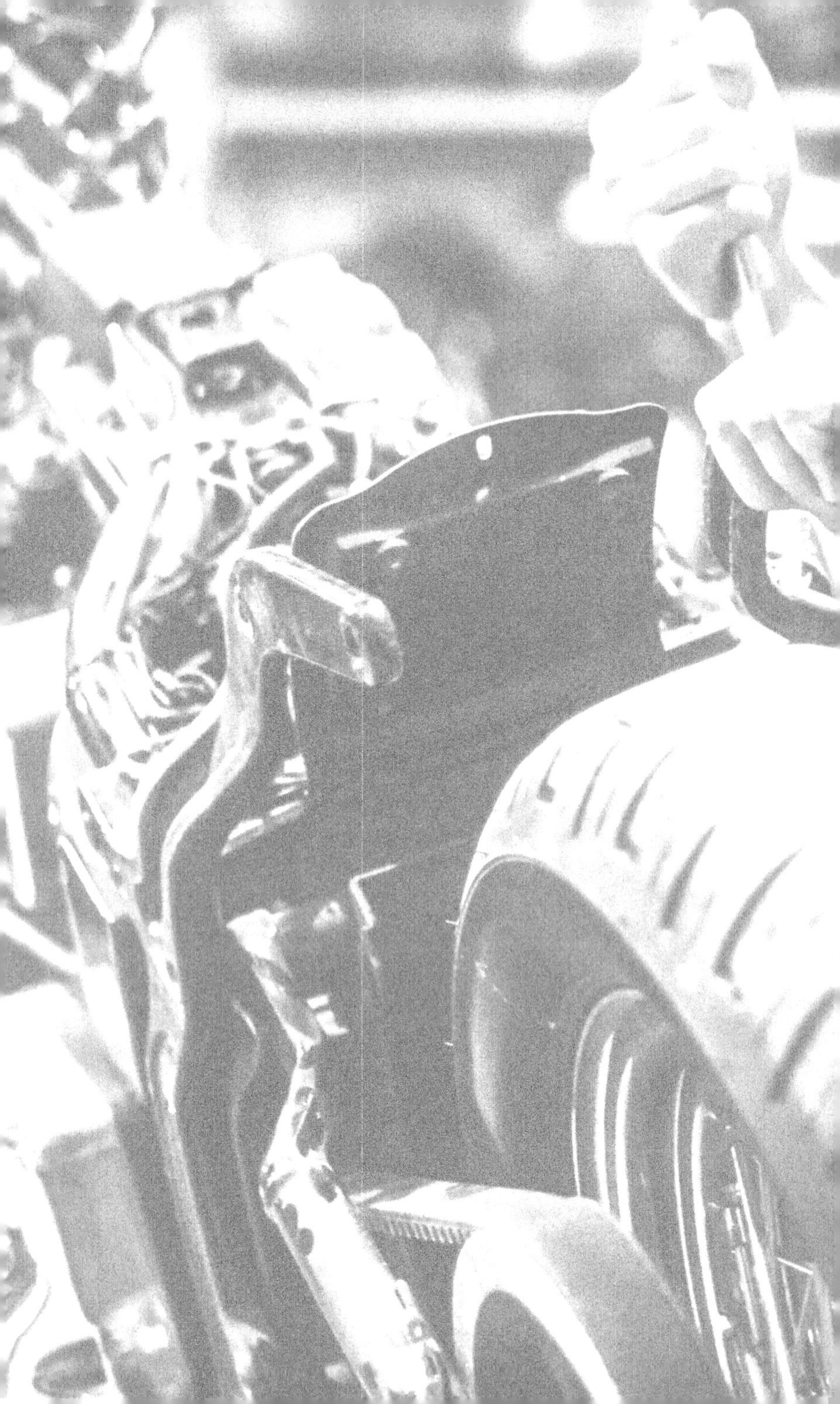

CHAPTER THIRTY THREE

AXLE

"The drop didn't go well," is all Cyrus says to me over the phone. He's rarely at the compound, preferring to be riding most of the time, but that's his own shit he has to deal with. He went with Luke to supervise his second-chance drop from a distance, but clearly Luke didn't manage to fix whatever happened.

"What does that mean?"

"It means we're lying low." I trust him to give me the necessary details when he can, but that's obviously not now because he hangs up in the next second, and I quickly type out a message to Knox and Vaughn.

Axle: You hear from Cyrus?

It's not long before my phone dings with a reply.

Knox: Handling it, Prez

Okay, I can live with that. I slip my phone into my pocket and look back up to see Isabelle leaving the cemetery. I didn't know how she'd be when she left Trey's grave, but I'm pleased to see she's smiling. It may be a little melancholy, but that's to be expected. It's her birthday, and her dad's not here to celebrate it with her—it's always gonna suck. Just means I'll have to make sure each is better than the last to make up for it.

She walks straight into my arms, and I bury my nose in her hair, holding her to me so tight I wonder if she can breathe.

"You good?"

She nods against my chest, and I relax completely. If she's good, then I'm good.

We get back on the bike, and I take us over to the compound. The main room is deserted when we get inside, but I don't hang around, dragging her behind me so fast she giggles as she practically has to run. I push through the double doors before bringing her in front of me just as the whole club hollers "Happy Birthday!"

She jumps back against me, but when I check, she's grinning from ear to ear as she takes in the banners and balloons they've decorated the pit with. People descend to steal hugs from my girl and wish her happy birthday, showing just how hard they've all fallen for her, and I graciously let them, standing to the side with Vaughn.

"She good?" He knew the plan for the morning, and we both hoped she'd be in the right frame of mind for this.

"Yeah." Either that or he's checking again she's not traumatized about what happened at the grave. He was *not* happy I'd done something so spontaneous and risky without the proper planning. For such a laid-back guy, he's got some serious control issues. It's why I didn't tell him my intentions if Gary was there in the first place. "You gonna fill me in with the drop?"

He sighs before taking a swig of his beer.

"Not tonight. That's Luke's story anyway." Good thing I trust my VPs.

I try to relax, knowing Isabelle's safe and having a good time as I watch her be passed around and chat to everyone here, but I still itch to have her in my arms. I can share, but I don't have to fucking like it. The only consolation is the fact that she searches me out too, meeting my eyes every so often to check I'm still close.

When I've had enough of watching her from afar, Vaughn and I join her, Kace, Jag, and some others. They were both relieved to make it back for her party and have spent some time catching up with her, but they're not going anywhere for tonight. She moves across to let me sit, but as soon as I'm next to her, I pull her legs onto my lap, my arm wrapped around her waist. She doesn't protest, relaxing instantly with a smile up at me, and my soul calms.

"So, you're the First Lady of the MC, huh?" Vaughn asks, and she tenses slightly, if just for a second.

"If you scare her off, I'll kick your ass," I warn him.

"Nah, she's presidential blood," Knox reminds us. "She's good." She beams under his praise, and he smiles back at her, looking way less scary than he usually does for everyone else.

"What do you actually know about an MC, spitfire?" Kace asks before taking a sip of Jag's beer, earning him a scowl.

Isabelle shrugs lightly against me. "You all wear the same jackets." Matching pained expressions cross the guys' faces, and I swallow back a laugh.

"Different jackets; same vests over the top. They're called cuts, baby."

She pulls a face before continuing. "You don't drive in cages," she adds, emphasizing the word with a lift of her brow as if they should all be impressed, making them all chuckle.

"I guess that's all the important things, then," Vaughn drawls, as Isabelle gives a satisfied nod, knowing she actually knows more than that. She knows what she needs to know. Of course, she can ask about her businesses whenever she wants, but the rest is irrelevant. She doesn't need to be involved in any of it. Her businesses are clean and always will be for her.

Needing an excuse to have her to myself for two minutes, to have my hands on her, I pull her flush to my chest.

"It's gift time," I whisper against her ear, before standing and pulling her up with me. I lead her back inside and through the main room to the parking lot out front, where a brand-new bike sits, plain and begging to be made beautiful with her talented hands. It stands out from the others due to the lack of personalization and the big red bow on the seat. She runs her hand along the leather seat and over the handlebars before looking up at me with wet eyes. "No, no tears," I say.

Instead, she throws herself into my arms with a huge smile.

"I can't believe this!"

"Believe it. I put it together myself. Now you need to paint it pretty, 'cause when it's done, I want you bent over it naked. That glistening pussy needs a suitable backdrop." Her eyes change from gratitude to lust, and I feel myself thickening just from that look. She rises onto her tiptoes and presses her lips gently against mine.

"How will I ever thank you?" she purrs, and I'm a goner, the evidence of what she does to me making itself known against her.

"It's your birthday. You don't need to thank me."

"It is my birthday, so I should get what I want, and what I want . . . is for you to fuck my throat."

I groan as I pulse against my jeans. "You're gonna kill me."

"Then I better make it worth it," she replies, squeezing my length through the denim. That's the extent of the torture I can take, so I remove her hand and bend, picking her up over my shoulder as she squeals. Marching back through the main room, I take her straight to her room—our room—and put her back on her feet. Except she immediately slinks to her knees and licks her lips, and I nearly combust right there and then. Flicking open my jeans and sliding the zipper down, her eyes widen as my dick springs free and bobs in front of her face.

"Isabelle—"

The words die in my throat as she licks a line straight up the underside of my dick. My fists clench at my sides, and I fight the urge to take control, letting her run this show. It is her birthday, after all. Sucking the tip into her mouth and hollowing her cheeks like sucking a lollipop, she looks up at me through her lashes then lets go with a pop.

"Don't tease," I growl, and she fights her smile before taking me in her mouth again, farther this time as she swirls her tongue around my shaft. Once she's got me nice and wet, she begins to bob her head along my length, using her hand to stroke the rest of me. My eyes are locked on her—the way her lips are stretched obscenely around my dick as it disappears into her mouth, deeper each time until I feel her throat around my crown and she gags.

The tightness around me makes me groan, and I tip my head back in ecstasy. She doesn't quit, still working my length with her mouth until she gags again when it reaches her throat. I flex my hands as they itch with the need to hold her. I don't know if she notices my need or it's hers, but she pulls her mouth away from me to speak.

"I want you to fuck my throat." The repeated request has me so close to losing control, and when I look down to see the sincerity in her eyes, I wonder how I don't lose it.

"Yeah?" She nods, and I finally thread my hands into her hair. "You need to swallow when I hit your gag reflex, okay?" She nods again as she licks her lips. "Tap my leg if it's too much."

Then I guide myself into her mouth, giving a few pumps to get her used to the feeling of me using her for my pleasure. When I reach her usual limit, her eyes widen slightly but she swallows like I said, and I feel the exquisite warmth and tightness as I slip down her throat. It's too much—the way she trusts me to use her, to give all control over to me. The way she looks on her knees with those huge eyes looking up at me, tears running down her face and pupils blown with desire as if she could come just from taking me deeper than she thought.

One of these days I'll come straight down that throat, but not today.

I pull away from her mouth, lifting her up and flipping her onto the bed on her front as she squeaks in surprise. Then I pull her shorts down before pulling her knees up so her ass is in the air, giving me a perfect view of her swollen pussy. I tug the wet lace away and slam into her—no finesse or warning, just the primal need to be inside her.

She screams into the comforter, and I hold her down with a hand between her shoulder blades. The fact that someone could hear me making her scream has me feeling like a fucking king, but I know if someone *did* hear her, then I'd rip them apart. Only I get to hear those sounds from her. The material muffles her cries as I pound into her from behind, knowing I'm only moments from exploding.

"You see what you do to me, baby? You drive me fucking crazy."

Her muffled moan sounds out as she tightens around me, and I know she's close too. Snaking a hand around to her front, I place two fingers against her clit before pushing her hips down so my hand is between her and the mattress.

Pulling her legs together as I continue to thrust in and out relentlessly makes the squeeze even tighter, and she rocks back and forth against my fingers as I do. It's a perfect storm, and I feel when she comes, her scream barely swallowed by the bedding while her pussy practically strangles my dick as I fight to get deeper still, filling her up with my cum on a groan.

Both of us slick with sweat, I collapse over her back, just managing to hold my weight off her by resting on a forearm. Giving one last deep thrust, she moans as I pull out gently before rolling her onto her back so I can see her.

"You good, baby?"

She hums a noncommittal agreement, but the dozy smile on her face reassures me. "Nap time," she mumbles, pressing her face to my chest, and I chuckle.

"There's a whole party waiting for you downstairs."

"Oh yeah."

"You wanna ditch? I'll happily take you home."

"No, I wanna stay. But I'll look forward to you taking me home at the end." My chest warms at the easy way she calls my place home—while she might be thinking of my cabin, I know that my home now is wherever she is. "I need to clean up first, though." I grimace at the inconvenience of not using protection, knowing we haven't actually ever discussed it. "Maybe we should start using condoms if you're going to jump me wherever we are," she says.

She's joking, but I still tense involuntarily at the idea. "Are you on contraception?"

"Yeah. I've had an implant for the last year. Don't freak out."

"I'm not," I say, placing a kiss on her head. "I'd happily fill you up every day until you're growing our baby." She gapes at my honesty, looking like she can't decide whether to laugh or panic. "Don't freak out," I parrot back to her, and she rolls her eyes at me, a smile tugging at her lips.

"Maybe we just enjoy each other for now," she gently suggests, and I'm more than okay with that. We've got all the time in the world for everything else. "But no condoms. I love the feel of you inside me bare."

I groan as I drop my forehead to hers. "Go and clean up before I make you even more of a mess." She grins and tips her face to kiss me lightly.

"Thank you for today." My brows rise at the change of topic. "It's exactly what I needed." I don't know if she's talking about the sex, the bike, the party, or the visit, but it doesn't really matter. "And thank you for bringing me home." Now I know she's not talking about the cabin, or the clubhouse. She means the club—bringing her back to where she belongs. I cup her face, stroking my thumb along her bottom lip.

"I'll give you everything I can for as long as I live."

"I believe that," she whispers, and my heart soars. As she fucking should.

"I love you, baby."

"I love you too." I press my lips to hers. Not a kiss to heat her, but a kiss to seal this—us—forever.

THE END

Also by Genevieve Jasper

RECENT RELEASE
Hardy
Combat knife: A smooth blade with backward serrated edges. Designed to slide through flesh easily, almost undetected, but causes irrevocably more damage once you try to remove it.

Sounds about right.

I think I'm going for a simple blind date, a favor for my best friend. Little do I know, my date is with the devil himself. The man who runs this city, and that tattoo of his is very appropriate.

Before I can even sense the danger, I'm trapped.

What happens when the time comes to extract myself? Will the pain be worth the pleasure?

Hardy is a contemporary romance novel, suitable only for readers 18+ due to language and sexual scenes. Hardy contains references to the mafia and violence as well as themes such as CNC and dubcon. A full list can be found in the front of the book.

THE GAMES TRILOGY
We Will Rule

The Guards rule this town—always have, always will. Getting rid of them isn't an option. I have to *become* one of them. And to do that, I have to win The Games.

I'll infiltrate their ranks with dedication, perseverance, and a whole lot of luck. No distractions, especially of the romantic variety. That means keeping to the pact Sawyer and I made years ago—to always stay friends, never lovers. It also means utilizing Nico's brain to learn what I need to know while keeping my ridiculous crush on him under wraps.

When Ezra moves in next door and sets off a whole chain of changes in our lives, I start to forget that I can't afford to be blinded by lust. Being hands-off doesn't sound so good anymore.

I've been preparing for The Games for years; I can't fall at the last hurdle. We're so close. Let's hope my heart doesn't overrule my head before we cross the finish line.

THE ELITE AT OAKVIEW U SERIES
When We're Alone

All my life I've been told "be seen but not heard," and I'm suffocating. Going through the motions to survive until I get my chance, my shot to prove I'm just as valuable as any man that my dad wants me to snare.

When my father dies unexpectedly, I'm free—until I'm not. With our finances and the business under another man's control, we're forced to move in with Dad's business partner and his son, Stone. He hates me, and I don't know why, but I won't take it lying down.

I just want to get through my last year of university unscathed. When Stone and the rest of the Elite continue to target me, I have no choice. The fighter comes out. They have no idea what I survived at the hands of my father. They won't break me.

When We're Alone is a contemporary romance novel suitable only for readers 18+ due to language and sexual scenes. This is an enemies to lovers standalone book with characters of university age. This book contains mature themes such as bullying and death, but our main characters will get their happily ever after (or for now). A full list of trigger warnings can be found at the front of the book.

What About Us

Traditional romance sells you the dream partner and the fantasy meet-cute. What they don't mention is what happens when lightning strikes with the wrong man. Not the respectable, reputable man that I should want, but the playboy friend who goes through girls like oxygen.

I'm looking for my Prince Charming, and I'm not planning on wasting my time with anyone who isn't him. So why am I drawn to Mason, the guy who only hooks up once then moves onto the next girl?

When he sells me the perfect illicit secret, I should walk away with my head held high and tell him where to shove his offer. He's not what I'm looking for. He's just the guy whose clothes I want to rip off; the only one who makes me feel alive. But what if, in some strange, cosmic way, he's been the Prince Charming I've been fantasizing about all along?

What About Us is a contemporary romance novel suitable only for 18+ due to language and sexual scenes. This is a standalone book with characters of university age. This book contains mature themes that may be uncomfortable for some, including discussions about consent and allegations of sexual coercion. Our main characters will get their happily ever after (or for now).

IRONHAVEN SERIES
Her Titans

I'm finally single again and am ready for my wild phase. Enter Atlas, the Viking God in a three-piece suit. I think it's a one-night stand; simple, no-strings fun, right? Now he wants me to be his girl. But can I really be his when I've also developed feelings for his two best friends? Together, they are the Titans——business flippers rumored to have a big presence in the criminal underground, and they are used to sharing. Do I follow my head, or my heart? Do I even have a choice?

When my house burns down, I discover someone is trying to warn the Titans away from me and claim me as theirs. Everyone in Ironhaven has secrets, and I didn't even know about my own. Can the Titans find my stalker before it's too late? I only wanted a wild phase, but it may wind up being the ride of my life.

Her Titans is a contemporary reverse harem romance novel, suitable only for readers 18+ due to language and sexual scenes. While the main characters in Her Titans get their happily ever after in this book, there will be other unanswered questions to be addressed later in the series. Her Titans contains references to gangs and violence and contains themes such as kidnapping, stalking, and grievous bodily assault.

Her Vipers

After 3 years in prison for a crime I didn't commit, I'm looking forward to getting my life back on track. That is, until I find out my 'accidental' incarceration wasn't so accidental after all. Somebody murdered my father and framed me. The only clue I have to find out who's behind it all is the Vipers Motorcycle Club, and the three legacies set to take over the throne. Caus, Echis and Kofi swear they had nothing to do with me being framed, and they want answers too.

When I find myself working in their bar and sleeping in their beds, I know I'll need to protect my heart and have my own back. They may say they are on my side, but the Vipers screwed me over once before. What's to say it won't happen again? I don't need them. I can figure out the secrets of my past and get revenge just fine on my own. They may know my twin sister, but they don't know me.

Her Vipers is a contemporary reverse harem romance novel, suitable only for readers 18+ due to language and sexual scenes. While the main characters in Her Vipers get their happily ever after in this book, there may be unresolved issues to be addressed in the final book of the series. Her Vipers contains references to gangs and violence and contains themes such as kidnapping, murder, prison, and grievous bodily assault.

Her Sentries

While my best friends each found love with gang leaders, my life spiraled out of control. Threats, secrets, even kidnappings. Ironhaven doesn't feel safe anymore.

I was forced to retreat, but now I'm ready to take my life back, starting with returning to Ironhaven. But moving on isn't as easy as I hoped. I develop feelings for not one, but three men.

Jeremy, who wants to protect me but nothing more.

Abel, the charming, sweet and funny guy who is just the distraction I need.

And Jackson, the asshole detective looking to bring those close to me down.

But the heart wants what the heart wants—and my heart is telling me there's more to him than it seems.

I want my happily ever after but it seems out of reach. With my heart belonging to three different men, how can I choose between them? And when I'm caught in the crosshairs of someone else's vendetta, who will save me?

Her Sentries is a contemporary reverse harem romance novel, suitable only for readers 18+ due to language and sexual scenes. This is the final book in the Ironhaven series and will have a happy ending. Her Sentries references gangs and violence, and contains themes such as murder, stalking, and grievous bodily assault.

STANDALONES
Christmas Eve Eve

"Come on, Mrs. Claus, if it's so important they can't do it without you, what great plans did the hot Grinch makes you miss?"

Eden

Finished up work for the holidays and ready to head home to my family, there's only one thing that could dampen my festive spirit: Rafael-bloody-Bennett. An entitled, self-important snob who thinks everyone is beneath him and work is more important than family. He's the last person I'd ever want to spend Christmas Eve Eve with, but when he ruins my plans and then offers to get me home faster than I would have originally, how can I refuse?

Rafael

When I spot a mistake that needs rectifying immediately, I know Eden Piper is the only girl for the job. Shame she's also an opportunistic pretty-girl who slept her way to the top. Plus, her festive spirit and Christmas cheer make me shudder. And yet, every time it comes to saying goodbye, I find another excuse to spend time with her. Christmas Eve Eve isn't really a holiday, but maybe she can convince me to celebrate after all.

Christmas Eve Eve is a fun and festive feel-good novella perfect for the holiday season. It contains spice and scenes suitable for ages 18+ only.

About the Author

Genevieve Jasper is a British romance author who loves angst, protective alphas, and *all* the spice. She adores reading just as much as writing and prefers to do both while cuddled on the sofa with her pooch.

You can find Genevieve on Facebook under Genevieve Jasper, Instagram @genjawrites, and Tiktok @genjawrites!

Printed in Great Britain
by Amazon